THE RAKE IS TAKEN

#2 LEAGUE OF LORDS

TRACY SUMNER

THE RAKE IS TAKEN

Copyright © 2020 by Tracy Sumner

All rights reserved.

Edited by: Holly Ingraham, Casey Harris-Parks

PROLOGUE

In a very loathsome part of the city...
London, 1855

inn had two choices. Which wasn't dreadful, as he often had none.

Trust the word of the men waiting in the alley outside his lean-to. Or run. When he'd spent all nine years of his life running. Dodging misfortune, grasping hands, chaotic dreams, and thoughts not his own.

There'd been a life before. He had memories. A girl with flaxen hair clutching his hand as they raced through a field of some splendid purple flower, her smile wide, her gaze focused on him in a way no one's had since. But those memories were as out of reach as Queen Victoria's blooming crown, as murky as the rotten, throat-stinging stew hanging over the river outside his door.

Finn wiped his nose on his tattered sleeve and shivered, a frigid gust tearing inside his shack and sending the city's stench into his nostrils. A reminder of how close to the bone he lived. All he *didn't* have. Opportunities he couldn't *afford* to miss.

1

The men, their promises, could be a *good* thing.

Against the better judgment of a world trying to beat that belief out of him, Finn hadn't given up on good things.

He glanced around the dark, dank warren he'd constructed beneath the back staircase of the Cock and Bur with scraps of wood pilfered from the docks. It was a piss-poor rabbit hole in London's most despicable parish, but it was *his*. His when he had nothing but what he'd managed to steal. A silver fork, a cheap paste brooch, a truly fine kid leather glove, a book, the stained pages nonetheless fascinating for what little he could read of the story.

Finn smiled, though it felt shaky around the edges. He was an incredibly good thief, of lots of things, and thank God for it, or he'd long ago be dead. Peering through a split in the timber, he inspected the two men conversing in low tones, their voices harmonizing with the howling wind. The posh bloke's words from moments ago returned to him. *Let me help you. I, too, have a supernatural gift I can't control. You can trust me.*

Trust.

Finn curled his hands into fists and slammed his eyes shut, tears pricking his lids. What he had—the ability to read minds—was no gift. It was a *curse*.

But he could use it. Would use it. Had used it every day to survive.

Calming himself, Finn let the men's thoughts ruthlessly worm their way through the ragged wood of his battered abode and into his mind. He couldn't always read a person without touching them...but sometimes, if they didn't put up a mental fuss, he could. One of the men, a giant the size one rarely saw outside a fighting ring, oh, his thoughts were there for the taking, a clear match for the pity shining in his eyes. Humphrey. Well, nothing cross about Humphrey, even if he looked like he could smash you into the cobblestones with nothing more than a crook of his pinkie.

The fancy one, upon close inspection only a few years older than Finn, was a harder read. Troubled and angry, emotions Finn recognized right off. Slowing his breathing, Finn worked hard to grasp the man's name, needing it for some reason. Needing the connection.

Julian.

He would love to tell the spit-polished Julian, who spoke with an upmarket accent no one got while living in this hellhole, that if Finn touched him, he'd unlock every secret. Twist Lord High-Class inside out with what he could see, no matter how hard a brain-battle the man waged.

Finn caught his reflection in the mirror shard balanced on a crate, and his heart sank. Another curse. Another limiter of choices. Prettiness that had so far been nothing but a disaster. Eyes so bleeding blue that once seen, they were never forgotten. An unfortunate circumstance for a pickpocket—being unable to slink away without being identified as that *beautiful boy.*

"*Beau garçon,*" he whispered, the words coming to him in French like they always did. A language he dreamed in for no reason he could figure. Part of his blank slate of a past, when all he truly knew was the name—Finn—scribbled on the foolscap delivered to the orphanage with him.

Through a serrated gash in the wood, he watched Julian place his hand on the lean-to and shudder with comprehension. The word immediately tripped from the posh bloke's mind to his.

Family.

Finn's deepest desire, and the one phrase with the power to break him when nothing else had. Not the edge of a blade dug beneath his chin, not a flaming cheroot extinguished on his wrist. Not rough handling of the worst kind.

Pitch-black, nightmare handling one never, *ever* forgot.

Remembering, Finn released a cry that sounded like it had come from a distressed animal and dropped to the filthy cobblestones, hugging his knees to his chest. The hulking giant tore the lean-to's door aside and pulled Finn into his arms, making hushing sounds as if he were a babe. Finn sagged against the beast's rough woolen coat, appalled by his weakness, embarrassed, ashamed, but unable to find the courage to turn away.

To run.

In the end, he let them lead him down the alley and to the waiting hackney cab. Lead him to an uncertain future. Of course, he wouldn't have accepted the offer, *any* offer, without a fight if the men hadn't already visited his twilight musings on more than one wretched night.

Because he only dreamed about those who mattered.

∿

In a very enchanting part of the city...

Her father was outraged. Again.

Victoria pressed her back against the nursery door and scrubbed her face free of tears. No use trying to leave the chamber when they'd locked her in. After the last incident, she'd gone two days without food. Now, there were crackers in the top drawer of her chest, secreted beneath her badly-embroidered handkerchiefs, and a slice of cheese wrapped in a linen napkin hidden underneath her pillow. Agnes, her companion, and lady's maid once Victoria was old enough to need one, always kept water in the room, just in case.

Victoria hadn't meant to ruin her father's party. She'd approached Lady Dane-Hawkins because the woman had whispered a rude comment about her to Lady Markem as they strolled from the dining room to the salon. Victoria *was* odd; she knew that. But she'd worked hard to appear normal, or as normal as a child could when they were, in fact, *not* normal. To have that gray-haired snipe say something that made her parents turn and look at her—as if to determine what precisely about their daughter was so strange—when Victoria tried valiantly to evaporate like morning mist when she was around them, was too much. Lady Dane-Hawkins had placed another crack in the cup that held their love, and Victoria felt it leaking away even faster.

She would have told them about her talent long ago if she wanted her parent's affection to wither like an aster bloom in the winter.

She'd only slipped her fingers around Lady Dane-Hawkins' wrist for one moment, long enough to erase whatever Victoria had done to make the woman think badly of her. A few minutes of the lady's memory obliterated. Maybe the entire night, but with a crowded social calendar, who needed another of those? Unfortunately, Lady Dane-Hawkins had fainted dead away, dropped right to the Aubusson carpet her mother loved, her glass of sherry going with her in a rosy-red spill.

Victoria's parlor trick, the ability to steal time,

was one she'd been employing since forever. Although it never worked out well for anyone.

A light knock sounded. A folded sheet of foolscap inched beneath the door.

Victoria opened the note, a tear rolling down her cheek and dropping to the parchment. She watched it bleed into the ink, fracturing the script into broken pieces. *You're not odd. You're unique.*

Charles.

Her brother, her protector. He and Agnes knew about her peculiarity when no one else did. No one else cared.

Her family was much smaller than it looked from the outside.

Dropping her head to her knees, she shivered. There would be no fire in the hearth tonight. No companion to read her a story. No food aside from the concealed cheese and crackers. No love, as expected.

She'd been told often enough that eccentric people usually grew to live solitary lives.

So often, she now believed it.

CHAPTER 1

Curzon Street, Mayfair
London, 1870

inn had two choices. Which was remarkable as he usually had many.

Continue to follow the woman he'd been dreaming of for months. Or surrender his pursuit. Only, he wasn't a runner. Hadn't run from a problem since Julian and Humphrey offered a new life as effortlessly as the baron's liveried footman offered champagne.

His smile was menacing, he knew. Because there was no choice. Not when the woman standing across the ballroom, his unwitting twilight partner, was the only person he'd ever encountered whose mind he couldn't read as easily as he did a copy of *The Daily Telegraph.*

Even touching her arm that time on St. James, as she rushed from a hatter's shop, had brought him naught. *That* was a first. A never-before-in-his-life first, because when he touched someone, the thoughts came. Added to the bizarre circumstance of not being able to read her, being close to her obscured his ability to read *others*, like she'd dimmed the flame on the gaslamp of his mind, leaving only his thoughts to contend with.

What was she thinking, he wondered?

What were *they*—the glittering mass of humanity filling the fragrant, brightly-lit space—thinking? It felt odd to not know.

Finn dusted the toe of his boot through a candlelit prism cast on the marble floor and lifted his tumbler, the brandy doing a reassuring glide down his throat. He'd never entered into a relationship of any kind— friend, enemy, lover—without a landscape of proba-bilities laid out before him. He knew from the get-go what everyone thought of him, what they wanted, what they hated, what they desired. It was an unfair fight, a gamble weighted entirely in his favor.

Always in his favor.

But not with her.

The dreams had tormented him for months be-fore he found a name to connect to the face. Victoria Hamilton. Lady, as in daughter *of*, because he wouldn't be lucky enough to dream of an aging widow. A chimney sweep. A seamstress. Someone of the same social standing as a mind-reading byblow of a viscount.

The lady currently stood by the terrace doors should she feel the need to flee, which happened on occasion, candlelight sparking off a gown so glacial he felt the chill from across the room. She had a glass in her hand but hadn't imbibed enough of whatever it contained to affect her, as she possessed the vigi-lant attentiveness of a thief.

Finn recognized this instantly as he'd once been a proficient thief himself.

He sipped and watched Lady Hamilton wiggle from the hold of an inebriated baron. Finn tilted his head; no, maybe a marquess. Though he cared little, he did lament the nip, slight but existent, that had him clenching his tumbler when the baron/marquess reached for her as she edged away, an unsteady, quaking grab. Finn's cock did enough of a shift in his fine woolen trousers to have him peeling out of his slouch against the pillar. What could he say? Troublesome women fascinated him. The only woman he'd ever loved, his sister-in-law Piper, was more than a handful and always would be.

He was much accustomed to feminine rebelliousness invading his life.

Lady Hamilton's defiance seemed insignificant on the surface—stolen kisses; midnight fountain dips; ballroom floors covered in glass, a diversion he'd created to give her time to remove herself from an unfortunate situation with a debauched heir to an earldom.

Insignificant, when the stuff of Finn's dreams was not.

In truth, the turmoil surrounding the lady captivated him. In his darkened midnight and outside it.

Perhaps he was lonely. Bored. Angry. Guilty. Emotions urging him to embrace chaos in a way he'd never felt the need to before.

Chaos. Which, in lethal tones of late, Julian claimed Finn was addicted to.

The thought of his brother slipped a forlorn cloak over Finn's mood. Humphrey, another brother of sorts, would be even more cross with him. They were allowed. It had been months since he'd been home, ignoring pleas from a family worried, and with just cause. Months spent trying to forgive himself for misjudging a situation and costing a boy his life. A boy who'd come to the League, Julian's community of supernatural outcasts, with the same challenge—saddled with a gift he couldn't control.

Finn shoved his hand deep in his pocket to keep from reaching for the scar on his chest, a throbbing reminder of his failure.

Failure that had injected fear in his veins for the first time since Julian and Humphrey dragged him from that filthy hovel all those years ago. Made him stumble when he'd previously sauntered. Revealed a man struggling to hide his true self under layers of sickening but accomplished charm, a convoluted package he couldn't take home to Harbingdon just yet. When someone loved you, they noticed things you tried to conceal. At least *his* family did. Julian, Humphrey, Piper...

They would see how bloody damaged he was, straight off.

As if on cue, Lady Hamilton gave the baron/marquess a jaunty half-wave and backed through the terrace doors. Finn smiled, lips curving against crystal, snagging the interest of Countess Ronson, who paused next to him with a wink. Although Finn warmly recalled her *very* talented mouth, he was already on the move, his focus solely on his prey. The crowd's hushed attention hammered him as he worked his way across the ballroom and out the terrace doors. A high-born bastard, he was considered acceptable entertainment, an appealing party favor.

The woman he chased seemed indifferent to him, however, having never once cast a look his way. Which was not the norm, he admitted with absolutely no pleasure. In any case, her disinterest made it easier to track her because she never looked back. That, and a gown the color of the hibiscus bush that bloomed beneath his bedchamber window at Harbingdon each spring. Would be blooming now, in fact. The hue glowed like a beacon, pulling him along in its silken grip.

The season was ending. It was time to retire to the country, to go *home*. The smell of cut grass and turned earth and pine sap flowed from his memory to his heart. He palmed his aching chest as he trailed Lady Hamilton around the corner of the townhouse, her gown flaring like a wisp of smoke behind her. Her scent, piquant, spicy, close to cinnamon but *not*, suffused the air, eroding the lingering note of cheroots, bergamot, and the moist promise of rain.

Mocking his endeavor, the storm chose that moment to announce itself with a soggy release that had everyone scattering, shrieking, through the terrace doors and back into the ballroom.

Not his lady, however.

Without hesitating, she slipped through a darkened servant's entrance and into the private quarters of the house. *Hell and damnation*, he thought and followed, the smell of hearth fires, boiled cabbage, and mold sucking him into a narrow, uninviting service hallway. He hoped to avoid another rescue, especially as the damsel was unaware of his chivalry.

Traversing the deserted bowels of the house, that wisp of pale indigo silk was his guide. Halting before the room she'd disappeared into, Finn nudged the door wide. Gas sconces spilled light across the faded Axminster rug and revealed Lady Hamilton, thumbing through ledgers scattered across the imposing desk centering the room, her back to him, unaware.

He corrected his assessment, no passable thief, this one. Just an impulsive girl in the midst of calamity. Tossed into his world for no reason he could fathom.

But he would take the time to find out.

A book lay in his path, and he'd just enough brandy to take the edge off his balance. It went skidding into the wall with a thump. If he were back in the rookery, he'd be dead after tracking anyone this badly. He'd gotten rusty, lazy because larceny was only for sport now.

When she turned, his breath seized. Amber light fell in a tantalizing waterfall over a body drenched from the squall. Sodden silk clinging to each subtle curve, she exuded tempestuous beauty, an incomprehensible expression, and not *one* thought he could capture. Slim as a reed, and *tall*. More so than he'd judged from their chance encounter on St. James. Almost able, with a searching tilt of her head, a nudge to spectacles he'd never seen her wear before, to look him in the eye. Which, because he was feebly constructed, made him wonder what it would be like to take her while standing, with less concern over the always-present difference in height.

Pushing the suggestive thought from his mind, he moved a step closer, but let his arms fall out in supplication. *Friend, not foe.* At least he thought this was the case. His dreams hadn't been completely clear on this point. "Searching for something?"

Adding additional appeal, curls the color of warmed honey had escaped her damp coiffure to gently frame her face. Light bounced off her lenses, drops of rain dusting the glass until he marveled she could see through them. He was impressed, he had to admit, by her calm acceptance of the intrusion. "I'm snooping since you barged in and asked," she finally said. Her gloved hand flexed once where it lay on the desk, her only nervous tell.

"Dangerous business. Anyone could come along." Finn brushed lint from his sleeve in what had become a habitual show of insouciance he wished he could jettison from his behaviors. "I wasn't trying very hard to conceal."

"Obviously," she murmured with a look thrown to the book sitting topsy-turvy in the corner. Then she returned to her task as if he'd not come upon her sorting through Baron Samuelson's correspondence. His gaze tumbled from her neck to her waist as she shifted, and he was no poet, but she reminded him of a sleek, meticulously crafted vase, delicate and tenderly rounded. Minute etchings waiting to be discovered if one inspected carefully. A crack, perhaps, to keep things interesting. Flaws you could run your fingers, your lips, and tongue over and settle in for the night.

At the continued silence, she lobbed a pointed glance his way. She had a mysterious look to her with the dark hair and eyes, until she appeared, except for the exquisite gown, like an urchin who'd stumbled in from a part of London she'd likely never even seen. He watched, mildly disappointed but not surprised, as she underestimated him with one painstakingly candid perusal, her decision rendered by the time she hit his polished Wellingtons.

Harmless rake who'd sought her out for the usual reasons.

A perfectly acceptable verdict about Finn Alexander, bed-hopping byblow of a deceased viscount. A role he'd perfected until even *he* was unable to separate fact from fiction. Which was noteworthy as his persona was a figment of his not-actually-blood-brother Julian's rather creative imagination. Julian's desire to protect Finn at all costs.

"Blue, since you're here, you can assist," she instructed and slapped a stack of correspondence in his hand. "We're looking for anything from my father, the Earl of Hanschel, or Baron Rossby, my intended."

He glanced at the letters, intrigued despite himself. *Blue.* So she knew who he was. Short for the Blue Bastard. Senseless, the nickname, but what could one do? He'd once been discomfited by his eyes, his looks because they seemed to halt people, not only women, in their tracks. Attractiveness that had made him somewhat infamous in the ton. Along the way, nonetheless, he'd found ways to use it. "I'm doing this, why?" he asked and slanted the envelopes into the light for better viewing.

She sighed through her nose, charm personified. "Would *you* want to marry Baron Rossby?"

"Quite right," he agreed and dug through the stack. The baron was a toad with alleged tendencies one did not discuss in polite company. Not at all a good match for this gorgeous hellion.

Finn considered asking for more detail about this investigation as he replaced the letters and circled the desk, dropping to his haunches to loot the drawers. He had no compunction, absolutely none, about robbing the man hosting this tedious soiree blind. Much of his moral fiber had been beaten out with fists, sticks, and the blunt end of a pistol before Julian and Humphrey saved him when he was little more than a five-stone lad. They'd gotten there too late to polish every rough surface. Rugby, and the later years at Oxford, hadn't *quite* killed the filching, wrathful ruffian inside him.

A foreign emotion, one he couldn't for the life of him place, crowded him as he glanced up to find Victoria Hamilton tangling with the baron's files, tongue peeking between her lips, her focus one of complete and utter resolve. He'd witnessed a disturbing episode with her father at the Marshton ball two months prior and assumed the knife pressed to her back was paternally placed.

Familial weapons were, after all, the trickiest to disengage.

"There's nothing here but promissory notes. Letters of debt." She tossed a scrap of foolscap to the desk with an oath he was surprised she knew. "Threats from creditors. Similar to my father's correspondence because, yes, I searched those as well. Samuelson introduced my father to Rossby, put the idea in his head for the marriage, I suspect. I don't know what they hold over each other, but I'd hoped to find something. A way to negotiate myself out of an unwelcome entanglement. Provide another solution, gain an element of control when I have none. If it's a liability, who is it owed to? And how much? I'm desperate, as you can see. Or rather, my father had placed his desperation on my shoulders." She sighed and blew a wisp of hair from her cheek. "Why I'm telling a virtual stranger this, I can't say. Perhaps I'm going the way of my great Aunt Hermione, who began her journey to Bedlam by talking to herself."

"Samuelson's up to his neck at the gaming hell, hence my invitation this evening. Keep your enemies close, as the saying goes. As if a glass of champagne and a puff pastry will keep me from his doorstep if I need to be there."

Interest, the first she'd ever directed his way, coated him like a ray of sunshine, the pleasure he felt proving he was an idiot. "So you do own it? The Blue Moon. The rumors—"

"A gift from my brother, Julian Alexander, Viscount Beauchamp. The rumors"—he dipped his head, hair sliding over his eyes and hiding anything he might want to conceal as his betting face, unbelievably, was not impenetrable—"I likely earned by honest means."

Curiosity raced across Lady Hamilton's delicate

features as she recorded the emotions he couldn't control crossing his, her hands squeezing the life from the sheet of parchment she held. In the end, she let it go, curiosity and parchment, society miss conquering sticky-fingered termagant. Finn felt a smile crack the solid set of his cheeks, a rare occurrence these days. Disconcerted, he took a breath that was all her, exotic but agreeable, a fragrance to fall into, when every verbena-scented bosom in the ballroom pushed one away. "Maybe you're wasting your time looking for a reason for the proposal. Maybe the baron simply wants *you.*"

"Oh, he does want me." She hesitated, her cheeks losing color in sluggish degrees. "My brother's gone. Almost ten months. I'm the only remaining asset not milked to the bone, and without a financially rewarding marriage, my father will be in debtors' prison before year's end. Or so he tells me. Heavens, what would some passionate fumbling in the dark add to *that* equation?" She exhaled on a gust, her chest rising and falling, and he couldn't help but track the movement.

Fumbling in the dark, indeed.

"Rash and reckless female. Unappreciative, puerile. I can read your thoughts," she said, slightly breathless as she uttered it at the close of the next exhalation.

But I can't read yours, he marveled with astonishment and not a little apprehension.

She palmed the desk, leaning down until he noted a tiny freckle on her cheek, as tempting a topping as a cherry on a cupcake. The urge to rest his thumb there, draw her close and roll the dice, was palpable.

The fierce shot of yearning was unexpected. Unwanted, truthfully. Her eyes, he noted at this distance, because he couldn't *not*, weren't brown at all but a deep, deep green. The color of lake bottoms and forest floors, nothing spring-like or effervescent.

Like his, nothing easy to forget.

"I've been thinking," she whispered after a charged pause.

From his position crouching on the floor, he gazed up at her, keeping his smile in place because it's what Finn Alexander did, but he could only think, *please don't.*

"You were standing by the drink cart at Braswell's dinner party when the glasses went down like a pyrotechnist's display. Affording me a handy escape from unwelcome mischief." She deflected, brushing at her own bit of sleeve-lint. "Strange that. Although it *was* entertaining to watch the Countess fling herself at you to avoid the shards."

Finn paused, hand buried in the baron's erotic curiosity drawer, if the contents—a garter with a dangling rosette, a scrap of pink lace, one aromatic stocking, and a scandalous daguerreotype, Finn turned it upright, of an actress currently housed at the Adelphi—were any indication. Two things occurred to him in rushed succession.

One, Victoria Hamilton *had* noticed him—although the accompanying dart of gratification had him shoving to his feet in exasperation with himself over the *need.*

Two, he was out of practice. At talking. To women. Using his brain, that is. He had loads of experience with conversations governed entirely by his cock.

Finn scrubbed his hand over the back of his neck, emotion simmering beneath the surface. Desire was misplaced in this godforsaken townhouse in a soot-soaked city he had no wish to inhabit. And he didn't believe in premonition. Though he'd never, not *once,* dreamed of anyone unconnected to the League. Anyone who wasn't, at some point, in danger.

He hated mysteries, was not a problem-solver.

He liked *facts*. Handed to him via nefarious means. Like reading minds.

His weeks of surveillance had taught him one thing: Victoria Hamilton was a nuisance. Truthfully, this whole caper was *bollocks*. But as much as he longed to, he couldn't remove himself. Not when he was dreaming about her. *Bloody hell*. He braced his hands on the desk, completely out of sorts, a headache beginning to pulse in his temples.

"Welcome to the party."

He glanced up to find her crimping her plump, darker-than-rose lips to contain what could only be a smile. He straightened to his full height, usually a lucrative intimidation tactic, questioning what she found so amusing. "*What?*"

She lifted a slim shoulder beneath ice-blue silk. "This is the first time I've seen you look like anything aside from frosting set to top a cake."

He tossed the baron's garter to the floor and slid his hands along the desk until they rested next to hers. In an inspired show of courage, she issued a measured blink behind spectacle glass but didn't move so much as a pinkie. A gust blew through the open window, sending the scent of coal ash between them and a strand of hair from her limp chignon against his cheek. Their gazes locked as muted gaslight buffed the tips of her hair amber and gold, a kaleidoscope coloring the potent awareness claiming his mind, his body.

The shift was noticeable, to him at least, that rough tumble into a deep green sea.

Something, *some damn thing* about this woman simply made his heart stutter.

She was reaching, and he was acquiescing, his lashes lowering to hide his desire when he felt the touch. Modest pressure as she wrapped her fingers around his wrist, her thumb seeking his racing pulse. A tiny shock hit his senses, not altogether pleasant, and for one moment, he lost thought. Then everything came rushing back like an enraged tide whipping the shore.

A struggle as he *dragged* it back.

"What did you just do?" he asked hoarsely and grasped her arm as she tried to scoot away. With a muttered oath, he was around the desk in two strides, his thoughts still bouncing off one another in a scramble to right themselves.

She turned her head when he reached her, chin digging into her shoulder, presenting the delicate curl of an ear he would like nothing better than to torture with his tongue and teeth until he had her on her knees.

"I ask again, Lady Hamilton, what *was* that?"

She hesitated with another press of those astounding lips, thinking through her story. *Oh, no.* His sister-in-law, Piper, had provided far too much experience in dealing with duplicitous women for this one to get away with anything. "A parlor trick," she finally said and traced the toe of her slipper along a silver thread in the carpet, avoiding his gaze. "Just this little"—she flicked her fingers in the air, a whimsical, inane gesture—"hidden talent."

He cupped her cheek, tilting her face into the light, that delectable freckle winking at him. Now menacing instead of charming. *Gorgeous goddamned trouble.* "What usually happens when you unleash this trick?"

He thought she wasn't going to answer, then she

whispered, so low he had to crowd in to hear her, "People forget."

Like gossamer, a scene from one of his dreams floated into his mind: her fingers slipping around his wrist followed by a smooth fade to black, a door clicking shut on a lampless room.

He stole thoughts, but she *erased* them.

"It's nothing," she stressed and wrenched from his hold with a stumbling step.

He let her go but held her gaze.

He'd wanted answers. Well, now, he had them.

"You couldn't be more wrong," he said with a weary sigh. "It's everything."

CHAPTER 2

*S*he knew she had a guardian angel.

Or imagined there was *some* benevolent spirit, a deceased relative, Grandmama Cecelia or Cousin Harold, who'd helped her escape quite a few calamities in a stomach-dropping pinch this season. Two occurrences came to mind without much effort behind the examination. Three, if she included the muddle with Lord Kellerson at the Epsom Derby.

She'd simply never guessed her angel was the man reputed to be the most beautiful in all of England.

"Cor, you foolish girl, the Blue Bastard's door you think to knock on," Agnes hissed with a shiver and a sniffle. Her maid's nose ran when she was nervous, something Victoria recognized because Agnes had arrived in her father's household while Victoria was still in nappies.

She'd heard that sniffle *often*.

Victoria ducked her head but, woeful truth, it was hard to hide from a person who'd wiped your bare bottom and witnessed every dreadful decision since.

"Trust me," she whispered. "Just this once."

Agnes snorted. "How many times have I heard that in my life?"

Victoria tugged her collar past her chin until only her eyes were visible. A drunken shout and the shatter of glass on the main thoroughfare had Agnes bumping against her until they were huddled in the gaming hell's side entrance like cornered animals. She felt cornered by Finn Alexander and his blasted presumption. The ridiculous invitation had arrived this morning and was burning a hole through her cloak.

Or maybe the heat was just anger.

She raised her hand, took a breath. Glanced at her feet, her slippers now splattered with grime. Moonlight registered as a slimy wash on the cobblestones beneath them, but just barely, and the smell—

She grimaced behind her gloved hand. No need to inventory the aroma.

A part of London her brougham typically increased speed upon entering for sound reason.

"Go on, girl, or we'll be getting right back in that hack. Paid him threepence to wait on Jermyn, we did." Agnes huffed a clove-scented breath that charged past Victoria's cheek as London's brume swirled and settled around them. "As if a lady of your station should be traveling in a *hired* rig in the *dead* of night to what is just one step up from a slum. Agree with this I did. Daft! My good sense be beat to death by all your shenanigans—"

"Hush, Aggie," Victoria whispered, resisting the urge to send her beloved maid's thoughts on temporary holiday. A swift pinch to her wrist would do the job. Agnes would return unsure of what she'd said. Better yet, of what Victoria had done. Except, after the last debacle, Victoria had promised not to incapacitate her ever again.

Regrettably, her parlor trick hadn't worked the

night before with Finn, a rare episode that had shaken her to her bones, though she'd hidden it well. "I'm not going to knock. I'm going to ring this delightful bell." The newest accessory in the locality, she'd bet, bright copper with nary a dent, it issued a single dull clang when she tapped it. The door opened almost immediately, the hulking porter taking one look at the shivering female package on the doorstep before slamming it shut in their faces.

"He's got the right of it," Agnes muttered.

Victoria dinked the bell again and was making a third attempt when the door reopened.

And there he was.

Out of breath, a miasma of moonlight and fog cocooning him as he leaned into the night, the magnetic eyes that were the talk of London highlighted in the splash. She wanted to deny their exquisiteness, as the man needed admiration like he needed a knock upside his head, however…they were extraordinary upon close study. Azure, cobalt, and as he tilted his head, a frown ripping across his face, *sapphire*. Stormy sunsets, twilight skies, shallow oceans. Eyes to lose oneself in, lose oneself over. As women did daily, tripping on loose stones and wrinkled Axminster, practically falling at his feet.

Victoria had laughed at their foolishness, but now that she found herself pinned by that stunning gaze, declaration, argument, and logical assertion were nowhere in sight. It was senseless. Almost as if she'd turned her parlor trick on herself.

Silent, Finn stared, the affable mien he usually sported replaced by cold determination, until sweat coated the nape of her neck and her knees began to tremble beneath copious layers. Or perhaps it was his lack of clothing heating her up like she'd pressed her back to a hearth. Dressed as informally as any man she'd ever seen, he looked like he'd been roused from bed. Flowing cream linen open at the neck, no waist-coat to conceal the sleek musculature of his chest or place barriers between them as directed, his hair a dark, desolate tangle, his cheeks covered in a light dusting of stubble. A ridiculously looped tie around his neck, the wrinkled ends dangling. Helplessly, she tracked a puckered scar severing the vee of his shirt, the only imperfection she noted on the man.

Patience incarnate, he studied her without moving a hairbreadth while she studied him.

What was he looking for? Dear God, what would he *find*?

He knows, is all she could think. *He knows.*

"I'm not going to yield, Blue," she whispered, a statement she hoped met his ears only. The words were ragged, her mind full of dread, but if she could only touch… *Ah*, a second of insanity as she followed the impulse to trace that angry slash on his chest. And do what after, she had no idea.

"Yield?" Stepping out of reach, he whistled through straight white teeth and tugged her by the braided edge of her cloak into the narrow vestibule. "As if I'd be so lucky."

With a gasp, Agnes shoved herself inside the en-tranceway with them and executed a shaky curtsy, as if to say, *you're not going without me.*

Finn's gaze snagged on the shivering maid, and he suddenly seemed to comprehend the indecency of his attire because he frowned, a dimple lancing his cheek as he glanced down. "Apologies for my casual attire, but you are uninvited—and on my turf." Then he qui-etly shut the door behind them and gestured to a staircase leading into the bowels of the building, as pretty as you please.

Victoria complied, Agnes a clinging vine by her side, as an argument in a gaming hell foyer would benefit no one. She took in everything as unobtrusively as possible, surprised despite herself. The carpet muffling her step was plush, the furnishings stately, not what she would have expected to grace a lower-level gambling establishment. Except for the sounds—the buzz of voices, slurred shouts and raucous laughter, a muted, manageable intrusion—she could almost pretend she was in the belowstairs of her home in Belgravia.

At the top of the staircase, Finn pointed to an open door leaking light into the hallway. Victoria stepped inside, halting so abruptly, Agnes stumbled into her. Pale moonbeams shot across the room, the lustrous wash revealing not a sitting area for visitors but a very personal space. *His* space. Housing a worn leather sofa big enough to seat five, overflowing bookcases, curio-stuffed shelves. A fire blazing in a bricked hearth. She turned a slow circle. Artwork. Rustic landscapes and portraitures covering every wall. Her gaze fixed on a side door. A bedchamber, she assumed, the postulation sending a warm spiral through her belly.

With a soft grunt, Agnes gave her a nudge as they were backed up in the entryway like carriages on Bond Street.

His fragrance immediately overtook her senses as she moved further into the study: leather, cardamom, ink, *man*.

While she tried to establish the most proper place in the room to settle, he strode to a narrow sideboard set against the far wall, elegance personified. An exceptional skill for a man of such breadth and height to move like a panther and look so adept while doing it. "Tea?" he asked and brushed his fingertip across a teapot to test its heat, as if she'd dropped her card with the majordomo and all was right in the world. As if they were preparing to discuss the upcoming regalia or the new apothecary on Pall Mall. "I fear it's cold. Guests were not expected." He glanced over his shoulder, one of the many smiles he held in reserve curling his lips.

She was coming to doubt the sincerity of those smiles, a hint of self-mockery bleeding through hadn't been evident before.

The realization was both intriguing and startling.

Stilling, he puffed his cheeks, shook his head. "On second thought, something stronger." He reached for a bottle and whispered, "For your long-suffering companion if no one else."

Oh, the nerve, Victoria seethed, hoping he'd catch her eye so she could throw a perfectly placed, acerbic dart. Although she had no idea what *that* might be, so thank God, he ignored her. Agnes—who'd scurried to a dark corner to hide, the seamed tip of a brown slipper all that was visible—was long-suffering. Everyone would agree.

But how impolite to mention it.

Tray in hand, he paused before her, his pene-trating attention issuing a challenge. She didn't want him to become a puzzle because no one loved solving a puzzle more. However, the varied pieces of him didn't quite fit. His expression, for one—irritation and concern. Her beloved brother's gaze had often held those warring factions. But Charles had cared about her, loved her when this enigmatic man was a stranger.

As expected, the thought of her brother unleashed a coil of torment and the prick of tears.

Swallowing hard, she raised her chin and took a

glass from the tray, the ample sip in response to Finn's nebulous dare sending a screaming fire down her throat. As she coughed behind her gloved fist, he slouched into an oversized blood-red armchair, extending his long legs until his heels brushed the lace edge of her skirt. What a portrait he made sitting there, lids lowered, clothing impeccably awry, glass dangling from slim fingers better suited to a sculptor, a relaxed state of masculine dishabille as accomplished as the art gracing his walls. The Blue Bastard on display. The man women came to fisticuffs over. At the opera recently, in fact.

Drinking him in from head to toe, she could see why.

However, behind the beauty, his solemn expression held nothing of the frivolous rogue. Maybe no one, not even while he towered over them in bed, had taken the time to really *look* at the man.

She loathed, absolutely loathed, that she suspected there was more.

Victoria liked nothing less than being outmaneuvered.

Placing the glass on the table, she reached beneath her knitted wool cloak. His alert gaze followed. Drawing the envelope forth, she tapped it once against crystal. "Unlike the colonel's wife, I brandish no pistol."

Finn took a leisurely sip and eyed her over the rim, firelight etching inky slashes beneath his cheeks. "Fortunately, she was a terrible shot." Dipping his head, his hair slicked over his brow. It was long, perhaps longer than any man's in the ton, although he was two steps outside society and the rules imposed. A surprising slash of gray near his temple spoke of wisdom she wasn't sure he'd earned.

Feeling the familiar rebelliousness rise within her, she yearned to fist her fingers in his dark strands and chase that impudent smirk from his face. Press her lips to his and erase it that way, no parlor trick involved.

She was quite good at erasing intent with kisses.

Flustered by the fantasy, she hurled the envelope at the jaded man across from her. It bounced off his open collar, drawing her eyes to the trail of hair snaking inside his shirt. She watched the cream vellum tumble to his lap, disliking herself and him. She would be *damned* if she fell in line behind half of London, waiting for the opportunity to do anything with or to Finn Alexander. "What is the meaning of this? An invitation to a summer house party at your brother's Oxfordshire estate?"

Employing the insouciance he was known for, Finn set his glass aside and picked up the envelope, spinning it between his hands like a child's top. "What would you like to be the meaning?"

She slid to the edge of the sofa until they sat close enough to drink in each other's scent, hear each other's rapidly-drawn breaths. His pupils expanded, the dusky ring leaching into indigo. *Not as calm as he appeared.* Because she was spiteful on occasion, his tension pleased her. "You didn't ask me at Samuelson's, as you could have. Instead, Viscountess Beauchamp directs the communication to my mother, a woman known to take tactless interest in all things society. With a minor"—she traced a nick in the table and glanced at him through her lashes—"addendum mentioning the Duke of Ashcroft's possible presence."

"God knows I don't make the rules." Finn sent the invitation skating across the table and against her hand. "But duke trumps baron any day of the week. Although we don't know what your beloved Rossby holds over your family. Perhaps nothing more than funds…and your dear father's wish to avoid a dank cell in debtor's prison. Money does tend to speak loudly and force hands. But we can find out."

Victoria popped off the sofa, then settled back with a huff. "This is madness. I have no baron. I simply signed an unwelcome, seemingly unavoidable betrothal agreement. And, yes, I would like to know why my father is indebted. But other than this, no one is *concerned* with me. Truly, not even my own family. I'm like one of the paintings lining these walls. An object. A duke showing interest, a man I've never met, is entirely implausible. If there's a reason for this"—she tapped her knuckle on the envelope— "I want to know what it is. Not this balderdash about supporting my marital pursuits."

His pupils expanded again, and she filed the tidbit. Amazingly, Finn Alexander, gambler extraordinaire, lover of women and mischief, was not wholly indecipherable. Cracks were showing in his façade.

There was a reason for the offer; he just didn't feel she needed to know it.

"I've never been introduced to your sister-in-law, a woman who welcomed me to her country home with such exuberance. Odd that."

"I forged the note. Piper will learn about the house party when we crawl out of the carriage at Harbingdon. Unless I get word to them first." He polished off his drink, did a stretch that brought his bootheel atop her skirt. A subtle trap. "The duke part is true, by the by. Ashcroft's looking for a wife for all I know—and he's often at Harbingdon. You certainly won't be more aggravation than he's encountered previously. What's the latest tattle? An opera singer, isn't it? His romantic entanglements are…untidy. But so is his life." Left unsaid: *mine is not.*

"Impossible. My mother will be otherwise occupied in Scotland and—"

"She sent a note of acceptance to my family's Mayfair home this morning. I believe your maid"—he nodded to Agnes—"was stated as joyfully accompanying in her stead. Almost a second mother to you or some such rot. The package is, shall we say, wrapped. Unless you'd like to go to the trouble of unwrapping it. Tossing aside a possible dukedom for a barony is the height of insanity, but what does a man of my marginal station know?"

A loud sniffle erupted from the corner, followed by grumbling Victoria thankfully couldn't comprehend.

Victoria jerked her skirt from beneath his heel and tried to concoct a sound rebuttal as the noose tightened around her neck. Her options *were* limited, her family's circumstances desperate, and London held no opportunity for her to stumble upon a better marital prospect as the ton was vacating the sweltering city like rats from a sinking ship. Baron Rossby was simply dreadful, agreed, but most in the ton needed funds flowing in, not flowing out. He was one of the lucky ones who was flush. And she'd not a farthing to her name aside from a modest amount of pin-money she'd been saving. She'd been told she kissed well and—

"Look at the thoughts churning through that exacting brain of yours. It's like watching a waterwheel," he murmured and yawned behind his hand.

Infuriating man, she seethed, and let herself take him in again from brow to boot while his eyes were closed. It should have been illegal to look so attractive without effort.

"Don't tell me it's propriety vexing you," he said after a tense moment with only Agnes's sniffles breaking the silence. "Not after showing up at a no-torious gaming hell's alley door in the wee hours. Conversing with me is even worse. You must know I'm untouchable for someone of your rank and situation."

"Unmarried being my situation. Widows of admirable birth seem to be *very* touchable in your world."

His lips quirked, the barest of smiles. "Will it anger you if I agree?"

She clenched her fist in her skirt. "I don't trust men who look like you."

His smile intensified, sending tantalizing creases from the edges of his eyes. "And I don't trust women with a brain."

"This is why I've seen you everywhere, isn't it? This campaign of yours, Blue, whatever it means. You've been following me. What I want to know is why."

He blinked, his gaze, when it met hers, far from sleepily unaware. Like the time on Regent Street when a cutpurse had robbed her blind, she experienced the sensation of being swindled. Rattled, she resisted the urge to check her pocket for the half crown, the only item of value on her person.

A tiny crinkle settled between his brows. "You noticed me."

She sighed and gave her skirt a yank, two times before releasing it from his dogged boot heel. "I have what is required: a pulse." Wading into his gaze, she prepared for the impact. "Tell me why you've engineered our association, and I'll accept the kind invitation to your family's country manor without dispute."

"You speak like an instructor I had at Rugby. An unforgiving crank." He flexed his fingers on the arm

31

of his chair. "Makes me fear for a ruler striking my knuckles."

She leaped to her feet, finished with his blasted nonchalance, his cavalier teasing. If he was going to tell her nothing, then to hell with him! And to hell with his blasted summons.

Mirroring her, he was up in an instant, his face, his eyes, ablaze. "I'll throw this in the hearth"—he crushed the envelope in his fist—"crisp it to a forgotten memory if your answer to the next question is 'no'. *Dreams*. Have you had them? Unusual, fantastic. If you have, I don't need to elucidate. You'll know."

Startled, she crossed to an escritoire desk shoved in a corner, as if work were a neglected duty. But evidence of effort lay in the open ledgers, books with pages bent to call the reader back to the location, the cloying odor of ink splashed across aged parchment. "I've used my parlor trick twice to make Baron Rossby delay our wedding. I told myself his submission was due to his desire to make me comfortable if not happy, not the pressure I was exerting on his wrist. Pressure that made him lose himself just long enough for me to slip from reach. Confuse him about the date we'd planned, the details of our arrangement. Etcetera." She glanced over her shoulder to find Finn standing in the same spot, watching her, his gaze intent, his famed smile absent.

The pronouncement was finalized right there: he was nothing like the man he presented to the ton.

The surety of the judgment chilled her to her toes.

She turned back to the desk, her gaze falling to a wooden box the size of her palm buried amidst the ledgers. It was lovely, geometric designs circling an escutcheon on the front. Bringing it close to her face —the only way she could read the inlaid script without her spectacles—she immediately located the hinge on the back and the lid popped open. She frowned. Nothing inside.

A floorboard squeaked as he stepped closer. "How did you…?"

"Puzzles are my passion," she answered. "I have a collection of boxes with secret compartments. One almost identical to this." She blinked, trying to decipher the text. "Is this Russian?"

He grimaced and streaked his hand through his hair. "My time at Oxford, before the expulsion, revealed a marginal gift for languages. French, in particular. But I also speak a little German, Russian, and Italian."

"Hmm…." She turned to him, propping her bottom on the desk. Better to face this challenge head-on. Victoria Hamilton was no coward. "Intelligence isn't the first trait you disclose. I can see why. Attractiveness is a reliable prop and presents no compulsion to dig deeper." She tilted her head, felt the internal shift as she placed Finn Alexander in the basement of her brain, where she kept puzzles, people, books she was interested in exploring further.

"It's a skill, posing as someone else. A skill I've worked hard to master. Not inborn, I assure you. Although it's made easy when you're surrounded by people lacking in self-awareness."

Fascinating was all she could think.

His jaw clenched, a muscle in his cheek jumping. "Let's get something straight, my lady. I'm not one of your damned puzzles."

She flipped the puzzle box lid open and shut, open and shut, before returning her gaze to him. "So, I'm to travel to Oxfordshire to summer holiday with a group whose acquaintance I have not previously made, without a rationale behind the invitation presented to me? Sounds delightful." She secured the box with a snap. "I think not."

He stabbed the crumpled envelope against his thigh, and she tried, valiantly, to evade tracking the move. Her heartbeat tripped against her better judgment. "You didn't answer my question. The *rationale*, as it were. Dreams. Have you had any?"

She knew the moment her face betrayed her—as his betrayed him.

Dreams, yes. Inexplicable, vivid, though none she was willing to share.

Not yet.

The flash of dismay that twisted his features had her sinking against the desk. He was across the room before she caught her breath, the invitation arriving in the hearth with a shockingly violent lob. It sizzled and popped, catching fire. The scent of burned vellum circled them as the muted tick of a clock, and Agnes's periodic sniffles rode the silence.

"I can't tell you what I don't know," he whispered, "but at Harbingdon, being there will make everything clear at—"

A soft thump and a giggle behind the closed door to his bedchamber arrested his explanation. He had the good grace, for an all-too-brief second, to look nonplussed. At the very least, his anger trickled out like water from a splintered pail as discomfiture trickled in.

So, he had just crawled from bed, the cad.

Victoria flipped the puzzle box between her hands, this embarrassing insight entirely what she deserved after showing up on the doorstep of a man who'd purportedly leaped from a second-story window to escape a marquess intent on doing him bodily harm for bedding his mistress. Who did he have in there, she wondered with the faintest throb of what she feared was envy.

The clock ticked off a minute, two. She found if she remained silent during a standoff, calm struck worse than words, and her opponent stumbled into a senseless explanation that typically led to her winning the argument.

Alas, there was nothing typical about Finn Alexander.

Halting before her, he took the box and placed it on the desk, his body brushing hers as he shifted. He radiated heat and smelled, *ah*…her nose twitched. Sandalwood and something dark, like chocolate but not quite. A hint of brandy. And ginger. His exhalations a gentle, consistent caress against her cheek, he held her hand for a lingering moment, his thumb sweeping the row of pearl buttons at her wrist. "It's not like I haven't seen you in a compromising position. Or three. Ruined a new coat with the spill I created so you weren't discovered behind that pillar, lips locked to Selby's." He halted over a pearl, and she had the panicked notion he was considering popping it free, seeking bare skin. "I wonder, does your intended know about your penchant for kissing strange men? Or the unhappiness that forces you into such perilous positions?"

She stilled to nothing but breath as he flipped her hand over and continued the caress, this time to her palm, a part of her body she'd had no comprehension of until this moment. Even through kidskin, she burned, awareness fluttering, shooting jolts down her arm and from her fingertips like a moonbeam.

"Victoria," he said very softly and shook his head, sending that tousled hair of his tumbling across his brow. "Victorias don't cause unbelievable amounts of trouble and glare at you like a boxer stepping in the ring. Tori has a nice hum to it. Toris are, conversely, quick-witted, surrounded by mayhem, and utterly enigmatic. A more interesting, if impudent, set. My choice, as it were."

She grunted, then wished she could call it back when his smile bolstered around the edges. What he preferred was a giggling bundle waiting behind a sealed bedchamber door. *Tori?* How common. She recalled a shopgirl in Haymarket who called herself thus. Her mother would loathe it. *Vulgar,* Victoria could just hear her say. The dart of pleasure that raced through her as she imagined that was absurd but unmistakable.

"I like the one you've chosen for me," he added. "Quite succinct and leaves off the insulting second morsel the ton loves to emphasize."

Blue. Yes, she had called him that. Twice, as she recollected. She yanked at her hand, deciding she wasn't the only quick-witted one. "I must tell you, I preferred the reprobate."

"Me, too. He's considerably easier to live with." Finn laughed, releasing her hand and taking the appropriate step back. "Never fear us finding common ground, Tori. I have a rainbow of secrets, one in every color. There must be crossover somewhere. You simply have to decide to share yours with me in return."

The moment drew out, suspended, an irretrievable step into a world, a part of herself, she had long denied. "Secrets bind us, meaning I should trust you because of them? Because you know about my parlor trick?"

Those arresting eyes of his sliced up, pinning her where she stood. "*No,* oh, no. Secrets are a chasm, a breach to cross. A complication. The parlor trick is why you belong in my world, which makes sense now that I know about your gift." His throat muscles rippled as he swallowed, drawing her gaze to the provocative sliver of skin exposed by his open collar. "I thought you understood. You should trust me because of the dreams."

She tripped into his gaze as the night closed in, sealing her in a hushed space where her pulse drummed, her breath caught, and this impossible, appealing man sought to lead her somewhere she wasn't sure she wanted to go. Sinking back, she grasped the edge of the desk and squeezed until her fingers throbbed.

"Mine have been full of you for months until I'm compelled, most earnestly, to ask you to give me time —at Harbingdon—to figure out why. My dreams, I will tell you from experience, *mean* something."

She palmed her stomach, her pulse jumping through layers of cloth to bump against her fingertips. Her dreams were surprisingly informative, particulars he might not want to accept once she exposed them. "If I go…"

"Enlightenment." He cocked his head, thoughtful, then entertained, she could see by the turn of his lips. A contained bit of theatrics. "About some things, in any case."

"Your secrets," she whispered, having no idea why this is what she said when there were so many questions she could have asked. Should have asked. Oh, she was as foolish as the rest of the flock when he'd stated in definite terms he wasn't one of her puzzles. But the extreme paradox of Finn Alexander—intelligence hidden behind astounding splendor hidden behind a gaze laden with contradictions—persuaded in a way she couldn't deny.

He stilled, shooting her a sidelong glance, the insinuation nothing her mind could determine, but her body...*betrayer*, warmed until she felt her cheeks sting, the skin beneath her bodice dampen. "Perhaps a trade will someday make itself known. My confidences in exchange for yours." He shrugged a wide shoulder beneath wrinkled linen. "Like the Rossby conundrum, there could be worse arrangements."

Curiosity drilled her to the bone. The one aspect of her personality that held sway above the pragmatism hammered into any aristocratic female from the time they were in leading strings. She was an inquisitive woman in an era when inquisitive women were neither appreciated nor admired.

He'd either made a grave error in judgment or a fantastically intelligent one by hooking her as nothing else could, presenting himself and this trip to his family's country estate as a mystery.

She knew little about him, while he'd directed her to reveal much about herself.

He knew about her parlor trick, the reckless kisses behind pillars, the dreaded engagement, her family's finances. With a sinking feeling, she realized she'd done the opposite of what she'd been coached to do, disclosing graceless personal information in uncouth fashion, while the man standing across from her, a byblow accepted because his brother, Viscount Beauchamp, demanded it, sailed his ship through treacherous waters with nary a tremor. Adroitly managing an assemblage set to gut him should he turn his back on them.

She threw a glance at his bedchamber door. Attraction wasn't the reason he'd been following her, which had been senseless to imagine for one *moment* as the line of women volunteering for the job stretched from here to Westminster.

He tipped her chin with a long, slim finger until her eyes met his. "Nothing sordid is connected to this invitation. You'll be under Julian and Piper's protection the entire time. Under *my* protection, should you be able to place value on it."

She drew back from his touch and lied without hesitation, "I never imagined it did."

"Consider this. Perhaps I can help you decipher your parlor trick. As a friend."

She felt her brow pinch. *Friend?*

His deep laughter brought her out of her deliberation. "It's possible, Tori. Or so I've been told."

"I've never had many friends. My brother, I suppose, but…"

His expression shifted, softening around the edges. "They're nice to have. Especially for those of us with, for lack of a more precise designation, interesting quirks to our persona. This sojourn provides the added benefit of a duke in residence, should he be entertaining the appalling notion of matrimony. At the very least, a country gathering with such esteemed members of society will be a boon for you rather than a set down. My participation omitted, of course. Or at least not emphasized any more than it need be."

Finn continued to watch her in his lazily penetrating way, as a violent gust shook the windowpanes and sent the hearth fire snapping. He didn't press, corner, or urge, giving her time to make her decision, a blessing no one had previously bestowed on her. In her world, freedom and friendship were almost nonexistent.

Maybe he could answer some of the questions about her *quirk*. And introduction to a duke in need of a wife was never wasted effort, she supposed. Her mother would undoubtedly agree to delaying the dreaded wedding to Rossby with such an opportunity having landed in their laps. More time to figure out another solution to her family's dilemma.

As she stood there mulling the invitation, Victoria knew she'd accept.

Although her foolhardy fascination with solving the mystery of the Blue Bastard surely meant she shouldn't.

CHAPTER 3

*V*ictoria peered from the window of the aging post-chaise as it settled with a squeal before the Beauchamp country estate, a sprawling chalk-brick manor surrounded by breathtaking lawns and miles of vast woodland that seemed to separate it from the rest of the world. Summer arrived differently here than it did in the city, and her gaze followed the scent of gardenias, roses, and daffodils to the blooming thicket lining the pebbled drive.

The estate was lovelier than she'd imagined, and imagination was crucial as she and Agnes had been given scarce information, aside from periodic updates on time of arrival from the footman seated on the outside bench. Surprisingly, her host had acted as subordinate postillion since they'd left the Cock and Bull—the quaint inn sitting midway between London, where they'd stopped to refresh themselves and change horses—managing the equine team with poise born from experience and following the shouted orders of the lead-boy with nothing more than amused replies. She'd never known a nobleman, or one close to it, to take orders from a servant.

Finn Alexander seemed to have no care for how others viewed him.

Or, she'd never witnessed a man being his true self.

Puzzle book forgotten on her lap, Victoria tracked a dirty streak on the window with her pencil and studied him as he alighted from his mount with all the elegance he was known for. Dusting his breeches and tugging at his sleeves, he ran his hand through his hair, seeming to prepare for inspection. One he would pass.

Unlike the night she'd ambushed him in his quarters, Finn looked the part of the patrician gentleman in shades of gray and black, sedate traveling attire, assuredly, but fit by the best tailor in London if she had her guess. An expert cut rounding out what was a singularly lean yet muscular figure, no padding required, unlike most of the men of her acquaintance. Sidestepping the whinnying mare, light burst from a crimson and teal sunset to streak across him, lighting the tips of his midnight-black hair like they'd been dipped in cinnamon. And those eyes, oh, they matched the brilliant blue sky to perfection.

Turning, he captured her gaze. She shifted, intent on breaking the contact, then tapped her pencil against the glass pane and thought, *I'm going to look all I like.*

Served him right for insisting on this expedition.

His chin dropped as delight roared across his face, glorious to behold even as she felt a pinch of irritation that he seemed to understand her in a way few ever had. She didn't know what to make of the man—and had spent a bewildering amount of time since their vexing encounter in the gaming hell trying to. For one, those smiles he unleashed, easily and so often. She'd no frame of reference to account for them.

Her father was aloof, irritable really with the gout and stomach condition, his taciturn nature her example of how men conducted, well, the business of *life*.

A business involving modest affection, stern lectures, and harsh commands. She couldn't recall her father hugging her. Not once. Or expressing love.

Consequently, when a crowd of people erupted from the manor to encircle Finn, Victoria's disorientation intensified. There were kisses and shouts, embraces and shoulder slaps. Not every family functioned like hers, it appeared, and she suddenly wondered how much she'd missed.

Wondered if ice encased her like it did her parents, never to be cracked or melted.

After all, she'd been formed by glaciers.

The snap of the step being forced into place shook the carriage and pulled her from her musing. She nudged Agnes from sleep and moved to exit when the door swung wide, and a footman's arm shot into the interior. A deep inhalation to calm her nerves, then she took the gloved hand and stepped into another world.

Finn Alexander's world.

The footman escorted her to the boisterous group gathered on the emerald-green lawn as if this was where she belonged. When she felt a solitary star, orbiting but unseen. No one of value, certainly no one who'd ever received a reception like this upon returning home. Why they were *emotional*. A woman Victoria assumed was Lady Beauchamp was clinging to Finn and dashing tears from her eyes. A tiny thing, head barely reaching his elbow, belly round with pregnancy, her grip on his arm fierce, as if she feared he'd disappear at any moment. A young man with a rather startling bruise on his cheek elbowed his way into the cluster, and Finn started, tipping the boy's face high and saying something urgent which the wind swept away before she could catch it—a very paternal display both men seemed comfortable with.

The crowd parted as a man she recognized as Viscount Beauchamp strode from the house, the ends of an open waistcoat batting his hips, streaks of what Victoria thought was paint smearing his sleeve. He halted before Finn, and they stared, lost in tense reticence. She'd seen them in a heated discussion at a racing event the season prior—easy to locate the tallest men in the room—and noted the affection flowing between them even during a disagreement. They made no apologies for their relationship, their unwavering connection, or the regrettable circumstances of Finn's birth. Indeed, the bond between them was legendary when most siblings in the ton barely tolerated each other.

Victoria clenched her fingers around her puzzle book. She and her brother had loved like that once, too. As if taking stage direction in a play, Agnes alighted from the carriage and bumped against her just as things got interesting, knocking her behind the group.

"I'm surprised you remembered the way," Julian Alexander finally murmured, his gaze never leaving his brother.

It was then Victoria realized the viscount was furious and not a little bit. His hands, also covered in specks of paint, flexed at his side as he took a rushed step forward. The viscountess moved between the men, a protector in miniature. Not surprising as her reputation was also legendary. Rescued from one scrape after another until Julian finally married her— a rumored love match—and from the tender look he sent her as he released a pent exhalation, it appeared

44

THE RAKE IS TAKEN

the rumor was true. The crowd of servants surrounding them, sensing discourse, dispersed with
quiet haste.

Finn's grin collapsed, completely wilting as he
watched his celebration evaporate like fog beneath a
brilliant sun. "We're going to do this on the drive,
Jule?"

Julian shook off his wife's hold and stabbed a
paint-tipped finger at Finn. "No, we're going to do it
in my study. Ten minutes, boy-o." Then he stalked
back the way he'd come, the front door slamming behind him. He never glanced her way, impolite but
captivating. And perfectly understandable. Finn
hadn't alerted his family to the theoretical house
party, and for all Victoria knew, he dragged women
of varying degrees of respectability to his brother's
country estate with unfailing regularity.

From the corner of her eye, she watched Finn
palm his brow with a pained expression.

Lady Beauchamp sighed and reached for his hand.
"Too many thoughts sliding into that nimble brain of
yours? I'm sorry the entire household felt the need to
swarm you, but it's been so long. I hadn't
considered—"

"It's not that, not right now," he interrupted with a
glance cast Victoria's way. "You said the children
were improving his mood, Piper. With one in nappies and another on the way, how can he still be so
damned controlling?" Finn ripped his hat from his
head and whipped it against his thigh. "Has he forgotten I'm a grown man?"

The boy with the bruised face snorted as he
flipped a farthing between his fingers, around and
back, in and out, much better than the illusionist at
Lady Calbert's vapid tea party. "Good one, boy-o."
The coin caught a glint of sunlight and sent it ca-

reening off a silver button on his waistcoat. "Viscount Beauchamp not controlling. That would be quite a feat."

Glancing curiously at Victoria, Piper sent her elbow into the boy's ribs. "Simon, *inside*. There'll be time for a reunion after dinner. We have visitors. Can you alert Cook, please?" As he ambled off with a sullen salute, she turned back to Finn. "Misguided angel who hasn't been home in months, let me explain your brother's exasperation. After the incident at Harbingdon last year and your accident just after—"

Finn squeezed Piper's hand—*stop, no*—then aimed a pointed look at Victoria, who was recording everything, saddened they'd noticed her, absorbed to the tips of her toes. Handholding, hugging, door slamming. This was better than the pedestrian play she'd seen last month on Drury Lane, better than any silly illusionist. *My.*

Finn frowned. "Not a riddle, Lady Hamilton. Remember?"

"That's what I brought this for." Victoria tapped her puzzle book against her hip, ignoring Agnes's loud sniffle. "However, do I look the type to ignore entertainment when presented?"

He grunted and glanced at the house, his gaze landing on a lower window she'd bet housed Julian Alexander's study. He looked torn in two, hopeful and anxious, so boyishly uncertain her heart lurched.

"Go on, Blue," she said, deciding to make it easier on him. Just this one time. "Go argue with your brother. Agnes and I will muddle along."

He did one of those needless tugs on his waistcoat she was coming to realize meant he was struggling to gain control of a situation. Because he was perfectly pressed, as usual. "You have this, Piper? I'll explain more later," he said vaguely, his attention having again traveled to that lower window.

"This," Victoria whispered as he stalked away without a backward glance. Now she was a *this*. Agnes harrumphed, clearly displeased by his insolence.

Lady Beauchamp had the perceptiveness to click her tongue against her teeth in chagrin. "I'm sorry my men are so rude today. Not unusual for Julian, I'm afraid, but I've never known Finn to be discourteous. Charm usually coats him like butter does toast. I can only say my husband has the power to scramble anyone's designs with that quelling stare of his." She stuck out her hand and laughed when Victoria stared at it, nonplussed. "I'm American. The incorrigible half anyway, which I'm sure you've heard. My official title is Viscountess Beauchamp, but everyone who counts calls me Piper."

Victoria took Piper's proffered hand, instantly liking the might behind the strange gesture and the petite woman standing before her. She was not American, but Victoria had been described as incorrigible many, many times. "Lady Victoria Hamilton, pleased to make your acquaintance. My father is the Earl of Hanschel, and Mr. Alexander and I...." She stumbled to a halt. How to explain? Her cheeks lit as she imagined what she was going to do when she got her hands on Finn, leaving her in the mortifying position of having to justify her presence to her hostess! She was going to parlor trick him to the devil, jumble his thoughts but good. Although her first attempt at that hadn't ended well.

Agnes disrupted the awkward moment with the delicacy of a lit torch. "Get your eyes in your head, girl," she said to a kitchen maid who stood with her mouth hanging open after having watched Finn cross the yard and enter the house. "A flibbertigibbet is what she is," she whispered for Piper and Victoria alone.

"My dear," Victoria murmured in agreement, "he needs no more adulation in this lifetime. Don't make a cake of yourself. Too, you're likely to swallow a fly."

Piper wrapped her arm around her rounded tummy and bowed her head in delight as the maid gasped and hurried into the house. "Leave it to dear Finn to bring me such a welcome gift during what is turning out to be a dreadfully horrendous summer of incapacitation. I'm going to like you very much. And you actually shook my hand. That was a test. I've not had anyone accept yet!"

Victoria smiled without comment—because what could she rightfully say when everyone knew you had to agree with expectant mothers on all counts—and followed Piper across the sloping lawn, Agnes trailing at their heels. The reason for the splatters on Julian Alexander's clothing and hands was apparent as soon as the front door closed behind them. The viscount was an artist, and his artwork lined the walls of the foyer and hallway in a scattered arrangement no museum would ever duplicate. It was a colorful explosion that fit the house, and the spitfire viscountess, well.

"These are like the paintings at the Blue Moon," Victoria said and crossed to study them. Vibrant landscapes and London street scenes laid out in bold strokes and a strikingly modern style, they were skillfully crafted.

Piper stumbled to a halt. "You've been to the Blue Moon?"

Victoria's breath caught. *Oh, that did not sound good.* Why would a lady, *any* lady, have seen the inside of a gambling establishment? "You misunderstand,

I'm not one of Mr. Alexander's..." She shook her head, searching for the word, mortification heating her cheeks.

"Doxies," Piper supplied with a laugh she tried valiantly to smother.

"Lightskirts," Agnes chimed in with.

"Paramour might be more apt. Or mistress." Her hostess's sputter of delight brought to mind the rumors about Lady Beauchamp and her scant regard for propriety. "Of which I'm neither."

We're friends, Victoria wished to add, but the statement sounded ridiculous. When had a woman of her station befriended a man of Finn Alexander's? And they weren't friends, at least not yet. Friends didn't orbit each other like fighters who'd unexpectantly been shoved into the same ring. Unnerved, she blurted, "He's been dreaming about me. Then I twisted his thoughts at Lord Samuelson's gathering, for a moment only, because it didn't really work, which is most unusual. He knew I'd done something, like a pinch to his skin, when no one ever does. My parlor trick, I call it. I steal little chunks of time. But it's more than a parlor trick or...so...he...thinks..." Her words faded as color leeched from Piper's face. Her hand went out to grasp the wall in support.

"Cor, girl, did you have to bring up your silly prank," Agnes snapped and grabbed Piper's arm, settling her on a threadbare settee that should've been tucked in a bedchamber above stairs. Or in the servants quarters below. "There, there, my lady, don't listen to my charge's foolish ramblings."

"If you faint because of what I admitted, he'll be vexed with me," Victoria pleaded, fanning Piper's face. Finn had spoken of his sister-in-law in extremely protective terms, brooking no question about his strong feelings for her or his family.

49

Dodging them by hiding out in London or not, which she believed he was doing.

"I'm a healer," Piper murmured, disclosing her own secret. Her eyes were serene when they met Victoria's. "And I see auras. Imagine witnessing someone's mood surrounding them, a visual cloud as colorful as Julian's paintings." She shrugged, offering a plucky smile. "I can't see yours, which has only happened once before. I'm quite astonished to imagine why."

"I don't know what that means." Victoria dropped to her knee before the viscountess, leveling their gazes. "I don't know what any of this means."

"He's never brought anyone home," Piper whispered, so softly Victoria wondered if she was admitting this only to herself. "And his dreams…"

"Will you explain them to me? What's special about Harbingdon? Why I'm here?"

Piper moistened her lips, shook her head. "Finn has to do that, I think. But I will tell you, you're surrounded by others with gifts. Everyone on this estate, in fact. Which makes for an admittedly interesting family. You'll be accepted here as you've never been anywhere else. As you'll never *be* anywhere else. You, my dear, are finally safe. We can protect you."

"Gift?" Victoria rocked back on her heels. "I don't have a gift. It's harmless. A meaningless bit of trickery." Her fingers twisted in her skirt. "Safe from what? No one knows about me. No one…cares about me."

"A silly prank," Agnes repeated in an urgent whisper. "Always just a silly prank."

"Then why is he dreaming about you?"

Victoria's cheeks flushed as her mind went in a base direction, fashioning images of Finn tangled in silk sheets, looking as endearingly rumpled as when he'd answered the door at the Blue Moon. *No.* Although she didn't know the details, his dreams were not sensual ones. The man could have anyone in England, *anyone*, at least for the night. He certainly wasn't attracted to her.

"Something tragic happened to a friend, and he's not been able to recover." Piper squeezed her hand, an impassioned plea. "Maybe there's a reason for your bond, as there often is in our world. For the patient woman, there's a wonderful, sensitive man beneath the charming patina."

Victoria's heart tripped, the revelation landing squarely on her chest, attracting her when she needed no lure. She'd never been able to trust any man aside from her brother, and he was gone. No one in her life needed her. She was a disposable commodity, a book placed on a shelf and forgotten—until the need for funds had arisen. A push into a bleak future without any care for what *she* wanted from her life.

She was utterly alone in this world.

The next thought left her breathless.

What if Finn Alexander, even with his family surrounding him, was alone in his world, too?

CHAPTER 4

"For God's sake, sit down. You have the look of a trapped animal."

Finn halted in the middle of his brother's study, a space he'd been roaming—window to bookshelf and back—since being permitted entrance five minutes prior. The silence was numbing, Julian's reproach threading childlike anxiety through him as if he waited for punishment for shattering an antique vase or spilling ink on a cherished rug.

No one could make a grown man cower like Julian Alexander.

Finn nudged a painting resting against the sofa with his boot. A charming portrait of Lucien, Julian's adorable two-year-old son. "I like living above the Blue Moon," he said, figuring the argument should start where it had left off six months ago. Although, he didn't actually *like* living there, but the reasoning behind his actions was a perilous pond he wasn't diving into this day. Not if he could avoid it.

Julian's paintbrush tapped a steady rhythm on the imposing desk he sat behind. "The gaming hell was an opportunity for us to further the League's contacts, gain information and entry into various levels

52

of society, develop negotiating power in certain circles, while you learned to manage a business. End of story. I never planned for you to be associated in the way you have been. I think part of its success is due to the chance to carouse with Viscount Beauchamp's infamous half-brother."

Finn dropped to a crouch before Lucien's portrait, a pang of what felt like homesickness flowing through him. Strange, as he'd just come home. "It's in the black, as you well know. A favorite haunt of every town dandy. The gossip sheets love us. Why, I'm scraping earls and barons off the sidewalk nightly, much to everyone's enjoyment. Gambling *and* theatre. After taking their money at the faro table, of course." He stole a glance at Julian, noting that discussion of their financial success had failed to erase his sour look. "Fortunately, reading their minds allows me to have them escorted from the premises before they irreparably change their lives. Hence being known as the 'friendly' betting establishment, the gaming hell where you lose, but not so much you feel the need to swim the Thames the next morning." Knowing it wasn't a good idea but unable to stop himself, Finn winked and added, "I'm simply doing my part to help society as they've always helped me."

"Using your gift for this idiocy is almost as bad as Piper posing as a medium. Remember how well that worked out?" He sighed, the paintbrush continuing its pejorative tapping. "This was far from my plan."

"My living in blasted, bland Mayfair was your plan, I know, I know," Finn snapped, his temper heating. His head was starting to pound from thwarting Julian's thoughts, privacy not afforded everyone. Control he didn't always *have*. Victoria had apparently moved far enough away for her blocking his reading to abate. At least a little. "The League is still top of mind, Jule. My first priority aside from breathing. Have you forgotten the translations I'm doing? The letters from our German contact? The concern you had, someone in Berlin that's far too interested in us, in the occult. It's almost spying, which was not Oxford's expectation when I sailed through those language classes. Their hope was a lifetime spent filling a library with the works of Heinrich von Kleist and Ludwig Tieck."

"My hope was *not* you being asked to depart due to unprincipled behavior. Rustication it wasn't, despite what you said at the time. It was expulsion."

Finn swallowed hard and scrubbed the back of his neck. "How was I to know the girl was engaged to the Vice-Chancellor's son? She never let a thought about the poor sod float through that stunning head of hers. I was as surprised as you were." *Though I would have done it anyway*, he wanted to add but didn't dare. She'd been very persuasive, very experienced, and he a green lad of nineteen.

Julian tossed the paintbrush aside and rolled to his feet. Wrenching the window at his back high, he leaned out into an enveloping, dusky twilight. "I don't understand your desire, after all we did to leave that life, to return to it. Creating intrigue where we pray there is none, living in that horror of a parish. We're not thieves any longer, Finn. You're accepted by association, and you always will be. As long as I'm alive, that is. It's enough. Embrace this life we've fought for."

"You were never *from* that world, Jule. You only stepped into the pit long enough to yank me out of it, then lie to society about our relationship after, which I'm eternally grateful for. Being born in the gutter is my history, no mind to how much we'd both like it not to be. The truth finally comes out in the end, doesn't it?" He took a fast inhalation, the scent of paint and turpentine stinging his nose. "My identity lies somewhere between what you created and what I *am*."

"I don't want your damned gratitude. You're the brother of my heart," Julian said between clenched teeth. "After the boy—"

"Freddie," Finn whispered and closed his eyes to hide what Julian might see, "his name was Freddie."

"Freddie's death wasn't your fault. The League stepped in as soon as we found out about him. You almost died trying to save him."

"Trying being the optimal word."

Julian cursed beneath his breath. "Being gutted on the wharf is your idea of your purpose, that it?"

"I don't know what my purpose is," Finn whispered too softly for his brother to hear.

"The League can't save everyone who has the misfortune to have a supernatural talent, Finn. It's not possible in this lifetime, and we'll both suffer greatly if we think it is. I've filled this estate with every single person I've found who is gifted and has no place. Wales, Scotland, Ireland, France. The new groom is from a small village in Italy, Finn, *Italy*. Those letters you translated last year, remember?" Julian traced a crack in the windowpane and shrugged his broad shoulder. "I can't save everyone. Nor can you. I'm truly sorry if I unwittingly placed that expectation on your shoulders."

The scar on Finn's chest burned as if the knife that had created the wound was again slicing across it. His mind, for the first time since Piper's near-tragedy years ago, was open to the dreadful possibilities. Julian's visions when touching objects; Piper's ability to heal; Simon's talent for seeing those recently departed from this life; the Duke of

Ashcroft's proficiency at starting fires with nothing more than a mental wish. These gifts placed the people he loved in a vulnerable position, one that shook him to his core. He traced the curl of Lucien's ear in the painting, praying Julian's son hadn't inherited any supernatural tendencies from his parents.

It was hard for him to explain, but Freddie had been the first person he'd lost—and the boy's death hadn't just broken Finn's heart, it had broken his *soul*.

It sounded maudlin, but his sense of self had flowed down the Thames with Freddie's lifeless body.

"I fear you're thriving on the chaos you're placing yourself in. And the threat isn't coming from the outside as it did with Piper and Sidonie, with the groom who tricked his way into our ranks last year and tried to steal the chronology, something, someone, I could influence. You. The danger this time is inside *you*." Julian beheld him for a long, tense moment, then he gave up, yanking his hand through his hair with a terse grunt. "If you're not going to let me in, who will you let in, boy-o? That's what I lie awake at night wondering."

All the asinine things he'd done to light a fire beneath society's arse since the accident flashed before Finn's eyes until he wondered what the hell he'd been born to do with his life. If he slipped up and anyone found out about his gift, the consequences for the League and the community Julian sought to shelter at Harbingdon would be dire.

Guilt slicing through him, he crossed to the sideboard and poured a generous amount of gin in two tumblers. He and Julian liked theirs dry and neat, no sugar, no lemon, as was presently the fashion. Upon his return, Julian seized the drink before Finn could settle it on the desk, his scowl communicating his irritation over Finn's recent activities.

Finn could list each cockup if asked, though he prayed Julian wouldn't. It was quite a feat. He'd taken his insouciant disguise, the philandering, careless bounder, and somehow made it real. When it wasn't real—at least he didn't *think* it was.

"Who's the girl?" Julian finally asked, the words thinly sliced, as if he preferred to address the divisive issues but had mercifully decided to start with the straightforward ones. "A momentous occasion as you've never brought a woman home. Should I have another nursery prepared? Lucien will still be using his for a bit. Arrange for a special license, perhaps, as the chit looked to be quality?"

Finn choked as gin shot down his windpipe. "What? *No.*" He dropped to the chair opposite Julian and thumped his chest, coughing. "I'm dreaming... about her, Jule."

Julian uncoiled from his slouch, his focus razor-sharp, Finn's foolishness of late blessedly forgotten. "Come again?"

"They started just after Freddie died. Dreams like those I had when Piper was in danger, every night, over and over and over. In living, breathing color." He let his head fall back, his gaze going to a streak of yellow paint on the ceiling he wondered how had ended up there. "Surrounded not by danger but lack of knowledge. No, no..." He closed his eyes, pulling the visions to the forefront of his mind. Victoria Hamilton in blinding brilliance, a nightly assault on his senses. "Lack of awareness. Solitude, this vast expanse of chilling solitude. Someone tied to me in a way I can't deny, *won't* deny, because I'm not losing another person. They weren't nightmares, like those with Piper and Sidonie years ago. These were almost calming, visions arriving just before you wake but gone by your first stretch. But they were relentless. A challenge, an appeal within them. So, I searched London high and low until I found her."

He'd been drawn to her long before he saw her across the ballroom that first night, in a dazzling lavender concoction that sent the room into sluggish rotations as dreams and reality collided. A connection existed between them—and not a trivial one. Imprinted like lines on his palm. Although he had no idea why. "I've been following her for weeks, and I'm telling you, she's trouble. Piper, and then some. Restless and unhappy." Desperately lonely, if he had his guess.

"A troublesome package but not a lover. Interesting. For you, anyway."

"She doesn't need a lover, she needs a husband," he growled, though his belly tightened as he imagined Baron Rossby touching her. Any man touching her. And he'd watched quite a few try. When no good could come from feeling possessive about a woman you could never possess. "I don't need the complication," he thought he should add in the event Julian was getting romantic ideas, as his intense love for Piper sometimes made him do. Complications, love specifically, made one vulnerable, and Finn wasn't up to the battle. He had enough people to worry about to last a lifetime.

Besides, he was a bastard, she a lady. End of story.

"You think you can trust her?" Julian exhaled sharply, his curse riding the air. "I don't have to tell you the complete and utter fear I felt months back, finding someone on the estate, someone who had a gift that reasonably brought them here, who wasn't our friend. Someone with incredibly brutal aspirations, to obtain the chronology despite any cost. Any harm." He tipped his glass high, his throat working as he swallowed. "He got close to Lucien, Finn. Near my *son*. I could have killed the man a hundred times over, although I only had to do it once."

"You can trust her, Jule." He tapped his tumbler against his thigh. "As well as you can trust me."

"You say this because you've invited her into your life, involved yourself in hers." Julian tapped his tumbler on the desk. Three hard pops while he ruminated. "Her gift, as I assume she has one?"

This was where Finn paused, trepidation, the same he'd felt since the debacle on the docks, seizing him. He was no good to anyone if he let fear manage him…but the enormity of Victoria's gift frightened him. Their enemies often had incredible abilities, a talent to see into the future and the past, their desire to use their gifts for nefarious means the difference. The League could never slumber, never rest, never disregard. "She seems able to erase memories. Short-term, brief, I'm not sure how far back it goes—minutes, hours, days—but erasure just the same. When she touched me, I took a mental stumble before I could right myself. I've never felt the like."

Julian slid his hands across the desk, scattering ledgers and sketch pads, paintbrushes and ink wells. "Something odd occurred when I entered the house after talking to you on the lawn. I touched the door-knob and saw nothing, Finn. Which has not happened to me ever. Not *once* in my life have I touched an object and not seen images of a person who touched it before." He drew a shaky breath, his fingers flexing into fists. "Is that because of this girl?"

Finn stared into his tumbler, wishing like hell more gin would magically appear. Why couldn't any of them have *that* gift? "I can't read her. Nothing. When she's around me, my ability to grasp her thoughts snuffs out like a flame in the wind. And it mutes what I receive from others. Sometimes more than mutes. She shuts me down."

"A blocker," Julian murmured in wonder.

Finn gave his empty tumbler another wistful glance. "Blocker?"

"Piper's grandfather detailed it in the chronology, long passages from a German contact we have yet to translate. He believed a blocker cloaked supernatural ability. Lessened or halted outright. Dulling the shine, he called it. A gift he considered more powerful than Piper's. There was believed to be another with the ability two hundred years ago. In Berlin, as I recall, hence the German texts. But nothing since."

Finn closed his eyes, a headache ripping through his temples. *More powerful than the healer*. Of course. After they'd barely been able to safeguard Piper when their enemies found out about her. Should their enemies discover someone with the ability to block a psychic gift, protecting that person would pose an impossible challenge.

Unbearable, Finn thought as his heart dropped to his knees.

"Her dreams?" Julian asked.

Finn squeezed the bridge of his nose, shook his head. *I don't know.*

"Will she work with you? With Piper? To test her ability, then cross-reference against what's written in the chronology? You can translate the text." Julian yanked a scrap of foolscap from beneath a ledger and starting scribbling notes across the page. "Does she need to touch someone to curb their gift or only be near them? Does one's ability simply diminish or completely fade? How far away from you is she before you're able to read minds again?"

"You think I know the answers to any of these questions?"

"We'll have to increase security at the gates, the main house, the perimeter. Employ the Duke's mercenaries in full force. You'll have to make Lady Hamilton understand why she can't go anywhere on this estate without someone with her. Not until Ashcroft and I have a chance to put a plan in place. It could be years, but at some point, she'll need protection. At some point, they *will* find out about her."

"She doesn't trust me," he whispered, loathe to imagine protecting her when the mere thought of losing someone else was intolerable.

Julian issued a brittle, humorless laugh. "With your shenanigans of late, would you?"

Finn spun the tumbler in his hands, shooting crystal prisms across the paint-stained Aubusson rug. He could tell Julian he was bored with the women, the drinking, the gambling. His pointless existence. By his own hand, he'd reduced himself to being an aimless commodity. "Do you know I've never had an honest relationship with a woman? One undertaken without knowing *exactly* what she's thinking? Fairly easy to manage expectations when there are no surprises." His encounters felt forged, crafted by knowledge he shouldn't have, didn't want, couldn't prevent from slipping through the cracks of his mind.

Now, he felt out of sorts because he'd met a woman he couldn't read as cleanly as the copy of *The Mystery of Edwin Drood* shoved in his portmanteau. For once, he'd been assigned a level playing field. Finn Alexander had no advantage in this game.

"Maybe she can help you experience a normal relationship. But be warned, you often have to give up one way of life for the chance at another. I speak from experience."

"Normal," Finn murmured, the word as foreign as the texts he translated.

Julian sighed. "Without reading her mind, Finn."

Finn slid low in his chair, balancing the tumbler on his belly. He didn't know how to be himself. And he didn't know *normal*.

He also didn't know what to do about Victoria Hamilton.

His lips curved in a cautious smile. The lady would be surprised to find she was what she loved.

A puzzle.

One Finn desperately wanted to solve.

~

Dinner that evening was a laborious affair.

Lady Beauchamp—Piper, as Victoria had again been urged to call her—had an infectious spirit, and it wasn't from her lack of effort to ease the tension in the room that the gathering wilted like a discarded blossom.

Finn, the person bringing them all together, skipped out on the festivities, the rat.

"Dodging life," she'd murmured when he failed to show, surprised when Viscount Beauchamp laughed in agreement. A sound filled with fondness and exasperation.

The viscount's gaze had touched her often, questions about her parlor trick almost tumbling off his tongue like a rock down a well, but his wife had simply given the slightest shake of her head—*not the time*—to hold him off.

She'd watched Julian touch items on the table more often than he needed to, his cutlery, his wine glass, the saltshaker, while throwing bewildered looks her way. Eccentric behavior, on a curious estate, a setting teeming with those with mystical talents. Victoria had tried not to look over her shoulder too often, wondering what supernatural trick the footman might be able to employ, the kitchen maid, the cook. Thankfully, the meal was casual, even by country standards. Limited to five courses with no entertainment after, which was a blessing as a musicale by a tone-deaf heiress, was the last amusement she'd been subjected to.

With a sigh, Victoria closed her bedchamber door and slumped against it. One night down. A new puzzle book and the glass of sherry she'd smuggled upstairs awaited. If that didn't put her to sleep, she'd sneak down to the kitchens and bake after the servants vacated the area.

"Didn't show, did he?"

Victoria gasped, nearly spilling the sherry when she wanted every drop to hit her tongue, not the Beauchamp's rug. "Who?"

"The scamp that drug us here, that's who." Agnes rose from the overstuffed chair tucked in a corner, hiding in wait for her mistress. She loved making disquieting entrances, and Victoria, after years of these contests, should have expected one. "Saw him climb into a showy landau, fancy crest decorating the side, and ride off into the night. Sneaking away from his brother's disdain and heading for trouble in that charming village we passed on the way here." Agnes crossed to Victoria, motioned for her to turn, then began unbuttoning her gown, a routine they'd completed a thousand times. "No good ever came from being that handsome. Just like no good has ever come from your prank. Scrambling thoughts and making people forget your foolishness, what kind of talent is that? A talent everyone in this house seems overly interested in, is what. I suppose because most of them seem filled with the spook, just like you. Takes one to know one. Peculiar, this entire place."

"It's a lovely estate, Aggie. Although the staff may be slightly unusual. Think of this as our last adventure before we enter confined servitude." She let her dress slither down her body, stepping from the pool of silk with a sigh. "As for Finn Alexander, don't let the face fool you. There's a clever man underneath all the glitter. Shrewd. He plays his cards close, that's his game. And you know, I love a riddle."

Agnes snorted softly through her nose and worked on Victoria's corset ties. "You play *any* game with the man, and we'll be in a fine muddle. I seen the way he looks at you. Rossby won't appreciate it if he hears you're messing with the likes of the Blue Bastard. He's dead-set on ownership before he owns. Neither will your mother, for that matter."

Victoria paused, her breath coming forth in a rush. How had Finn looked at her?

Are you going to be one of those senseless girls after all, Victoria Hamilton?

With a whispered curse, she waved Agnes away and strode to the wardrobe, pulled out her night robe, and slipped it on, cinching the crimson ribbon around her waist. "If I can find another solution, maybe Rossby would be relieved if I begged off."

Agnes brushed past her, Victoria's dress and corset twisted in her fist. "Don't you believe it. When Rossby looks at you, his gaze is fiercer than the Blue Bastard's. Gives me the chills, it does. Your mother's not a proper judge if she thinks the baron is fit for you. And your father—" She whistled sharply through her teeth and hung the dress on a peg in the wardrobe, placing the corset on a low shelf. "Not every woman has prettiness and intelligences. Rossby tiptoes around you like a boy who stole a jewel and has it jammed in his pocket. Not your fault he's a snowflake and you're sunlight. You'll melt him, and he knows it. But he craves that sunlight." She shut the wardrobe door with a final snap. "We're stuck, bugs in amber. Tossed out on the street if you don't save this family. And soon. Your father already let the house in Belgravia for the summer, did you know that? Nowhere to go should we dash back to London."

Victoria moved to the window and flattened her hand on the cool pane. Harbingdon's rolling lawns and vast parklands stretched to the horizon in smoky, surreal twilight. The scent of cut grass and woodsmoke, evergreens and azalea blossoms, drifted in on a tender breeze. It was a peculiar place, yes, but it was also beautiful. Peaceful. And as Piper has said, *safe*. Especially for someone who had nowhere else to go. "I could talk to my father again. There must be another way. If he'll give me time to find another way."

Agnes came up behind her until they were shoulder to shoulder, as they had been for most of her life. "I love you like my own, girl, you know that. But the truth is, they don't have it in them to love anyone but themselves. Neither of them. Your mother sending you here, without a care except for the hope that a duke might flutter by, with me as your only protector, almost no funds, is proof of her indifference." She reached for Victoria's hand and squeezed it. "You have to get over it, harden your heart to them. Love isn't always given where it should be. Sharing blood should force a river of affection into their hearts, but it hasn't. I've been waiting for it since you was in nappies. Charles, too. I finally gave up and think you should as well. At least on them anyway. Save your hopes for better things. Better people."

Victoria ran a knuckle beneath each eye, knowing Agnes was only trying to make her accept the truth. Then at some point, it would no longer pain her so much. "Is Rossby better people, Aggie?"

Agnes snaked a hand around Victoria's waist and pulled her into her side. "No, darling girl, I don't think so. But where you go, I go. We'll work it out."

Victoria closed her eyes and rested her cheek on her treasured companion's shoulder.

Was Finn Alexander better people, she couldn't help but wonder?

CHAPTER 5

*L*ater that night, Victoria heard the wheels of the carriage grinding over the pebbled drive before the conveyance emerged from a misty shroud. A landau, the Beauchamp crest emblazoned on the side, two sleek horses stomping and snorting in the lead. Stationing herself behind a pillar, she pressed her cheek to the cool stone and shivered. Her shawl lay in her bedchamber beneath the puzzle book she'd been trying since dinner to invite into her mind.

She should have gone to the kitchens to bake, her secret pleasure. Instead, she stood in the shadows of the veranda, waiting for Finn to come home.

He exited the carriage as it lurched to a stop, more of an expulsion. The coachman rushed to assist when his boot awkwardly hit the metal step, but Finn waved him off. Somehow he kept his feet, though his route across the sloping lawn looked as if he were trying to write his name in the stalks of grass.

By the time she reached him, he'd made it to the top step of the veranda and lay sprawled on his back, one arm flung wide, his hand cupped as if to catch a snowflake. The other lay over his stomach in a protective curl. His frock coat hadn't made it home with him; his waistcoat spilled wide like the pages of a book, exposing lean but significant muscle beneath snowy-white linen. His neckpiece lay in a limp twist, the ends dangling. Someone had tangled his hair beyond hope of repair. A streak of oil, no doubt from the coach's seat, split his brow in two.

He looked vulnerable, younger than she suspected him of being, and impossibly appealing.

Knowing that aiding the inebriated toast of London in the dead of night in nothing but her night robe was a dreadful idea didn't stop her. However, she did whisper a reproachful, "This is a dreadful idea," as she dropped to a squat beside him. With a sigh, she reached, halted, rounded her fingers into a fist, and let it sink into the folds of her skirt. As a friend, she could assist another friend, a completely foxed one from the look of it, into the shelter of the house. But there was no call for gratuitous touching, despite the overwhelming inclination to do so.

Tipping her head, Victoria gazed at the murky spill inking the sky, the stars startlingly brilliant pinpricks nestled inside opaque folds. Aside from the distant call of an owl and Finn's soft breaths, the world was blessedly silent. Bucolic, far-from-town silent. Glancing back at him, she reminded herself that an attraction, when he and his family held answers she should have sought out long ago, was enough of a barrier. If the pending marriage required to save her family from financial doom was not.

When a summer romance would mean nothing, less than nothing, to one of the most profligate scoundrels in England.

"So," he whispered, his words elegantly slurred, "are you going to help me up? Or shall we ruminate on the loveliness of a country evening...from what is turning out to be shockingly cold marble? *Le plus in-*

confortable." Very uncomfortable, he added, switching to French for no reason she could fathom.

She reeled, losing her balance, landing on her bottom beside him. "Are you mocking me, Mr. Alexander?"

"Do I seem the mocking type, Lady Hamilton?"

Yes, he did. But she laughed, unable to check the impulse. She didn't want to like him. Was trying hard *not* to. Partly because every female he encountered liked him too much. "Let's get you sitting up. Then, if I have to call a footman, your incapacitation won't seem as dire as it currently appears."

His smile grew, but his eyes remained closed, a detail she was thankful for as she assisted him to a resting slump against the pillar. Settling in beside him on the step—far enough to prevent them accidentally touching but close enough for a shimmer of awareness to dance along her skin—she wondered if she should start a conversation or merely endure the charged silence for as long as she could stand it.

"What are you doing out here at this time of the night without that rabid-eyed duenna of yours?" he finally asked as he dug around in his waistcoat pocket. Gesturing to the cheroot he extracted, he anchored it between his lips.

Victoria nodded, charmed by his graciousness in light of the impropriety of the situation. "I couldn't sleep. Agnes always can. At the drop of a hat. It's so quiet here, except for the occasional creak of a floorboard or rattle of a windowpane." She traced a crack in the step. "I suppose I'm used to the commotion of the city. The stink and bustle, the feverish pace. Even if one suspects they don't like it, one becomes inured."

He exhaled a wisp of smoke but didn't comment.

Then, in an outrageous offer, he offered the cheroot to her.

"Oh, no, I—"

"You can do anything you want, Tori. You left the vipers behind in Town. It's just you, me, and the crickets." He tilted his head, gazing at the sky. "And a thousand stars. Just look at them, will you? Besides, I know you to be a very bothersome package, up to a dare."

Releasing a huff, she took the cheroot from fingers more suited to sculpting clay than smoking stubs and lifted it to her lips. The tip was moist, which sent a dart of heat straight through her. No way to deny it. "It doesn't taste good," she whispered with a grimace.

"Why, no, it doesn't."

She coughed and handed it back to him. "Then, why do it?"

His gaze caught hers, sapphire dialed down to onyx in the shadows. "Because I can." Then he laughed, an enchanting sound that wrapped around her as handily as her missing shawl. And she found herself laughing with him. "There's that wicked smile. I feared the prospect of spending your summer here had forever altered your disposition. Broken your courageous spirit." He gave her one sweeping glance. "However, you're here, cavorting around in your nightclothes. That's courage in action."

She rested back on her elbows, marveling at her ease with a man she barely knew. With his patient air and unruffled manner, he was gifted at making people feel comfortable. Even if being comfortable was not in anyone's best interest. "Are you going to tell me why I'm here, or shall I wait for the explanation over kippers and toast?"

Finn stretched his legs out with a sigh. Long limbs

that took time, there and back, to complete the study of. His boots were polished, his breeches pressed, shirt neatly tucked. What immaculate stylishness he had, even in this state. Another of his gifts. "What did Piper tell you?"

He needs a friend.

Victoria dug the tip of her pinkie deeper in the cracked marble. "Nothing, actually."

"Many thanks, Pip," he muttered beneath his breath.

"I believe the interpretation was, she's your problem."

He gave the cheroot a twirl, the flaming tip shooting a crimson glow over his skin. "For the first time in my life, I'm challenged." He was silent for a thoughtful moment, his hand going to his brow and pressing. "But earlier today, while you were away from the house on your walk with Piper, thoughts just flowed through me like a rushing brook, and this is what I surmised. Without intending to surmise anything, I should add. One of the kitchen maids is worried about her mother after a recent illness. A footman, a fairly new arrival at Harbingdon, is obsessed with his cousin. Although I can't say if it's a man or a woman suffering from the footman's admiration. Cook broke a tureen she worried she might need to prepare the roasted lamb. The guard at the gate"—he frowned and flicked the cheroot into the azalea bushes lining the veranda—"oh, Lord, never mind that one."

She rolled to a sit and turned to face him, tucking her night robe around her. "How do you know these things?"

He tapped his temple. "*My* parlor trick."

She gasped and brought her hand to her head.

Chuckling, he drew his knees up and rested his

forearms on them, a boy's stance in a man's body. "Relax. For some reason, I can't steal a damn thing from that fascinating brain of yours. Believe me, I've tried. Besides, you clog the pipes when I'm close to you. It's bloody weird. A temporary but astounding respite. I don't hear anything. Which I'm not sure how to fathom."

"You read thoughts? Minds?"

He made a checkmark in the air. "Yes, yes."

She clenched her hands in her robe, her palms dampening. "All those events. Balls. Horse races. The gaming hell. Musicales. Bond Street during the apex of the season. I saw you there once surrounded by a veritable flock. How can you stand it?"

His smile dimmed, his charm tumbling off the edge of a cliff, and leaving what she supposed was a truthful expression. An extremely weary one. "Judging from tonight's performance, the last year's performance, perhaps I can't."

"But not me," she whispered, her gaze drifting across the lawn and to the golden glimmer of a lake she could see in the distance. "You steal thoughts, but not mine."

He balanced his brow on his folded arms and was still for so long she wondered if he'd fallen asleep. "I would pinch them if I could, I can't seem to help myself. I'm a born thief, Tori, I'm laying that right out there. A rake the likes of which you've never encountered. But, somehow, you're blocking my gift." He exhaled through his teeth, cursing softly. "*Gift*. What a tidy word for a disastrous burden."

"How long...?" She gestured inanely to her head, to his.

"As long as you've been able to nick chunks of time. Forever, am I right? I used to have to touch people to capture their thoughts, mostly anyway, but as I've gotten older, I've gained more control. Much due to working with Piper. She's quite talented in helping one strengthen their ability. I can shut it off, or rather, turn it down. Sometimes. But in a crush, it's impossible. Walking down a crowded street is like going to war."

"Healer," Victoria breathed, recalling Piper's word from earlier. Lady Beauchamp was indeed afflicted, just as she and Finn were. His request to come to Harbingdon for the summer was starting to make sense.

"She isn't a medical doctor. It's more a healing of the soul." He rolled his head to look at her, shadow and light playing across his high cheekbones, his firm jaw. "I send my mind out like a dog to hunt. Then I'm brought back thoughts, along with a face to connect them, usually, which is helpful. Thoughts no one wants to release, thoughts buried deep. People have unwittingly shared clandestine affairs, murderous dreams, ghastly degradations, fantastical aspirations, heartfelt fantasies. I journaled for years, my hands covered in ink, pages and pages of notes because Piper said it would help clear my mind but…"

"Your mind is full, but you're empty," she whispered in a ragged voice.

His gaze snapped to hers. "Except when I'm around you. It's like I'm dipped in mud, and you're the warm bath, allowing me to cleanse myself, hear myself." He sounded accusatory when none of this was her fault. She didn't want a preternatural gift any more than he did. And she surely didn't know what to do with it. "You're changing me. An important role for a person I don't know very well."

His profound admission, uttered in an entirely leaden tone, a man on the verge of giving up his mission, sent a surge of panic ripping through her. What was she doing, sitting in the summer nightfall with the most gorgeous mind reader in England, telling him her secrets and letting his roll over her, roll *through* her? Twist her up until her heart hammered beneath her breast, her bodice sticking to suddenly moist skin. "I don't want this. I want to be—"

"*Normal*," they both said.

Finn grasped her wrist when she would have jumped to her feet, another burst of French tumbling from his lips, too complicated for her to translate. Awareness shimmered, wrapping them in gossamer, an intimate estrangement until it felt she stood with him against the world. His eyes were liquid pools, deep, dark, and unfathomable, nothing like the witless charmer who'd rescued her from several humiliations during a dreary Season. Her pulse skipped, her breath rushing forth as she imagined pulling her other trick and kissing him to make them both forget.

When kissing meant as little to her as it likely did to him.

"Don't start designing ways to distract me, Tori darling. I can see the wheels spinning. Understand this. I've never dreamed about anyone unconnected to the occult. Unconnected to the group of misfits my brother has assembled and calls the League. *Never*." His glittering gaze sliced away. "I don't know why we're linked. I don't. I usually—" He swore roughly and tugged his fingers through his hair, the enticing streak of gray glinting in the moonlight.

She flinched, and his eyes widened, apparently stunned to find he still had a hold on her. Something, the stark sadness in his gaze, his painful effort to explain himself, the way his thumb was drawing deliberate circles on her wrist, made her heart bottom out.

He released his grip and slumped back against the

pillar. "I've never conversed with a woman, or more when the occasion warranted it, without knowing what she expected from the involvement. Placed like a bouquet of daffodils at my feet. It's part of the reason for my success, as it were. The knowing. I'm given the answer before the question is asked."

Victoria scoffed and gestured to him, head to toe. "*You're* the reason for your success, Mr. Alexander. Although I'm sure reading minds means you deliver superbly."

He brought his hand to the bridge of his nose and squeezed, his lids sliding low. "Can I tell you a secret? The first of those I promised to share if you came with me on this journey. I'm fatigued. Discontented. I yearn for my family, my home. The boy I let slip away on the wharf one horrible, stormy evening. Simon, the boy living here, who needs me when I can't quite let myself need him back. Julian's growing the League without me when I once wanted nothing more than to be a part of building it. Not managing a gaming hell, quite successfully, I might add. I find myself playing a role I no longer want to play, yet I'm not sure how to crawl out of the furrow. Julian stamped this life all over me with that heavy hand of his, a good life, but the toddler who showed up in a rookery orphanage with a note stuffed in his pocket listing a first name and nothing else was lost in the process."

"Is this secret number two? That you're not the late Viscount Beauchamp's byblow?"

He closed his eyes with a groan, his cheeks flushing. "I've never admitted that to anyone before. I sometimes forget Julian and I are not actual brothers, and I, well, the blood part doesn't matter." Yanking his neckpiece off, he stuffed it in his waistcoat pocket, popped two buttons on his shirt, and breathed deep. She tried to avoid looking too closely at the golden skin exposed by the open vee, she really did. "I must be losing my mind, or all that brandy is doing a number on me. I don't usually drink heavily. I've found it to be very unwise for a man with my talent."

The poignant burden of his confession landed on her chest, suspending her breath as she searched for a reply that wouldn't break the fragile bond they were constructing. She chose humor, as this seemed to be one of his standard fallbacks. "You're simply fatigued from climbing trellises and leaping from windows with furious husbands in pursuit."

He opened one eye and pinned it on her, a reverse wink. "That goddamn window was two stories up. And the trellis, which is a true story though I wasn't fleeing an incensed husband but rather an overeager baroness, didn't support my weight." He threw his arm out, traced a pale scar on his wrist that twisted like a crooked river up his arm. "I bled like a stuck pig all over the baron's shrubbery and down Curzon Street. Upon reading the broadsheets, Julian immediately sent Humphrey to fetch me, our fixer-in-residence, so I had to face his censure as well, which is, if you can believe it, and you will when you meet him, worse than my brother's."

She covered her mouth and leaned into the laughter, feeling slightly tipsy when she hadn't had anything aside from that measly glass of sherry. How she could be amused when her family didn't care what she did as long as she surrendered her future to save them, *and* she'd come to find she was even more peculiar than initially thought.

"Care to discuss your misbehavior? What was the latest on-dit? Lord Kilroy's fountain? Or was it the Earl of Trotsham's musicale? The fiasco at—"

"Excellent diversionary tactic, my guardian angel, but perhaps a suitable plan for the summer would be for you to consider what else there is to Finn Alexander, if you're set on forging a new path. Aside from the obvious attributes, of which all are aware. A necessary break from the hordes tripping over their feet to get a second look at you." Although the kitchen maid earlier had been sufficiently dazed, so it might be impossible to escape attention even in the country, but no need to mention that when the man looked utterly demoralized, his loneliness so palpable it seemed to be inhabiting the scant space between them.

She sympathized with every woman whose heartbeat raced when faced with one of his smiles. It wasn't like he didn't make her knees tremble, she was only human.

But *she* could control it.

"What else is there, aside from..." He looped his hand in a lazy circle, signifying all kinds of things that made her stomach heat and twist. Speechless, he frowned, an absurdly captivating fold popping between his brows. His scent, bergamot and brandy, drifted to her on a steamy breeze, sliding along her skin like the gentlest of caresses.

"I'll help you if you help me," she proposed with more courage than she felt. "We step back from Town mischief and find out who we really are. This supernatural predicament, notwithstanding." She gestured to whatever lay beyond the house. "In the wilds of Oxfordshire, no less. As a betrothed woman, I'm safe from your charms. And you can't read my mind, so falling back on your old standby won't work. An exchange: enlightenment for friendship. As we explore my gift and you forget, at least in my company, about yours."

"I know I suggested it, but I'm coming up blank on the friend thing. Experience with, that is." He blinked sleepily, his lids fluttering. "Forgive me, the brandy has befuddled."

"What a shock," she whispered, recalling the women she'd seen hanging on his arm, the rumors printed in every gossip rag, the stories tripping off the tongues of those who wanted the piece of him they were jealous they weren't getting. "Who needs friends when lovers are so abundant?"

"True," he concurred and lay back, his arms going beneath his head to cushion. She couldn't help but record every inch of him as his eyes drifted shut, his cheeks smoothing out, the stubble lining his jaw sparking gold in the moonlight. Broad chest, flat tummy, lean hips, long legs. Boots polished to a high sheen. Perfection.

He yawned, his throat pulling taut. "Friendship, and this engagement mess of yours, mean I have to ignore my attraction. That's what I'm hearing. Which is, of course, the prudent plan. New beginnings, stepping back from Town mischief, etcetera, etcetera."

She wrenched her gaze from him, seeking the glimmer of the lake's surface in the distance. "Attraction is habitual, it means nothing. You go there without trying to encourage a cerebral connection. I'm no better. I've thrown out kisses like rose petals to men who don't deserve tribute of any kind. Better I should give them the thorns. Maybe it's time for me to find another way to manage life, too."

"No mind reading, which is a relief." His lids lifted slightly, his gaze catching on her mouth and holding, an intense look as sure of feeling as if he'd brushed his finger down her cheek. It was a clear break in his promise to keep his charm contained. "No flirting, which is not. Cerebral, is it? This friend thing sounds monotonous as shite."

She pressed her lips together to will away the imagined sting of his touch, longing pulsing through her body in a sturdy, betraying rhythm. "The League, Finn? Can you tell me more about it? And the chronology? And why I'd ever be in danger because of the parlor trick?"

"Tomorrow, I shall tell all," he murmured, lashes settling against his sun-dusted skin. "Now, Tori, darling, I'm going to dream. Maybe of you." He sighed softly. "Maybe of you."

Then he drifted to sleep, the frustrating man, right there in front of her, a Greek god laid out on marble. As the promise of her dancing through his dreams surrounded them.

CHAPTER 6

*S*he liked watching him.

A suitable pastoral diversion, Victoria concluded, leaning over the balustrade and bringing the eyecups close to her face. Finn Alexander was her bird, an enchanting cerulean one presently racing his mare across the woodlands like disaster nipped at his heels. Agnes had taken her dogged inspection of Harbingdon's lawns and gardens as a burgeoning interest in nature and the like—a relatively innocuous activity when exposed to such harmful ones in London—and requested assistance as her charge's eyesight was weak. A maid by the name of Long Sally arrived in her bedchamber after breakfast—opening and closing the door without touching it—and presented a set of mother of pearl opera glasses in a citron velvet purse, wholly over and above what she needed to spy on her *friend*.

Nevertheless, Victoria decided with a twist of the glasses' center wheel, they did bring the man into sharp, glorious focus.

A daring rider, this she knew from the first sight. As she'd once been a daring rider herself.

Heels down, thighs clenching the horse's flanks

with just the right amount of pressure, which was to say, not too much. Refined poise, all told, precisely as she'd have expected of him. However, the old fear gripped her as Finn jumped a hedge as if attacking it, without a care to the muddy depression on the blind side. She tipped her gaze to his hands as he cleared the obstacle with room to spare, a soft hold sending the reins sliding through his cupped fists like water, allowing the horse to control his balance, not the rider. Richmond, her family's groom, would have been pleased.

Victoria had often taken too firm a hand herself.

Her riding style said a lot about her.

Finn back-armed sweat from his brow and settled his mount with a reassuring glide of his palm across the horse's neck, his untucked shirt riding high with the movement and exposing a minute strip of tawny skin above his waistband before linen resettled over his lean hips. A tantalizing encounter she would have missed without the aid of Lady Beauchamp's marvelous—and apparently little-used—opera glasses. Missed if he wore a waistcoat or topcoat, which he did not.

Curiously, it wasn't Finn's undeniable beauty or lack of clothing that held her captivated. Instead, it was his continued effort to hide behind an aimless veneer, his countenance melancholy, his ready smile locked away when she caught him unaware, like the night on the veranda. A man grossly different than the one who'd wooed society with such wicked carelessness. There was nothing careless about his soulful glances, the impenetrable, shimmering intelligence held deep within.

She wanted access to *that* man more than she should.

Only she didn't know how to ask for access. Not

when he seemed to be struggling to settle back into family life and had avoided her for two days, despite his promise to *tell all*.

Through the open window, the sound of a pan striking the kitchen floor had her turning, the glasses dropping from her hands to dangle from the wrist chain. Her heartbeat stuttered, her mind blanking for a brief moment. Turning back, she found Finn's riderless horse standing beside the hedge, her head twisting as if on too short a lead.

Victoria's terror was immediate and impregnable.

Her shawl flew from her shoulders as she raced down the marble steps and across the lawn, her hair plunging from its delicate coiffure to streak her cheeks and tangle in her mouth. Her slippers were dew-soaked when she reached him, the hem of her dress soiled beyond repair, but she cared little, dropping to her knees and grasping the arm he'd flung out when he'd tumbled from his mount. His hand still clutched the reins, which she released, allowing the mare to settle. Finn's chest rose and fell in a slightly staggered rhythm, but unlike her brother's after his fall, it rose and fell.

He was covered in grass and earth, staining his clothing and his face. The side of his lip was cut. She dabbed at the blood with a wild glance thrown over her shoulder, a fruitless search for a footman, groom, maid. She'd finally come to understand Finn's comment to her on the ride to Harbingdon about *magical attendance* by the staff. The estate operated on the unpredictable sovereignty of those gifted with a supernatural ability, upper house to lower, garden to stable, sitting room to parlor. Doors opened before she reached them, gas lamps flared without her touch. Formidable, yet no one seemed trained for even the most straightforward household position.

"Finn," she whispered and gave his hand a squeeze, her brother's still form lying beside his horse, the awkward twist of his neck, roaring through her mind. She closed her eyes and concentrated, finding the racing pulse at Finn's wrist and smoothing it with her thumb. Like she would if she sought to steal time. Perhaps she could shock him back to consciousness.

"*Stop*. It's beginning...to hurt to hold you off." Finn's lids fluttered, his hand shifting in hers. His hair was a dark spill across his cheeks, the strands much longer than current style endorsed, giving him the look of a ruffian, and effectively hiding his expression. "I landed hard...on my back. My breath..." He inhaled shakily. Twice more before trying to speak again. "The reins, thank you for taking them...as I'm guessing no groom is around. Someone who sees the future could have helped in this situation. We have one of those, you know. Edward, the footman, but I guess this tumble escaped his purview. Or maybe it's Old Neddie. No, no, he sees the past. Edward, definitely Edward." He dragged his tongue along his teeth. "Blast, I think I cracked one."

Victoria rocked back on her haunches, tossing his arm aside, irritated to the soles of her leather slippers. Indeed, he'd chipped the edge of his front tooth, a minor imperfection, the first she'd found on the man aside from his unaffected arrogance, his lackadaisical indifference to *everything*. She was finished with men who gave less than a farthing about their futures, less than a farthing about their families. Rising to her feet, she wiped his blood on her skirt. "They're right, Blue, you don't care what happens to you. Go to it, then."

He blinked hard and elbowed to a wobbly sit.

"What the hell does that mean? And who, exactly, is *they?*"

She shook her head, thoughts piling up on each other like mud sliding down a slope. All that came out was an aggravated oath as she turned and marched back to the house, the opera glasses beating a rhythm against her hip. *Imprudent, conceited toad...*

He was beside her in three strides, out of breath, disheveled, dogged, blood dotting his lip and cheek. "Explain that comment to me, will you, my lady?"

Oh, would she. She halted so suddenly he had to skip back to reach her. His gaze, when it hit hers, was running as hot as hers felt. "Have you considered what it would do to those who love you should something dreadful happen? The carriage races, the brawls, the slums. Second story windows, gaming hells. Where is the care for your family, your future?" Her brother had lost his wife and infant son to illness, and he'd given up. Victoria had tried, but she'd been unable to save him. Now she was left with nothing, alone without her closest ally. She wasn't walking that joyless path again, not even for the enticing man standing before her.

"The women," he snarled, the first time she'd seen him act anything but bored. "You forgot about the women. The lightskirts, the demimondaines, the jaded widows. I'm jumping out of those windows for a reason, my dear."

She tapped his chest, right above a rip in his shirt and on the edge of that wicked scar, tears of sorrow and frustration pricking her lids. He was so tall she had to stretch to reach him, and the fingertip she trailed across his bare skin burned. "You forget *yourself*, Mr. Alexander. The women don't matter, the slums and the faro tables don't matter. The clubs and the fisticuffs are meaningless. Your family—"

Her words dissolved, and she turned away from him.

Or tried to.

He seized her chin, his fingers trembling against her jaw. "What is this?" he asked, a soothing tone ironing out his earlier ire, a cloud of heat and recognition unfurling around them. He tipped her gaze high, his regard penetrating. "Did this little tumble of mine truly upset you?"

She pressed her lips tight, a tear she couldn't contain spilling free. His fingers were scalding her skin. Add to that the glorious pain of being able to, for the first time in forever, talk to someone about something *real*. Even as she knew talking about real things brought her closer to Finn—when being closer was a danger to her future and her heart. Swallowing, she whispered, "My brother, Charles. He reacted thusly, caring nothing for life after his wife and child died of scarlet fever. I couldn't save him from himself, although I tried. At least, I think I did." She shook her head as if she could shake away the memory. "He died in a riding accident."

Finn stepped back, gradually relinquishing his hold as if he'd rather step in, comfort she feared she'd gladly accept in her fragile state. "You're quite adept, in the most unsophisticated way, at making me feel a cad. I've never known a woman to be candid and gain so much through such a lack of artifice. A solitary tear enough to rip my heart from my chest." He fingered a gash in his trousers and exhaled, gazed across the distance, then, finally, back at her.

Yanking a stalk of grass from his hair, he said softly, "I don't ride often, or as often as I'd like due to the persistent drumbeat of thoughts in my head. It makes for a distracted trek, I realize, even though I love it. Dangerous not only for myself but the mount,

85

a risk with a beloved beast I wouldn't take. But you've been blocking, clear across the lawn, across every sitting room we've shared, the breakfast parlor this morning. Even from another floor in the main house, the whispers in my bedchamber are muted. I've been testing distances, making notes. Today, for instance, a hundred yards, maybe one-twenty. I reached the edge of the pine thicket before the voices started flowing back in. But something happened, you got sidetracked, or I did, and a thought shot right through my skull. I tried to cut it off, which is quite shocking for the person whose mind I've entered, hence her dropping the pan...me misjudging the height of the hedge. Bad timing all the way around."

"There was a kitchen maid quite taken with you upon our arrival. Was she daydreaming, I wonder, while you were riding? Shocking you when you received her lurid thought—shocking *her* when you tried to give it back. It's possible that I was far enough away from you for them to enter your mind."

His lips tilted, a confession in dazzling sunlight. "If I said yes, I don't think it will further our friendship. So I shall remain mum on the subject."

He was so bloody gorgeous standing there, mussed and apologetic, shuffling from one glossy boot to the other, covered in dirt and blood and ignominy, that chip in his formerly flawless smile winking at her. How could she renounce a lovesick girl, right now cleaning up whatever she'd dumped out of that pan when Victoria wasn't thinking about the man in strictly polite terms herself? "Are these the start of our experiments then?" she asked and blew a lock of hair from her face, exasperated with him and herself.

He shook his head, his lips falling open. "*Pardon?*"

She dropped her gaze to the opera glasses dangling from her wrist, sunlight bouncing off the gilded metal and throwing glints at their feet. She'd have given a gold sovereign to know what he was thinking, a clue to how she'd managed to disconcert the Blue Bastard when most failed. With 'unsophisticated candor', no doubt. Her lack of charm. "My parlor trick. The testing of distances. Your promise to enlighten me, Blue. The chronology, the League. The danger surrounding me. Is this where my education starts?"

He walked back a distancing step, tugged another reed of grass from his hair. "Are you willing?"

It depends on the request, she wanted to say with an adoring look. Artifice in spades, a playful glance fired through what she'd been told were fetching eyelashes. She knew how to flirt, how to captivate. She'd kissed three of the most eligible men in the ton, at their request, although she hadn't enjoyed it. They were destitute, unable to assist with her financial predicament, and she unable to assist with theirs. But she hadn't wanted to waste everything on her intended when she and Rossby created less spark than a damp fire.

Anyway, she'd be damned if she cried again if it caused this exquisite mindreading goat to look at her with pity. She wasn't used to being on the receiving end of anything but admiration herself, she'd love to tell him.

"That dark look has me almost frightened, but I must ask about the dreams. Tori, I need to know about the dreams."

She found his gaze, an opaque flood as vibrant as the sky. She wondered if Julian Alexander had attempted to capture the color on canvas. Unique. And familiar. Even before she'd met him, a secret she wasn't sure she should divulge.

The mystery of his past was unfolding in the gentle twilight of *her* sleep—but the answers might be disturbing.

At some point, and soon, she'd have to tell Finn about the dreams.

After all, they were, in essence, *his.*

"I'm willing," she said. *But you may not be.* Then she reached out, later she couldn't have said why, brushing a strand of hair from his cheek. It was as silky as it looked, dark as coal, streaking amber in the sunlight, the ends curling slightly. She gave it a gentle tug before releasing it to the wind. His reaction would have been gratifying, the hushed intake of air, hand clenching into a fist at his hip, the subtle lean. If not for her own overriding it. Desire, blistering and heavy and terrifying, sending her heart to her knees. She shrugged, admitting, "I used to cut my brother's hair so he could ride without it whipping in his eyes. I could do this for you, for your safety."

"I'm willing," Finn murmured, gaze fixed on her even as he took a halting step back, firmly out of reach. The air around them shimmered like waves of heat over a barren desert. One breath, two, then he strode to his mare and swung gracefully into the saddle without looking back.

She watched him ride away, wondering what they'd agreed to.

Wondering how in heaven she was going to survive a month of gazing into the saddest eyes in England.

The situation was beyond complicated.

Finn stacked his hands behind his head with a sigh that cut through the numbingly silent predawn.

She was complicated, more so than any female to enter his life to date, even Piper. He slid deeper beneath the counterpane to escape his sudden unease and the chill in the air and ran his tongue over the chip in his tooth. No fire in the hearth, he noted. No pot of tea or warm cocoa waiting on the sideboard. The maid set to do those things could likely turn herself into a dog and fly over the estate or some such inspiring sorcery—but prepare a fire in an empty hearth, no thank you. Considering his preference for sleeping *au naturel*, maybe Harbingdon's domestic disregard was a good thing.

I'm willing, he'd told her. A senseless declaration and they both knew it.

Of course, he was willing.

His compulsion was stronger than mere willingness, dominating his aimless norm of being swept along halfheartedly in a flood of debauchery and conceit.

Attracted.

He was attracted to Victoria Hamilton and then some. Profoundly. Incomprehensibly. When, despite his reputation, he rarely experienced honest longing. Most of his associations were a performance, that Blue Bastard fellow fulfilling expectation and nothing more. Not one step more.

Not one step.

Alone in the semi-darkness, he'd admit to being enthralled by her fiery temper, and what he suspected was a wholly generous heart, one she concealed almost as well as he concealed his. Enthralled by that willowy body and the raw intelligence shimmering behind spectacle glass. By the star-shaped freckle beside her lip. By the enchanting hoyden he imagined she'd been growing up, still showcased in the woman who didn't care about getting dirt on her face or blood on her skirt. Someone he could teasingly roughhouse with before sliding inside her warm, welcoming body. Most of the women he'd tupped were temperamental and resentful, using him as revenge against a feckless husband or a world that seemed to be passing them by. Their attachment fragile as gossamer, he never really touched them. Not with his mind or his heart.

Fleeting in every way that mattered.

Victoria, *ah*, the fantasies centered on her were ones he'd never considered. He wanted to tangle his hands in her hair, destroy every weak coiffure that looked one breath away from detonating in a spill down her back. He wanted to record the sound she made when pleasure overtook her, only to call it forth later while pleasuring himself in his darkened bedchamber. He wanted to find out what she was afraid to ask for. What she *craved*. What would make her skin catch fire in seconds. He wanted to leave her so well-loved she wouldn't be able to crawl from his bed for days.

He wanted to make love.

An act he never, ever thought he'd share with a woman.

But how could he ask this of her when he had no way to repay her for anything she shared with him? When she looked at the world from those amazing hazel eyes as if isolation was exactly what she expected to receive.

As if she didn't deserve more.

As if she didn't deserve love.

Dangerous, she was dangerous. And the first woman in ages, maybe forever, who didn't know it.

Any effort he made was much more than alleviating a tenacious erection, mild embarrassment every time he was within a hundred yards of her. The dilemma of a doggedly hard cock he could quickly solve on his own. In fact, he likely would before he climbed from this bed. Laughing at his idiocy, he watched the last vestiges of moonlight ripple across the ceiling, realizing it was anger coursing through him.

When he didn't often allow himself to become angry—because the boy in the rookery had been nothing *but*.

Gross emotional displays weren't his chosen method, too much loss of control. Why chance cracking his well-crafted façade? Still, it had been a long time since a woman had managed to unsettle him. Steal his breath with a single, unexpected tear coursing down her cheek. Dissolve the world around him, he suspected, should he give in to temptation and touch her.

"Tori," he murmured, letting the name drop like a coin into the yawning depths of his soul. "What am I going to do about you, you troublesome package?"

Finn closed his eyes, coveting blessed calm for another moment. They were set to begin research into Victoria's gift this morning at nine o'clock sharp. Unless he wanted to encounter the wrath of his brother, he'd best arrive at the library ten minutes early.

She thought she had him figured out when his experiences were changing him. Like clay being shaped into a different form, a cynical, temperamental man was emerging. Maybe he couldn't escape his history after all. Those who crawled from the sewer eventually crawled back in.

He didn't want to involve Victoria in his mess of a past. His mess of a future.

He kicked the sheet away with an oath. As if he *could* involve her.

Bastards were not an acceptable choice. Too, the

League was going to need her if her gift was as powerful as Julian suspected, and Finn would never stand in the way of progress with the organization his brother had sacrificed his life to build. Victoria, in turn, would need their protection when it came to light a blocker existed in their world. And someday it would.

A romantic relationship that ended badly, when they *always* ended badly, would have her running—and he couldn't risk her safety when he had nothing to offer. He grimaced in the darkness. Not when she had a baron, even one as loathsome as Rossby, on the hook.

Furthermore, and this is where it got tricky, he'd begun to *talk* to her. Unload the ballast of his life in minute chunks, lightening his burden, bringing about the unfortunate but irresistible desire to unload more. Worse, she'd begun to share her secrets with him.

He liked listening to her. He liked talking to her. Why it was…it sounded like…

Finn laughed and scrubbed his hand across his jaw. He and Victoria Hamilton were becoming friends.

Friendship. With a *woman*.

A beautiful, infuriating, insanely capricious woman whose mind he couldn't read worth a tinker's damn. What could go wrong with that?

CHAPTER 7

*H*e was late. Twenty minutes, to be exact.

The tea cool, the biscuits untouched, the library hushed, the conversations complete. Julian, Finn's brother of love-but-not-blood glanced at the mantel clock for the fifth time and tapped a paintbrush Victoria hoped was dry against the bookshelf he leaned against. Tap, tap, tap. She brought her puzzle book close to her face, hoping to appear engrossed in wordplay when all she wanted to do was study the fascinating interaction between Lord and Lady Beauchamp. She'd not been given many opportunities to witness genuine affection, a living, breathing example of a love match. It was almost unheard of in the aristocracy. Nudging her spectacles high, she watched the lady cross the room, settle her hand over the lord's paintbrush while flashing an adoring smile that would melt butter.

Or melt viscounts, as it were.

"I'm not planning to kill the boy, Yank," Julian whispered with a glowing look thrown his wife's way, a lingering sweep of his thumb across her wrist emphasizing the unusual sobriquet. "Just bash his head in a bit. Humphrey will track him down. That's worse than any piddling punishment I would dole out."

"He's not sleeping well," Victoria offered, the need to defend him making her want, in turn, to howl with laughter and hurl a book across the room. Maybe she'd start with the hulking chronology lying open on the desk, though she wasn't sure she could lift the volume, much less heave it.

Julian settled his long body against the window frame, tucking his very pregnant wife by his side, muted morning sunlight flowing around them in dust-specked streaks. The viscount presented an intimidating portrait, broad shoulders and fierce glower, a titled thug manipulating his paintbrush like a weapon, his spouse curled against him like a protective kitten. "I'm curious how you came to this deduction, Lady Hamilton."

Victoria repositioned herself on the tufted sofa, her gaze meeting Lord Beauchamp's with calm ease even if her knees shook the tiniest fraction beneath her skirt. Her relationship with her father had prepared her to handle sullen men with the steadiest of regard. "Not in an untoward manner, I assure you. I suspect I'm the only female in London who can claim *lack* of that dubious honor." She sighed and folded the edge of her puzzle book back, realizing only hoydens and lightskirts discussed bed partners in mixed company. Mercy, who cared at this point? The entire situation was beyond the pale in a disastrous way, and her reputation was likely to crumble and blow away in the wind after this summer. One floor above, she imagined poor Aggie was sniffling her head off. "The dreams he's having about me. Disruptive is all I'm suggesting," she muttered and slapped her book to the floor. "But what do I know," she murmured, hopefully for her ears alone.

Julian popped the paintbrush against his thigh, the first smile she'd noted twisting his lips. She could see what his wife found attractive in the strong jaw, the patrician nose, the eyes as gray as smoke. A solid, handsome face. A strong body. A commanding presence. "What a surprise. Every woman in this library, nay, the entire estate, begs me to go easy on my appealingly beddable little brother. The darling boy. Can't extinguish the brightest light in London, now can we?"

Before she could retract any protective gesture she'd made because, truthfully, she felt Finn's light should be dimmed slightly if not extinguished, he was there, being jostled through the library's doorway by the largest man Victoria had ever seen.

Finn sidestepped, wrestling his sleeve from the brute's grip. "You sent Humphrey to find me because I was five minutes late? Really, Jule? What am I, thirteen?"

Julian pointed the paintbrush at Finn, his smile growing. "Going on twenty-five minutes. And I don't know, are you?"

Humphrey sighed and threw himself into the only chair in the room that would hold him, a monstrous leather affair that could house a small family. "Found him in the kitchens surrounded by a pack of squawking geese, and I don't mean the bird kind. Lounging like he had all the time in the world, waiting for one of the flock to brush crumbs off his lip or offer him another morsel, and of what, I'm not going to say. Delaying the inevitable, he was. Again. Like I don't dread this research project myself."

Piper rapped Humphrey on the shoulder, and he

started. "Begging pardon, ma'am," he said with a nod in Victoria's direction, "because I can't *wait* to see what magic you're about to pull out of your lacy sleeve. I'm sorry to say, after years of miraculous arrivals, I don't know if I have anything left in me to be impressed. Unless your talent is procuring the finest Irish whiskey known to man with a wrinkle of your nose. That I'd be impressed by."

Finn expelled a breath through his teeth and circled behind the sofa, seating himself at the opposite end, as far from her as he could get. "I simply went to get another crumpet. Crucify me, but Cook makes the best in England. I was trying to escape the kitchen when the big heavy here found me."

Victoria swiveled her head and pierced him with a droll look. "Crumpet?" she mouthed. She'd tasted one this morning, and they were stale. She could whip up a pastry in ten paltry minutes that would have him crying in his soup.

Wordlessly, he crossed his long legs at the ankle and balanced his chin on his knuckle, the very picture of impudent negligence. But she could see his jaw muscle ticking in time to Julian's paintbrush taps. So much more going on beneath the surface than he liked to admit. Exhausting, she imagined, the daily battles he fought to allow the caricature to rule the man.

Victoria moistened her lips and swallowed, the click of her throat cracking the silence. "I don't make magic. It's a parlor trick, sleight of hand. Nothing more. Nothing monumental. From the little Mr. Alexander has told me, you invite people here who have true gifts. Sight and touch and sense. This, mine, is largely"—she flipped her gloved hand over and back—"an annoyance."

"I'll go first, Lady Hamilton," Julian said, "as we provide insight into your annoyance." He motioned to his brother. "Finn, something from your pocket, please. A coin, anything. Although I fear what I may witness during this test, I fear it much less than I normally would."

Finn tunneled his hand in his waistcoat pocket, coming up with a silver penknife, which he tossed to Julian. The teasing hint of cardamom drifted to her like a caress, and she wondered how he managed to smell edible and entirely masculine at the same time.

Julian traced the engraving on the front of the knife. "You still have this? Must be going on ten years since I gave it to you."

Finn stacked one glossy boot atop the other. "My thirteenth birthday, so going on twelve."

Victoria was unable to contain her surprised murmur as she did a quick calculation. Finn was her age, maybe even a few months younger. For some reason, this fact made her crosser than anything had since receiving his bloody invitation. With his innumerable extravagances and the beguiling bit of gray in his hair, she'd imagined him to be thirty at least.

She sank back against the cushions, seething.

The cheeky smile Finn shot her was filled with such genuine delight she wanted to pinch him—like she had her brother when he vexed her.

"Old enough, Tori darling," he whispered for her alone. Then he danced his fingers through the streak of silver at his temple. "I like it. Makes me appear older than my years, handy on occasion. Nothing so remarkable as your wild tangle, curls fighting to escape those distressingly feeble arrangements. If anxious Agnes can't assist, you'll not find a maid at Harbingdon who can. Make you disappear and appear on the other side of the estate, maybe, but construct a simple coiffure? Alas, we're not equipped."

Her hand rose to smooth her hair. As if she could help that the strands were as unbiddable as her nature and that neither she nor Agnes was skilled enough to confine them. With effort, she tore her gaze from the reclining boor taking up too much of the sofa's acreage and focused it on Lord Beauchamp. "You mentioned providing insight, my lord?"

Julian stared at the penknife he smoothed his thumb over as if he sought to polish it to a high sheen. When he lifted his head, her breath caught at the intensity of his expression. "I see visions when I touch objects. Visions of someone who touched the object previously. A day or a week before, I have no choice in the visitations. Vivid, often disturbing scenes best left unobserved. This gift has complicated my life beyond what I'd wish on anyone, changed it beyond what I'd planned. As yours likely did, my mystic ability started when I was too young to realize I should hide it, and when I exposed it, my father reacted, shall we say, violently. So I ran to Seven Dials, the nastiest slum in London, where I knew I would become lost. Our butler had grown up there, and I never forgot the stories he told me about the place. How you could disappear, never to return. How you could become another person." He tipped the penknife the hulking brute's way. "Humphrey found me, saved my life truth be told, and a year or so later, I found Finn, his gift making him notorious in a hell-hole where no one wants notoriety, a gentle boy swimming in a sea of sharks. I don't think I'm telling you anything he hasn't, which in itself—I dare say your appearance at Harbingdon at all—is most unusual."

Her attention shifted to the gentle boy, but he'd

closed his eyes. Although she knew he was listening from the pulse drumming a fierce beat just below his ear, a delicate spot she had the sudden urge to press her lips to. When her lips had never traveled beyond a man's mouth—and she'd never wished them to.

Julian placed the penknife on the window seat with almost solemn reverence, a dull click that resonated through the room like a church's bell. "I've never encountered an object, not once in my life, without images—soft and muted or fantastic and grotesque—storming my mind. More vivid than any painting I can create, and trust me, I've tried. Laid out what I see on canvas as a way to expunge the illustrations from my mind. This has happened every day, with every touch, every doorknob, every spoon, every teacup, except for four instances." His gaze circled back to her, blazing with enough emotion to send her to her knees had she been standing. As outlandish as it seemed, he looked like he wanted to drop to his knees himself. She'd suspected this man to be taciturn when he was anything but. "Four instances when you and I have shared the same space."

"Blasted, bleeding hell," Humphrey growled and shoved to his feet, stalking to the sideboard situated at the back of the library. "I had a deadly feeling about this summer."

"Calm down, Rey," Julian murmured. "This could be a very good thing."

"A fine predicament is what it is. We'll need an army to fortify the estate because once they find out about her, we're at war. You'd better get word to Fireball." The carafe clinked as he poured, the glass smacking wood after he drank. Apparently, the startling admission meant morning refreshments would be served, at least to handsome beasts who rescued viscounts from rookeries and genuinely detested the occult but chose to live amidst it.

Victoria frowned. "Fireball?"

"The Duke of Ashcroft," Finn replied from his drowsy repose. "A story for another day."

Ashcroft. She flinched, kicking her puzzle book beneath the table, so bewildered her teeth were beginning to ache. "I'm not doing anything to weaken your ability, my lord. I'm simply...*being*. My parlor trick involves stealing time. Brief, insignificant spans of time. I make people forget trivial events, often things they've seen me do that I, in all honesty, shouldn't have done." She felt Finn's searing gaze strike her, the judgmental oaf. "I present a change of plan when it suits, paltry misdirection. I persuade people to take certain paths, a harmless nudge."

"My lady, misdirection appears to be your side gift. However, your main one is astounding in our world, and as you've just entered it, I understand your lack of awareness. You see, you're not weakening my ability, you're halting it in its tracks. Not to sound disrespectful, especially in front of my cherished wife, but if you were a timepiece, I'd never remove you from my pocket. Around you, I am *ordinary*. As it is, I've spent two mornings in a dining area not of my choosing but one that brings blessed relief from the constant visions. Have you not noticed the crowd in there, servants and family at one table? Have you seen that happen at any aristocratic home in England? Scullery maids and the lord of the manor dining together? But I can't deny them what is so wonderfully rejuvenating to me as well. You diminish the chaos in their minds, if not outright erasure. *That* is your gift, one that places you in grave danger should our enemies ever, *ever* know of your existence. And someday they will, make no mistake."

"What enemies? I have no enemies."

Julian flipped the penknife to Finn, who caught it with a one-handed snatch. "Leave it to you, boy-o, to bring home the second most obstinate woman in England. As it seems I've failed to convince her, Piper darling, queen of obstinacy, you'll have to try."

Victoria scowled as Finn slipped the penknife in his pocket without meeting her gaze. The graceful cur was doing nothing to save her from this interrogation when she'd protected him earlier.

Piper staggered to her feet with assistance from her husband. "Excuse me, everyone, while I roam the room. I can't sit for long periods without my back spasming, because he or she is a very, very active babe." She laid her hand over her rounded tummy and smiled, her eyes glowing as fiercely as the emeralds in Victoria's favorite brooch. A family heirloom sold long ago to pay one of the many creditors pounding on their door.

Victoria settled back with an inward sigh, and an acknowledged cautionary prickle dancing along her skin. She would leave this library with more understanding than she'd ever been granted about herself if she let them continue. But did she genuinely *want* to understand? Why change her life over a chess move employed to divert select interactions, an innocuous exchange always in her favor? Altering little except to postpone a marriage she didn't want. Hide reckless kisses she'd mistakenly thought would ease her loneliness. Buying time by stealing it. Why complicate the future with talk of blocking supernatural gifts and being someone's shielding pocket watch when she could muddle along with some normalcy, the ordinary life Julian Alexander spoke of with such reverence.

This entire country sojourn was inviting the abnormal into her existence.

Piper circled the sofa, halting before the chronology. She flipped a page, two, before she looked over her shoulder. "My grandfather, the Earl of Montclaire, started the League after he realized his wife was afflicted with an unnatural skill, a skill I unfortunately inherited. Healing, not in the medical sense, more an ability to...calm. Strengthen. Provide control. I help mystics find their way." She smoothed her finger over the lines of text. "He died protecting this, a book containing everything he knew about the occult. And in his final moments, he placed responsibility for the organization, responsibility for maintaining the chronology and protecting his granddaughter, at Julian's feet. To be honest, lobbed all three like explosives when my husband was little more than a boy himself. In the ensuing years, we've grown from a scattered collection of enthusiasts into an organization spread across many countries, with contacts at every level of society, sheltering those at Harbingdon when dire need requires it."

"This is why the gaslights flicker, doors open and close without touch. The haphazard way..." Victoria paused, twisting her hands in her lap, remembering a lady never commented to her hostess about the disorder of her home.

Piper flipped another page and laughed beneath her breath. "Harbingdon does run a bit like a carriage with a missing wheel most days. Everyone employed on the estate is a member of the League. Either personally affected or a family member of someone who is. So you see, most are placed in positions they were never trained for. But this effort has created an environment of acceptance and, frankly, safety."

Humphrey grunted from his position guarding

the refreshments he'd had yet to offer anyone else, clearly unimpressed by this aspect of Harbingdon's management.

"Like you, I have another gift in that I see auras, as I told you the day you arrived." Piper drew her hand through the air as if she were painting on a canvas. "Colors surround everyone I meet, ones that tell me quite a lot about their state of mind. You're one of only two people I've not been able to record this portrait for. Combined with Julian's lack of touch and Finn's inability to read your mind, I predict we have much more to discuss."

As if on cue, Finn rolled off the sofa and strolled to the chronology. So, he hadn't been asleep. She watched his lower lip slip between his teeth as he began to flip pages, searching, his long body angled over the imposing leather-bound volume, his hair a tousled mop he had to repeatedly sweep from his vision. He trailed his finger along the lines of text, whispering in a mix of English and German. "There's mention of someone with the ability to"—he leaned in, brow creasing as he translated—"place obstacles in the path of a mystical corridor. As closely as I can interpret, as the script is quite dated." He tilted his head, his frown sending that enticing little dent between his brows. "This references an obstructer, though the earl called it a blocker as he's noted in the margin." Pausing, he glanced back at Victoria, his regard as tangible as a touch. "But you should think of this as a puzzle, Tori, if it makes the investigation into your gift more palatable."

Their gazes met as a jolt of awareness passed between them, keen emotion she feared was closer to desire than friendship. Which would just be her rotten romantic luck when all of England lay scattered at his feet. Finn's eyes were highlighted in the muted light cast from the window, so penetrating she had trouble wading from their depths. Proof of his intelligence, entirely at odds with his lackadaisical demeanor, it brought a hot pinch to her stomach and a shot of anger to her mind. *You hide this incredible intellect behind carriage races and feckless mistresses*, she thought but let the critical observation remain unspoken.

"Who knows about you?" Humphrey asked from his shadowy corner. "About this?"

Victoria tore her gaze from Finn's, able to provide an answer she suspected would ease some of the tension in the room. "Aside from my companion, Agnes, who's been with me since birth, no one. I've shocked more than a few governesses into silence, true enough, but the stolen time only left them befuddled. I never felt the need to confess what I considered a ridiculous trick of nature. Of course, I told my brother, he knew, but now he's...gone." She picked at a loose thread on her skirt, avoiding the pitying gazes sure to arrive with the next revelation. "My mother wasn't directly involved with childrearing, distasteful business, or so she stated on many occasions. My father was unconcerned about anything aside from his horses. So I was left to my own devices, easily able to hide anything that made me different. And when I was introduced to society, my outspoken demeanor and insignificant dowry sent me like a boulder over a cliff. Straight down and out of sight. Not many were tempted to befriend me."

"Your frightful temper couldn't have helped," Finn murmured and negligently flipped a page. "Or your astounding penchant for trouble."

Victoria yanked the thread free and swallowed what she'd love to say if not amid unfamiliar company. If the trace of a smile lighting Finn Alexander's face grew any wider, she was going to lose the scant hold she had on her frightful temper. "My intended, Baron Rossby, has no clue about my parlor trick, will never have a clue. Our agreement, funds to save my family in exchange for an heir, does not require me to share my life." Which sounded miserable, she knew. However, the reality surrounding aristocratic marriages was often ugly.

"Rossby," Julian echoed in an unenthusiastic tone.

She nodded, eyes on her lap, refusing to confront the criticism sure to make her feel worse about a situation she had no control over. "Yes, the Grape. It's an unfortunate moniker, although he does slightly resemble—"

The door to the library burst open, and a little boy raced across the room and piled into Finn's legs before Victoria had time to draw a proper breath. Finn laughed, swinging the boy into his arms without a hint of the discomfort she'd always felt around children.

"Fig, Fig, Fig," the scamp chanted.

"Finn," he corrected, sliding his forearm under the lad's skinny bottom to hold him up.

The boy presented a crooked smile and a jam-covered hand which he flattened over Finn's cheek, leaving a smear of what looked like raspberry preserves. The spiral of heat in her belly as she imagined licking the jam from his skin was not good. Not good at all.

"Careful with your injury, Finn. Lucien will sock you without knowing what he's doing. He's a strong little bugger."

Finn recoiled, his cheeks leeching color before he gained control and let a placid smile bleed through. "It's healed, Jule. Quit worrying."

"You take more care, boy-o, and I'll do less worrying."

A maid burst into the room, her cheeks rosy from a race she'd lost, the interruption ruining any chance Victoria had to ascertain if Julian was talking about the nasty scar on Finn's chest. And how, exactly, he'd acquired it.

"Lucien, you wee devil! I told you mama and papa were busy. You'll get no cookie with these antics. Apologies," she panted and bobbed her head to the room at large, "but he's as swift as a Whitechapel cutpurse, he is. Running me ragged, and that's the truth."

Lucien perked up. "Cookie?"

Piper laughed and wagged her fingers at her son. "Oh, Minnie, give him his cookie. How can you resist that brilliant smile?"

"Spoiled rotten is what he is," Minnie grumbled as a cookie lifted from her apron pocket, two tries before it floated into the boy's hand. She frowned and brought her fist to her brow. "It's hard to do that with her in the room, you're right, my lord Julian. She's bringing the quiet to my mind, deafening quiet. Like trying to run through butter."

Victoria clicked her tongue against her teeth. *Ah*, this was the lady's maid who moved objects with her mind.

"Fig," Lucien said around a mouthful of cookie.

Unable to tear her eyes from boy and man, her heart squeezed as Finn brushed crumbs from Lucien's bottom lip with a tender touch.

They were a family, this odd assortment of people, unconnected by anything as lofty as blood. When Victoria had found blood to be a most tenuous connection herself. Her marriage to the Grape could produce offspring, an adorable little thing like Lucien. Maybe two, if she could endure the process to create them. She was terrified of children, of course, but assumed she'd very much like her own.

Though she wasn't looking forward to seeing a naked Grape.

Finn glanced at her, his gaze pensive, that subtle way he had of reading her—when she knew he wasn't reading her as he was accustomed to. A new experience for them both. He nodded to the boy in his arms, shrugged a broad shoulder, his smile for once posing a genuine offer. *Would you like to hold Lucien?*

The envy was robust and shocking. She shook her head wildly and crowded into the velvet cushions. He blinked slowly, thoughts churning, the shift to indigo as sympathy filled his eyes apparent across the short distance separating them. Recognition erupted like champagne bubbles beneath her skin and scrambled dangerously along her nerve endings. He had the disturbing ability to reveal her until she felt stripped to her drawers, a sensation both embarrassing *and* arousing. She released a fast breath through her teeth.

There was no place in her life for what he made her feel, no place at all.

"You've had your treat, young man. It's off with you now," Minnie commanded and took a wiggling Lucien from Finn.

"Fig," he repeated as she carried him out of the library. "Bye-bye."

Fig, Victoria thought and felt her heart not just sink but crumble. Like the biscuits she'd baked last night to calm herself, one of which was clutched in Lucien's tiny fist.

"I'll do it," she said when the door closed, without touch, behind them. "Research, notes for your chronology, assessment of my parlor trick and how it can help the League, whatever best suits. I'll be an able soldier, all in for the cause. One month, then I must return to London. I've already put off the Grape for as long as I dare."

And the dreams, she added silently when Finn turned with a raised brow.

She would gather her courage and tell the charming Fig about her dreams.

Even if he hated her for sharing them.

CHAPTER 8

This day was getting worse, Finn decided as he watched Simon pace the library in one of those adolescent moods that took hours to recover from. "You can't possibly go with me to London when I return. Your life is here, your tutor is here, your family is here."

"You don't know how bad he gets," Simon threw over his shoulder. "I'm in prison!"

"You jest. I know *exactly* how domineering Julian is, God do I. Still breathing down my neck even at this age. That's what you have to look forward to, by the way. Although you must remember, the undue attention is given with love." Brandishing his penknife, Finn fractured the seal on a letter he'd selected from the pile the domineering man in question had left for him to parse through. Dispatches arriving from the League's contacts spread across the continent, warnings of threats to someone in their community, most written in languages Finn could translate with at least moderate proficiency. He'd appropriated the library, covering every surface with ledgers, language primers, and correspondence related to the management of the Blue Moon, a surprisingly time-consuming business to keep afloat even if Julian felt he'd stepped down a level by taking too great an interest in it. "I survived, and so will you. Or rather, I am endeavoring to survive."

Simon mumbled a curse, then closed his mouth at Finn's sharp look. "If it's the women," the boy said in an aggrieved tone, "I'll ignore them like I do every dead soul who follows me through life. The trollops *and* the classier ones, mum's the word. I won't tell Julian a thing. I can sleep through all sorts of racket, aside from the haunts. Come home blotto for all I care. I've seen the inside of a gaming hell, you know. Picked more than one pocket in the Devil's Lair back in the day. Went through an entire room in minutes and left with a king's ransom, best in the East End."

"Except the time you were caught and beaten to within an inch of your life."

Simon rotated a coin between his fingers, sunlight glinting off the metal and casting sparks on his striped waistcoat. At one time, he'd been the most renowned cutpurse in London, to this day able to perform sleight of hand better than any magician could hope to. "You're starting to sound just like him. A boring, old toff."

Finn felt his second sizzle of temper, the first occurring when Humphrey dragged him from the kitchens. He rarely got angry in London, but his family had the uncanny ability to rouse him in seconds flat. It broke his heart to imagine the 'racket' Simon had to sleep through before the League found him living in St. Giles, a hellhole even worse than the one he, Julian, and Humphrey had escaped from. The fact he had to endure daily conversations with ghosts —or *haunts* as he called them—had made for an unbearably troubling childhood. Losing patience with himself and Simon, Finn ripped into an envelope like

he was slitting a throat. "Do you imagine my disso-
lute lifestyle is a suitable model for a young man to
witness? We're trying to separate you from depravity,
Si, not draw it closer."

Simon's face took on the rosy shade of a beet as
he shoved to his feet. He gave his nose a vicious
swipe. "You could change your life if you wanted to.
Less debauchery, less everything, for your family.
Find a wife and make a proper home, then take me
with you. You're my brother, too, not just his, and
you left when I needed you! Do you think it's easy
with all these people in my head, standing by my
side? Living life with me! Telling me things I don't
want to hear?" With a hand that trembled, he shoved
the coin in his pocket. "But the blasted women mean
more than I do, I guess," he said on a tear-laden
breath and sprinted from the room, slamming the
door behind him.

"Brilliant," Finn ground out and yanked his hand
through his hair. The tender age of fourteen was
proving to be a difficult one for Simon to navigate.
The scar on Finn's chest chose that moment to throb,
reminding him of Freddie and the *real* reason he'd
been keeping his distance for months. One boy reminding him of the other. A venomous circle of guilt
and worry, and then more guilt.

It was frightening to love someone and still be
unable to make everything better. Make everything
perfect. Smooth their path so they'd never stumble.

When Simon joined their family, he'd been a
filthy, willful eight-year-old rescued from a flash
house crawling with thieves, vagrants, prostitutes.
Abused and tormented, he'd trusted no one. Stolen
almost every piece of silver in the house, picked
every lock, every pocket, told every lie, before finally
letting someone—Finn—into his heart. Two or-

phaned gutter rats who recognized something desperate in the other.

Simon mistakenly believed Finn would choose anything, *anyone*, over his family, when he loved the boy like a son, with his every breath. Finn swore and hurled his knife at the door, where it stuck deep, quivering.

He was on his feet to retrieve it when the knock sounded. "No," he snapped, caring little who stood on the other side. Although he knew who stood on the other side. He could feel the ripple beneath his skin, the warning squeeze in his gut. And no one's thoughts intruded. His mind was clear. *Damn her.*

She knocked again, tenacious to the end. "Let me in, Blue," she pleaded. "I need a moment without a roomful of people staring at me with dreamy eyes. Oh, here they come. Just five minutes without being anyone's savior. Please, I beg of you."

He pinched the bridge of his nose, groaned, laughed. *Hell.* Opened the door to find Victoria Hamilton, fetching in a gown the color of the roses crowding the estate flowing over her supple, elegant body. Her skirts brushed his legs as she passed, a delicious tickle, her perfume—delicate and dreadfully feminine—trailing just behind. It astounded that nothing came to him but the look and scent of her. Not one private thought, not one. Like a normal, pathetic man, he was left to figure out what a woman was thinking for the first time in his existence.

She watched in enthrallment as he yanked the knife from the door, snapped it shut, and slid it neatly in his pocket. "Our research appointment with Julian isn't scheduled to begin for another half-hour," he said.

"Yes, yes, I know. I'm early. And remarkably, you're here." She tipped her shoulder toward the door. "Close that, will you? Maybe then they won't find me."

Following her directive, he closed the door and rested against it, knowing he shouldn't but doing it anyway. "How untoward, Lady Hamilton. What would poor, devoted Agnes say about you shutting yourself in a library with a man of my reputation?"

"She would faint, more than likely. Although with my reputation, maybe *you* should be frightened. As it is, she's in bed with a garlic poultice. The peculiar inhabitants of Harbingdon are giving her the vapors. A saltshaker slid across the table by itself at breakfast, and that was that. She's having none of what she calls the spooks at the moment."

Finn lifted off the door with a startled chuckle. "Oh, my, is she going to have a horrendous summer. Wait until Simon tells her about the haunts who reside on the estate, the ones likely sitting beside her at dinner."

"Indeed," she agreed, her gaze tracking him as he circled the desk and collapsed to his chair with a squeak of stiff leather. Her regard lit him up, a modest glow, a sensation he didn't remember feeling before. Possibly because thoughts were rampaging his mind, and they'd dulled his reception.

Not comfortable being honest with her, he released a practiced, flat smile. The Blue Bastard's façade firmly in place, which made him feel secure and dejected.

What do you want, Tori? Rest assured I may not care. I'll undoubtedly act like I don't.

She gave her spectacles a boost, pinched her lips together, contemplating her words, sweetly nervous, which perversely made his cock stiffen even as a dart of dread at what she might say pierced him. She was patient, a thinker. A strategist, as he was, even if he didn't look the part. Evidently, intelligent women appealed when he'd been settling for senseless ones all this time. "You seem troubled," she finally decided on with a pointed glance at the gash in the door.

His erection wilted. Solid choice of topic, he thought grimly. "Family matters."

She walked to the bookshelf, freed a slim book of poetry, and turned it over in her hand. "Troubled, when I would give anything to have so many people care about me. You're the most popular person in Oxfordshire. Sincere affection, too, unlike the rabid thirst in London. That's not a burden, it's a godsend."

The third jolt of anger this morning raced through him. "Did I say it was a burden, my lady?" Swallowing tightly, he smoothed his hand over his chest, the thought too close to the one he'd had when he threw the damned knife.

She pivoted to face him, her eyes highlighted in the sunlight, a mix falling somewhere between the color of spring soil and autumn leaves. They were changelings, altering with her mood. As they stared, lost, a gust raced through the window and sent papers drifting about the room like snowflakes. "Would you like to talk about it?"

It. The scar. She'd seen the mark that night at the Blue Moon. Her gaze had lingered on the open collar of his shirt and the angry slash beneath for long enough. "Not without a lot to drink, no, I don't think I would."

She replaced the volume and circled the room, stopping before a stack of books he used when translations were getting complicated. "Medieval Latin," she murmured. "I have to admit, Blue, I'm impressed. What a mind you've been hiding. A fantastic gambit. You've fooled them all."

His skin heated—no way to admit it was anything

but pleasure—just enough to let him know what a daft fool he was. Enough to let him know how much he liked this snappish, enchanting, clever woman and her incidental observations. "Not bad for a gutter rat, I suppose."

Signaling an impending storm, another breeze lashed the room, ripping a strand from her wobbly chignon and slinging it across her cheek. England surely couldn't let them have more than two hours of sunlight without recompense. Tipping his head against the curled tuft of the chair, he let his lids slide low though he could still see every delicious inch of her. "Your hair has a mind of its own. As feral as your temper."

He watched her reaction unfold, fascinated to his toes. A slight lift of her hand to smooth the errant strands, then stubborn denial of the impulse. Brave girl. With a playful smile he'd give a thousand pounds to be allowed to decipher, she crossed to the desk, steepled her fingertips on the edge and leaned in. "Now that you mention it, do any of those desk drawers hold a pair of scissors?"

Scissors? But he found a pair readily enough, offered them with the sharp edge flattened against his palm. No need to encourage treacherous behavior.

"Turn," she ordered and drew her finger in a tight air-circle. "And take off the jacket."

He rose, his pulse doing a fiendish dance beneath his skin. Her voice held a rough thread of longing if he was not mistaken. Because he stole thoughts to confirm his suspicions, he usually wasn't. But not this time, no hints for him—and Victoria's face showed only serene vacancy. Talk about gambits. Without question, he followed her directives, shrugging out of his coat, one arm, then the next, giving it a neat fold and setting it on the desk. When he went to sit in the chair, she halted him with a light touch that was pure torture, spirals of pleasure racing down his arm and out his fingertips. "Perch on the edge. Back to me. I'm tall enough, and the height should serve well."

Serve well for what he wanted to ask more than he'd wanted to ask anything. In. His. Life. Did she realize you could command someone like this in bed and have them eating from your hand? Have them *begging*.

Higher, lower, faster, harder...more.

Arousal flooded his body, his cock digging painfully against the bone buttons running the length of his trouser close. He dropped his arm to cover it and breathed hard through his nose. Then he remembered. A memory propelled by the fingers dipping into the hair framing his nape and skimming his scalp, the teasing, cinnamon-scented breath streaking past his cheek and diving into his senses.

The haircut.

His lids slipped low as the scissors made a metallic hiss next to his ear. She would do this when they'd agreed to friendship? Agreed to a denial of their attraction?

When she knew who and *what* he was?

My God, she was a reckless bit of baggage. Or mad. Or both.

He'd not consented to touching. Standing so close he could almost taste her. Feeling enticement of this magnitude without his gift tainting it, turning his feelings in upon themselves until they were a twisted mess. Emotion, honest and pure, and overwhelming, with nothing to suck the life from it.

"Don't be alarmed. I used to do this for my brother. And some of the household staff when funds got ridiculously tight, and we had to reduce wages." She tugged on his hair, pulling the strands taut as she snipped, and he barely contained a groan of delight. Goosebumps erupted along his arms. His chest constricted. His heartbeat raced. "I'm quite proficient. Steady hand and all that."

"What?" he asked breathlessly, his concentration held captive by a raging erection and the air trapped in his lungs. She thought he feared the *haircut*? That he cared if she had a steady hand? A jolt of humility hit him, the Blue Bastard brought gutter-low. He wasn't sure how experienced she was, what with the hasty kisses she tossed out like torn stockings, but this effort pointed to it being less than he'd assumed. Much less.

Because her touch was setting him on fire.

She went on talking like nothing momentous was occurring. Although the chatter did somewhat diminish the impact of her hands roving all over him. "How is the Duke of Ashcroft involved with the League? I believe the giant called him Fireball."

Finn suppressed the shiver that pleaded for the opportunity to work its way up to his spine as bits of hair fluttered to his lap. "Um…" He struggled as another sweet breath blasted past his ear. Why did she always smell like biscuits? "This stays within the confines of this estate, but he has a rather unusual talent for shooting fire from his fingertips. Rather, he can start fires at will. It's quite extraordinary. Or bloody frightening, take your pick. Because his control has not always been tip-top. It's why he's known to favor pyrotechnics. A solid excuse for the accidents at his estates."

The scissors snapped shut as her gasp circled the room.

"It's true. I have the singed clothing to prove it."

"He's part of the League," she whispered.

"For years. Since he helped us resolve a kidnapping incident with Piper before she and Julian were married."

"Kidnapping?"

"We have enemies. I tried to tell you." He suppressed a shiver, curling his hands into fists to keep from running his fingers through his newly-shorn hair. "Ashcroft's contacts have broadened our reach in ways we'd never have without him, while Piper has helped him gain modest control. An equitable trade. Also, he's a former soldier with mercenaries on his payroll, ones Julian likes to plant like shrubs around the estate. You've seen them, the ones with stern expressions and scarred faces. Julian's increasing them around the perimeter, with you here. In the future..." Finn clenched his jaw to keep the sentiment from spilling free.

The Grape couldn't protect her.

But the Duke of Ashcroft could.

And he had the funds to save her family, save a thousand families. A destitute aristocrat, the duke was not. Although Finn made no mention of it, thanks to Julian's sound investments and his own of late, he could save a few families himself. But money could not change *fact*. Finn would never be more than a noble byblow—and the actual truth, which he'd want his wife to know—was even less palatable.

He would never be a suitable choice for an earl's daughter.

Despite the challenge his body was issuing with one standing behind him smelling of sodding flowers and sweets just pulled from the oven, her attentive little breaths racing past his ear, her fingers having stilled to rest lightly on his shoulder. He'd never before felt like he might, with an innocent, grazing touch, spill in his trousers like a randy adolescent.

Christ, being this close to her was torment of a

variety he was unaccustomed to.

Because he usually took what he wanted. Was *offered* what he wanted.

Following a blind impulse, he swiveled to face her. Her gaze was the glazed, cavernous color of a forest at midnight, her bottom lip swollen as if she'd been assaulting it. As he watched, holding himself as steady as he had in his life, her cheeks lit, a vivid wash followed by an unsteady exhalation.

So, he wasn't the only one affected by the haircut.

"I didn't enjoy the kisses," she whispered. "Three to be exact. March, Lyle, Somerset. Oh, well, four counting Rossby. Although his was painful. Bruised my lip. I dare say I'm not looking forward to that again." She smiled, but it didn't reach her eyes. "That will make having offspring rather a problem, won't it?"

He blinked, releasing his own unsteady breath when he wanted to smash his fist into the Grape's face. "Why tell me this?"

Her pupils flared, chin lifting, gaslight winking off her spectacle lenses. "Because I think I'd like yours."

The devastating confession held him captive, boxed in on all sides, his heart bumping against his ribs until he was sure she could hear it over the ticking mantel clock, the call of a Whippoorwill outside the window, the clang of a washbasin down the hall. Like a translation, he was uncovering obscure pieces of her one word at a time. Lashes so long they dusted her skin when she blinked, a delightful sprinkling of freckles across the bridge of her nose, the one next to her mouth that had called to him from the first moment he'd seen it.

She held his gaze, accepted his regard with quiet courage. A formidable partner should he be looking for one.

He recalled her warning at the Blue Moon. *I'm not going to yield.*

Evidently, neither was he.

With judicious intent, he slipped her spectacles from her face, gave them a gentle fold, and placed them on the desk. "You're right," he agreed, sliding his hand up her cheek and into her hair, guiding her body into position between his spread legs. "You will like it."

"What are you doing?" Her voice was frayed at the edges.

"Breaking our agreement."

Then with a soft sigh, he pressed his lips to hers.

Touching him had been a mistake.

Tendering such an intimate gesture as trimming his hair had been a mistake. All she'd done was free the strands to curl adorably about a face that needed no further introduction. Gambling with herself and him for some irrational reason. Likely because, hellion at heart, she couldn't help herself. Backing down from a dare, even her own, was not a skill.

Now, his lips were covering hers, his head tilting to adjust the fit, the hand at her nape squeezing as he released a hoarse sound that ignited her blood, sending a river of fire through her veins. He was as tied up by their attraction as she was, this unbelievably handsome, brilliant man.

"Let me in," he pleaded, his thumb drawing her bottom lip down until she had no choice but to follow his command. Follow every forbidden one whispering through her mind.

Step in until your hips meet.

Tangle your fingers in his hair.

Angle your head.

Touch his tongue with yours.

Clash, engage, *explore.*

It was a kiss unlike any she'd ever experienced—and she tumbled into it with abandon. It wasn't born of domination or teasing flights of fancy, an effort to persuade or negotiate. An endeavor built around running from trouble or into it.

It wasn't soft. It wasn't gentle. A typical first-try experiment.

It wasn't even perfect.

It was fierce.

His tooth bumped hers, the one with the chip. When she ran her tongue along the ragged edge, helplessly digging her fingertips into his scalp and bringing him closer, he reacted with a moan and a hip shift that brought his shockingly stalwart erection into play against her thigh. She shouldn't have known what it was, a gently bred young woman, yet she did.

And it, *he*, felt magnificent.

She sighed in yearning as astonishing discoveries ripped through her. His breath teasing her lips as he repositioned his mouth over hers and dove deeper. The moist flush of his skin beneath her questing hands. Broad shoulders, muscular chest, lean hips. Brushed cotton caressing her cheek as he wrapped his arms around her. The enticing scent of spice and chocolate clinging to his hair, his skin, his clothing. His hands moving lower, grasping her hips and settling her against him as she went up her toes to secure the fit. The world spun, racing at high speed, and locking them in its fiery center.

What a kiss was all she could think.

What a *man.*

What a *find.*

She was sliding his brace off his shoulder, having already tugged his four-in-hand from about his neck when voices in the hallway suspended rotation of the clandestine world they occupied. With a wrenching, awkward movement, he gripped her shoulders and pushed her back, blinked hard, and met her gaze, presenting as bewildered an expression as she guessed she'd ever see from him. She watched, waiting. It was seconds, long, measured seconds, before the room they stood in, their being locked in each other's embrace, before everything—good, bad, indifferent—came to him, riding on his sharp intake of air. "Fucking hell," he whispered, brushing his knuckles across his lips as if they stung.

This won't end well, her mind taunted. Not when such a grim expression was seizing his features, his eyes darkening to a thoughtful, complicated, hands-off indigo. He uncurled her fingers from his brace and slipped it back in place, then went to a knee to retrieve his necktie from where it lay crumpled on the carpet. Appalling, perhaps, but she, Victoria Lane Hamilton, disregarded daughter of an earl, had been in the process of undressing Finn Alexander, celebrated bounder, in his brother's library.

Victoria took two steps back and slumped to the sofa they'd shared a mere twenty-four hours prior with their attraction admitted to but not acted upon. A disastrous difference. Finn was set to deny everything—she could see this from the stiff set of his shoulders, the downcast eyes, the way he yanked the tie about his neck, and created the ugliest four-in-hand she'd ever seen with fingers that, thank you very much, *Tori darling*, shook.

"Fine," she whispered, dropping her brow to her hand and squeezing. She could play this game. She'd played any number of games with any number of gentlemen. Forlorn but fine in the end, she wanted to tell the Blue Bastard but didn't dare.

In that fantastic world we stepped into, we were normal.

Did you feel it, Finn? Normal.

Maybe that was what unnerved him, because he looked unnerved crouching there on Julian's faded Aubusson rug, collecting hair she'd clipped from his head and placing it delicately in his cupped palm.

After all, the poor man had never experienced normal.

"You're a virgin in this area. Is this the source of your discomfiture?"

His gaze hit her, the ire in his eyes—and just who the devil he was angry with she'd love to know—a surprise. *"What?"*

She tapped her temple. "For the first time, you can't steal someone's thoughts. Did I like it? Was it better than the others? Do I suspect you're a most extraordinary lover? You've bedded half of the women in London, so why the tumult over a simple kiss? Because you can't read the mind of the accomplice? Join the rest of us who have to make an insecure guess, Mr. Alexander!"

"Don't believe everything you hear. It's far less than half." He gave his neckpiece a solidifying jerk and rose to his feet, dusting at his shoulders, hair flying. She tried to ignore the bulge in his trousers, she really did. Inelegant of her, but it was too impressive to ignore. *He* was too impressive to ignore. "I'll tell you this much, no simple kiss I've ever participated in included the accomplice removing my clothing one tantalizing piece at a time. That's reserved for the complicated kisses. My bright idea, this whole debacle, true enough, but you ended it close to climbing atop me." He dropped to the chair, dumped the hair on a stack of letters, and gave her spectacles a dink that had them sliding across the desk and against a ledger. His firm jaw was set like stone. "And if you've ever had better, I'll eat my goddamn hat. I've seen a few of them, remember? Those graciously-offered-behind-pillar kisses extended to every loose-lipped fop in town. Truthfully, they looked inhospitable and not much else."

"You don't wear hats," she snapped, insulted by his riposte when his reputation was beyond horrendous. Had she ever had a better kiss? Of course not. Not when she'd never dreamed there could *be* a kiss like this one. Inhospitable? True. The others had been boring and brief, no tongue or teeth, for heaven's sake. No strangled breaths batting her cheek and clenching fingers curling around her hip. No full-body flush that was still warming her to her toes.

She straightened her spine and raised her chin, prepared to fight. Why save all her enthusiasm for her intended when the Grape couldn't possibly put it to good use? If her technique was lacking, it would be excellent with a little practice. "Is this how charming you are after every romantic encounter? Why, I'm relatively faint with delight."

He grunted and yanked his hand through his hair, sending the liberated strands into elegant disarray. He made a face that had his dimple swooping in, should she have forgotten about it, denting his cheek like she'd poked her finger against his skin. "Your hair looks like a bird built a nest in it, Tori darling, and I'm terrified to imagine what mine looks like. Did you even finish the trim?" He threw a circling glance around the room. "Never a mirror when you need one."

Finn Alexander would be bloody gorgeous if he shaved his head, she seethed while struggling to reassemble a coiffure he'd ruined with his eagerness. She'd *darling* him. He'd almost pulled her atop *his* body. She wouldn't have had to climb anything. Would he like her to point that out?

"We have to face Julian in fifteen minutes," he said and dropped his head to the back of the chair, "and my hands are shaking. I'm not good at hiding things from my brother. He'll know the minute he sees me that something happened. Kissing you, the blocking, the League, he won't like it. I can just hear him, 'Boy-o, this is a remarkable conflict of interest'."

"What about the other"—she eyed his lap—"issue?"

He glanced down, frowned, not even trying to act like he didn't understand her question. "Still apparent. I shall remain seated."

In for a penny... "You said I could be different here. Free. What's the harm?"

His head jerked up, color rushing across his cheeks. Unbelievably, for such a skilled libertine, he wasn't good at hiding his emotions. "No. Oh, no. No way. This kiss was it. *Finito*. A fleeting lapse. A moment's insanity. Masculine idiocy." He half came out of his chair. "We're doubling down on the friendship bet. You'd be mad to consider anything else. I'm not for you, for any proper lady, in any way but one. A road you and I are not traveling. You know this. You *know* my story. The rookery, the orphanage. Isn't that ignominy enough of a detriment?"

She rose, walked to the desk, leaning over it until her face was inches from his. He didn't move a muscle, but he drew a staggered breath as his arms tensed. Interesting. Finn Alexander was only comfortable when he was in control. "Has anyone ever said no to you, Blue?"

His eyebrow rose, just the one, an excellent recovery. "It's rare."

Lowering her lashes, she smiled, then laughed at the fascinating mix that crossed his face. Curiosity, suspicion. "Most of us mere mortals hear it all the time, so we quickly find ways around it. Lots of ways."

A choking sound ripped from his throat. "Good God, is that a dare? Hell's teeth, are you one presumptuous piece of baggage."

She moistened her lips, pleased to see his gaze sharpen, his hands clench where they rested atop the desk. "I'd say it's more a statement of fact."

"You can take your statement of fact and jam it—"

This kiss caught him off guard, threw him off balance, which is where she wanted him to be. She missed his mouth trying to reach him, but the spontaneous reaction from earlier raced back in even with her lips pressed to his cheek, tangling them in need and blinding desire. She shifted and popped up on her toes. If he would just move a little to the—

He broke away and circled the desk in three strides, caught her shoulders and walked her back, almost lifting her from her slippers. "You love puzzles, Tori. And as I'm coming to find, so do I." Then he slanted his head and captured her lips, crowding her into the wall and pressing his long, lean body against hers until she couldn't tell where hers ended and his began.

The kiss was punishing, filled with two parts retribution and one part rage, finally fully exposing the man beneath the cavalier façade. Overlord of a gaming hell, mind reader, gifted interpreter. Intelligent, furious, passionate, perplexed. Going against his anger, his hand rose to cradle her jaw, a tender, trembling touch that softened the assault. Softened her heart until her weakened knees failed, and she had to grasp his forearms for balance, only his broad chest and the wall holding her up.

"Incorrigible," he murmured against her lips. "Mischief-maker."

"Very," she agreed, looping a gloved hand around his neck and pulling him closer, her body unfurling like rose petals dipped in dew as his tongue swept in and engaged. His arm coiled around her waist and tugged her in tight, up high on her toes until they fit, lock and key, against each other. His body was more muscular than it looked beneath his beautiful clothing she found as she began to explore. He ended the kiss, and she thought to argue when his mouth trailed her jaw, nipping, soothing each point he touched, to the shell of her ear and back. Goosebumps dimpled her skin like raindrops striking a pond.

I'm yours, she thought as the door to the library burst open, and a startled exclamation shattered the silence.

Edging back, she glanced over Finn's shoulder to find Lord and Lady Beauchamp standing in the doorway, echoing expressions of astonishment on their faces.

Finn banged his head against the wall and sighed. "Julian. Piper."

She nodded, letting her arms slide free and giving him a shove that sent him stumbling, all his delicious magnetism moving away with him.

His eyes when they found hers were a dogged blue-black, darker than she'd ever seen them. The look in them alarmed and aroused. "You owe me for this one, Tori darling, and you should know I *always* seek payment."

CHAPTER 9

The first taste of her had felt like Finn's brief but frenzied experience with absinthe.

After Freddie's death, he'd spent many a predawn surrounded by starving artists, butchers, cobblers, earls, actors, barons, princes, paupers—even a doctor who'd kindly attended to his chest wound when he'd torn the stitches during an unfortunate brawl—crowded in the back room of the Mon Plaisir, the lowliest back alley club, during the infamous *l'heure verte*. The green hour. Only to be expelled like a heedless gasp into the wretched London miasma when the curtain of darkness began to fade. He'd stumbled through those twilight streets night after night with a blessed sense of detachment.

Which, at the time, he'd needed to withstand one day rolling into the next.

He'd not felt that sort of separation from mind and body until he'd stepped away from Victoria a half hour ago, forced apart by intrusion, a good thing, as his awareness had compressed to only the points where their bodies touched, like poking holes in a sheet of paper and trying to see the world through it. The nape of her neck, his hip, her thigh, his bottom lip, her cheek, the rounded curve of her breast. Scalding points of contact drawing them together as if they'd been connected with needle and thread. Coming back to find himself surrounded by the scent of moldy books and ink, stacks of letters and open ledgers, the sound of his breath rushing from his lips to mix with hers, had been as bewildering as a blow across the jaw.

He'd never lost himself in a kiss. Not once.

Not ever.

Had never imagined he could when his attention was centered on the thoughts. This time, amazingly, the ones crowding his mind were his and his alone. He'd found that to be, indeed as he'd always imagined, quite wonderful.

From his view out the library window, Finn recorded Victoria and Piper's progress across the sloping lawn. At this late stage of pregnancy, Piper waddled, to put it kindly. They paused at the fountain to rest on the carved stone bench adorning it, Victoria's gaze not once roaming his way, although she knew Julian was monitoring how the increasing distance affected their gifts—observations to be recorded in his blasted chronology.

Finn tapped the letter he held against his thigh. It was a simple kiss. Two, he supposed, if precise calculation signified. Nothing he and Tori hadn't experienced many times with other people and walked thoughtlessly away from. Kisses were weapons he often retained to create distance, not eradicate it when he wasn't even sure he liked the amusement all that much. Too intimate an effort when reading someone's mind was the very definition of dispassion.

Victoria was quite skilled at using kisses to remove herself from tight spots, conversations she wanted to divert. He'd seen her in action. Saved her from letting the ton see her in action.

Because being caught in a compromising position was more damaging than anything she could do aside from marrying *him*.

He crushed the letter in his hand, wondering where the hell that thought had come from. *Simple, Finn, remember?* Nothing to this. Just another girl. Same old. Except simple was an unfair categorization for an interaction more carnal then ones he'd had with someone's legs locked around his hips.

"Incredible," Julian said from his place beside Finn, shoulder wedged against the window frame, folio balanced on his arm as he scrawled notes across the page. "I don't even get the sensation of a vision from this pencil until she's more than a hundred yards away. She and Piper made it to the garden before the images starting floating in. So faint I could almost overlook them, and I had half a dozen people touch it at breakfast, something that would've had me retching in the rubbish bin on a normal day after holding it this long. The most curious element? It seems to draw nothing from her to impede our gifts, like she holds them off with a sword that weighs less than a feather."

"Minnie was able to perform while in the same room. Remember her giving Lucien the cookie? Different effects on different abilities."

"True enough," Julian agreed and scribbled another note. "We'll test everyone on the estate. Distances, interpretations of potency. She and Piper, for instance. One gift strengthens, the other calms. How do such divergent abilities work together?"

Finn shrugged, the occult not nearly as interesting to him as it was to his brother. The chronology was Julian's religion. What was fascinating to *him* at the moment was watching Victoria hold her arm aloft for a passing butterfly to land upon. Her smile could light the darkest of souls should one tear down the walls and let her in. "Test her with Simon. It should be interesting. Can Lady Victoria's fantastic gift repel the haunts? They seem to multiply with every year that passes. I think they talk amongst themselves and decide Harbingdon is a nice place to visit, then they never leave. God, would it be wonderful for Simon if they'd leave him for even a moment."

Julian flipped a page, paused. "You test her with Simon. He's your boy. Always has been. Attached at the hip since we dragged him here. Or in the past six months, did you forget that fact?"

Finn muttered an oath and turned his back as Victoria struggled to pull Piper to her feet, their warmhearted laughter trickling in the open window. Not a surprise they'd become fast friends as both were obstinate and attracted to trouble. Nevertheless, he'd no time to stand there mooning over a woman plainly out of reach. There were letters to translate and invoices for the gaming hell to pay, enough work to keep him sequestered in this library, should he be hiding from anyone, which he was *not*, for days. "Broach the subject with Si. He's a bit perturbed with me at the moment." He extracted his penknife from his waistcoat, slid the blade beneath the envelope's seal and shredded, relishing the obliteration.

Julian's stinging gaze landed on him. Suggesting there was discord in the Alexander household was like waving a crimson flag before a papa bull. "Meaning?"

"Meaning he wants to live in London. With me. Above the Blue Moon, where he'll graciously ignore the women *and* the drinking, all for peace. From you." Finn dropped to the worn leather chair behind the desk and gave a halfhearted salute with the penknife. "Congratulations, Jule. You continue to suck the sunshine out of your brothers' lives, one cloying gesture at a time."

Julian hummed beneath his breath, signaling advice was about to be offered, a marked expectation of obedience attached. "I don't usually get involved in your liaisons. Except for the one with the Earl of Kilmartin's daughter. Couldn't just stand by and let that work itself out."

"How was I to know she'd brandish a pistol? And proceed to shatter every window in the earl's ballroom shooting at me?"

Julian glanced out the window and closed his eyes —still testing the visions he was receiving from the pencil against how far away Victoria stood. "You don't have to tell me anything, boy-o. The broadsheets described the destruction in detail, ink bleeding over every society matron's fingers the next morning. We can only thank God Lady Esmerelda has horrendous aim, and Baron Fredricks was besotted enough to marry her the following week."

"I paid for every window from my funds."

Julian laughed then for some bloody reason, tapping his pencil against his knee in time to an internal clock. "Your adventures have kept me young, Finn. Should I have desired a quiet life in the country with my beloved wife and babies."

Finn released a sound somewhere between a snort and a laugh. "Piper's never given you a peaceful day in your life, and she never will. But you love her too much to notice. And speaking of serenity, who's on the docket to arrive this week?"

Julian had the good grace to flush, halting the tapping of his pencil. "A young groom from the Marquess of Ardmore's estate. His communication with animals is unparalleled, but he's being thrashed daily by the villagers because he made mention of his gift. There's scant information about such a talent in the chronology. Most intriguing. We have Piper to help him, and maybe now Lady Victoria, too."

Finn looked to the wiry mutt who never strayed more than ten feet from Julian. Henry lifted his head, yawned, then let it fall back to his crossed paws with a contemptuous sniff. "Superb. I can't wait to finally find out what he's thinking."

Julian sank into the chair across from him; a gleaming mahogany battlefield laid out between them. "Lady Victoria's talent is inconceivable, so formidable it makes Piper's look dull in comparison, a statement I never thought to hear myself make. Especially when I wondered, to the depths of my soul and back, if I'd be able to protect her. Now there's another. A blocker, which I didn't even believe existed." Julian trailed his finger over a drop of dried green paint on the desk. "Until someone from the other side infiltrated the League last year, a man we had no knowledge of until he arrived here seeking asylum, I thought we might be safe for longer. For my lifetime and yours. For Lucien's. But now…"

Finn directed a veiled glance to the envelope he clutched—sent from a Parisian friend of the League with deep-seated contacts in the supernatural world, a man who'd had word of menacing rumblings—hoping Julian didn't see the tremor travel down his arm and into his fingers. "You're going to propose she marry Ashcroft."

Julian braced his forearms on the chair, set to rise. "She must be further from the house than I thought if you're able to dip back into my mind. Let me check on the distance so I can note—"

"Jule, I can't read anything." Finn tapped the envelope against his head. "And no blinding headache trying not to. Trust me. They're giggling by the fountain, dreaming up mischief. Their thoughts, and yours, are closed to me."

Julian settled back, frowned. "Then, how did you know?"

Finn unfolded the letter and smoothed his palm over it, diving into the lines of text. French came easily, too easily he thought. He woke from dreams with the language heavy on his tongue, spilling from his mind like an overfilled mug. "It makes perfect sense. Ashcroft makes perfect sense. Title. Money. Protection. Everything she requires. And when she sucks the fire from his fingertips the first time"—Finn made an inelegant crease in the foolscap, barely containing the twist of irritation the purposely suggestive words sent through him—"he'll throw himself at her feet in supplication. Even if he has to give up the opera singer, reported to have the most talented lips in London, by the by. A wonder he hasn't burned down his Mayfair townhouse." Finn smiled but kept his eyes on the page. No need to invite Julian into whatever might be written across his face. "You just know he's caught more than one bed on fire."

"Glass houses, brother of mine, glass houses."

Finn flicked away the critique, struggling with a line of colloquial speech in the letter he wasn't sure how to interpret. "It's a perfect solution. Wish I'd thought of it myself. Oh, wait, I did. Now you just have to get Victoria to agree." He spared her spectacles, sitting almost within reach on the desk, a hard look, vexed for no reason. Or no reason he wanted to admit. "Good luck with that."

"It isn't perfect in any way if you care for her, Finn."

Finn folded the letter with two neat tucks and slipped it inside the envelope. "You know how it goes. Women can't seem to help themselves, and apparently, neither can I."

"The kiss Piper and I witnessed was nothing, that's what you're saying."

"A bit of boredom. I'm used to the excitement of Town, and so is she. Consider it a country pleasure among friends."

Julian was silent for so long—a painful, drawn-out hush—that Finn was forced to look him in the eye. Lord, did his brother know how to employ medieval torture.

Finn tossed the letter to the desk, feeling his temper notching higher. Yanking open a desk drawer, he nudged Victoria's spectacles into it and slid it shut. "It would be ruinous for her to consider an association with me."

"From the ton's perspective, I agree." Julian flipped to a blank sheet in his folio and began to sketch, his hand whipping across the page. An artist since he was a child, he often drew while he talked. Finn had long-ago gotten used to it. "If that's what she wanted, however, who cares what they think? You don't owe society a thing, Finn. I've made sure of it. You have funds and a family. A home. Your wife won't have anyone to challenge, please, or enrage but *you*. Choose for love and only for love. That's my advice. Above and beyond this weird realm we find ourselves thrust into, find the person you can't live without."

"I'm not cut out for marriage, Jule. Mind reading presents too many complications. And would place too much strain on the one relationship where my gift *isn't* a concern."

Julian paused, did another hum beneath his breath, then added a stroke to the drawing. "I used to think that about my gift, about Piper. Too much responsibility. Too incredible a task to protect and love her at the same time. While growing the League, being the man I wanted to be. Only when I allowed myself to do just that without thinking about it so hard did the world right itself, was I able to find my home, my place. Fear kept us apart for years. My fear, not Piper's. I still wake some nights in a panic, thinking I let her go, let Lucien go, because of my stubborn belief that *I* knew better. When I knew almost nothing except that I loved her." He glanced up, then down, and Finn had the awful realization that Julian was sketching him. "In the end, I just blindly went with my heart."

Welcome anger washed over Finn, and before he could stop himself, he sent his hand across the desk, hurling papers and ledgers to the carpet. "I don't even know who I am, Jule!" With a choked inhalation, he slumped back, realizing he'd spoken in French. Rage flowing from his soul in a language a rookery orphan shouldn't know.

Shouldn't dream in. Shouldn't adore.

With the calm composure he was known for, Julian knelt and began to tidy the mess Finn had made of his correspondence. "You know, you did that often when we first pulled you off the streets. During what I called the night terrors, when Humphrey and I had to hold you down to get you to sleep, you'd slip into this perfectly-accented French mixed with the most dreadful cockney. You went from street thug to refined toff in the blink of an eye while telling me exactly what I was thinking. It was terrifying."

Finn searched the ceiling for a crack, a spiderweb, anything to keep from looking at his brother. Losing control wasn't a reward he normally afforded himself. "I don't remember."

"Probably beneficial that." Julian slapped two neat stacks on the desk. "I hope Humphrey has children of his own someday. He was so good with you. Had all the answers when I was hopeless, little more than a boy myself. You and I would've never survived without him. His gruff exterior is as contrived as your glib charm."

Finn gestured to the mess he'd made, his smile weak around the edges. "Apologies. It seems I left my glib charm in London."

"Thank God for something."

Finn laughed, affection for his brother overwhelming him. A frightening sentiment that had kept him hiding in his maisonette above the Blue Moon for months.

Being home was splendid and unbearable.

Julian perched on the edge of the desk, traced his finger along a jagged score in the wood. Subtlety wasn't his strong suit. "Maybe French is part of your history. Why you picked up languages so quickly."

"*No*, Jule."

"We could hire an investigator. Bow Street has worked well for us in the past."

Finn's heartbeat kicked into a ferocious rhythm as the scant memories of his time in the orphanage, and before that, if he tried very, very hard to recall, coated him like a bracing winter mist. He looked to Julian, letting everything work its way to the forefront. Coloring his eyes, twisting his features. Of all his talents, and they were many, hiding his feelings wasn't one of them. "The past is staying in the past. I can't go there. I don't want to go there. Not now, not ever."

Julian waited the appropriate amount of time, letting silence smooth a coarse path, the best man Finn knew at not rushing in. "It doesn't change anything with your family, *this* family. That you want to know about the other one. Or need to. I know everything about my past, although I wish I didn't. But it's not a blank canvas. I know why I am the way I am, and in some respects, that brings solace. And grief."

"I'd like to engage an investigator, actually." At Julian's surprised look, Finn rushed to add, "To look into what Rossby holds over Victoria's father. And if they can't find out, I'll go directly to the source and steal the unquestionably captivating thoughts in the Grape's mind."

Julian blinked, clearly stunned. "You'd go that far for this woman?"

Finn clenched his jaw and looked away, to the window and the hint of yellow he could just make out in the distance. Victoria's gown was a golden shimmer on the verdant lawn, the exact color of the buttercup that bounded the lake's edge during summer. If he'd had her opera glasses handy, he would have taken a closer look.

She needs to ride again, Finn suddenly realized, the notion as bright as a friction match being struck in his mind. She'd been watching him these past mornings with longing and fear. He'd felt both emotions shimmering off of her, remnants from the accident with her brother. He could help her in this one small way. "The stable is well stocked, Jule, am I correct?"

Julian nodded, his gaze also going to the women on the lawn. "We have a new groom who's a most talented clairvoyant. He'll provide a suitable mount while telling you when you're set to pass into the great beyond. Why, may I ask?"

Finn tapped the desk drawer holding her spectacles, marveling at his fierce urge to touch them. Thoughts from a maid on an upper floor were leaking in, the dreaded return of his gift. Victoria had moved far enough away to break their bond, and in a moment, he would tell Julian and watch him spark like a hot ember. "A gift for a friend," he murmured, "just a gift for a friend."

∾

Victoria halted at the woodland boundary, the hum in her ears increasing in volume until it sounded like a train roaring down uneven tracks. Closing her eyes, she let the disturbance overpower her senses and shove everything else out. Her skin tingled as a feeling, a *force*, rocked her where she stood. She was falling before she realized she'd lost her balance, landing on her hands and knees with a jarring thud.

Piper gasped and dropped beside her in an awkward half-kneel. The viscountess's hands were covering hers as she murmured soft words of comfort. Of *healing*. A calming rush swept Victoria, lowering the muddled drone, the sensation of a knife scraping her skin until it was raw. A flash of perfect, wondrous ease.

"I'm fine," she said in a hoarse voice she barely recognized. Forcing herself to a shaky sit, she wondered what, exactly, had happened. Shoving her hair from her eyes, she blinked into the bright sunlight. One moment she'd been recalling riding through fields like this with her brother, the next, she'd felt someone opening the door to her mind. An invasion she'd forcefully rejected, which had caused the world to tilt.

Finn. Sneaky, adorable scoundrel.

Piper groaned and flopped to her bottom next to Victoria. "Oh, goodness, I may not be able to get up." She wrapped her arm around her protruding tummy and balanced her chin atop it. "This baby is getting too big for me to manage. You may have to summon the field cart to bring me back to the house."

Victoria turned, horrified. "Are you well, Lady Beauchamp? I'm so sorry. You shouldn't have thought to tumble down here with me."

"Piper, please. I'm fine. Fat, but fine." Sprawling back in the grass with a sigh, she stacked her arm beneath her head. "And I love tumbling. Ask Julian."

Victoria sputtered a laugh and waved her hand before her face, the wobble in her knees finally starting to retreat. If she waited a moment, she'd be able to stand. "You're far from fat. I'd go with ungainly. Lovely but cumbersome?"

"Dashed if that doesn't sound worse."

"You were able to heal me," Victoria murmured, recalling the tranquility Piper's touch had brought, the instant stillness. "When I thought I blocked your gift."

"I tried, but I didn't know it got through. Though I can't see your aura, which is most unusual, I must be able to partially reach you." Piper plucked a cornflower from the ground and twirled it between her fingers. "Wait until we tell Julian. He'll record about a thousand pages of notes in his excitement."

Victoria laid back as well, grass tickling her cheek as she turned her head toward the viscountess. "Don't tell Finn. About my fall, I mean. I felt him intrude, and when I pushed him out, the world just spun on its axis. For a second, it was like we were out of rhythm with each other, and I had to run to catch up. I wonder if I didn't do my little parlor trick on myself, stealing time, just enough to recalibrate."

"That makes sense, I suppose."

"I don't know how to explain it, but I feel...*more* here. At Harbingdon. It's like tiny abrasions on my skin. A prickly sensation, no, more a vibration. All these abilities flowing through me, leaving bits and pieces like flotsam caught on a branch in the river. I'm not sure how much control I have or that I even know how to channel this." She shrugged her shoulder against the ground. "I don't understand how I'll be able to help anyone when I can't help myself."

"We'll work on that. It's going to take time. You're powerful, and you don't realize it." Piper pointed with the cornflower to a hawk circling overhead. "Supernatural talents require exploration. There are no easy answers, often no answers at all. Julian is extremely focused on providing them through the chronology, but it's not always that simple. There are so many variables that come into play. Which is frustrating if you want conclusive evidence, as my husband does, exhilarating if you consider life an adventure, as I do."

"Opposites attract," Victoria said, wondering how long she'd have to wait before Piper asked about the kiss. "You and Julian, I mean."

"So, you plan to keep this little episode from Finn?" Piper asked when the silence had begun to chafe.

Here we go.

She wasn't sure why she didn't want him to know his gift had affected her. Maybe because this *one* thing—that he couldn't read her mind—set her apart from the parade of women in his life. Which was foolish pride talking when she wasn't a woman in his

life at all. Unless two errant kisses placed her there. "I
haven't told him everything," she admitted. About the
dreams, about her gift. That she was starting to feel
herself obstructing mystical lines of communication,
turning down the glow on mental gaslamps all over
the estate.

Because she didn't trust him. Or rather, she didn't
trust *herself*.

She'd never responded to a kiss with everything
in her.

Falling in love with the Blue Bastard would be an
unadulterated disaster. Worse than marriage to a
man she not only didn't love but was repulsed by. At
least *that* situation she had control over. When she
had control over little else.

"Maybe sharing isn't the best route, at least at
first. I told Julian absolutely everything, and it took
me years to land him. Our love story could aptly be
titled 'Chasing the Viscount'."

Victoria gathered a pine needle and tied it into a
tidy knot. "You misunderstand. I don't want to land
anyone. He has his pick of women, and I'm betrothed
to—"

"The Grape, yes, I know."

"It's a financial obligation." Victoria felt the need
to stress this when most marriages in the ton were
based on a business arrangement, not love. But Lord
and Lady Beauchamp had a legendary connection, if
the gossip was factual, which after seeing them together, she wholeheartedly believed it was. "I was
baiting Mr. Alexander, and he accepted the challenge.
What you witnessed is the unfortunate result. Both
of us, I'm abashed to admit, are known for tossing
out kisses like we would dirty bathwater. It's an insignificant occurrence, I promise you. One and
done."

"You being at Harbingdon is momentous. There's no need for a kiss to make it more so."

"I'm only here so Finn can interpret the dreams. And now, so Lord Beauchamp can pick my brain like a lock."

"The dreams. Is this what you're keeping from Finn?"

Victoria came up on her elbow, dusting at the dirt clinging to her bodice. She yanked a piece of straw from her hair and sighed. If Aggie should come upon them rolling around in the grass like children...

She turned her head to hide her smile. Piper was a radical influence when Victoria needed no incentive to misbehave. However, she felt a heartfelt zing of affection that surely meant she'd found a friend. "I'm going to tell him," she promised. Piper likely thought she'd kept quiet to protect herself when the dreams were going to change Finn's life, not hers. It felt like protecting *him* to keep them to herself. Plus, she was a little worried about his reaction.

"Perhaps you should wait until tomorrow," Piper said with a yawn.

Victoria glanced anxiously over her shoulder, wondering where in the dickens that field cart might be. She couldn't very well carry the lady home.

"Time enough to let your lips cool off, that is."

Victoria clapped her hand over her mouth with a hoot of pure delight. "You are unlike any viscountess I've ever encountered."

"I'm recreating the role one uncouth deed at a time. For the betterment of society, of course." Piper clutched her belly and groaned softly. "He or she is kicking in agreement. Oh, my. Would you like to feel?"

Victoria stilled, joy and dread racing through her. "Oh, well, I don't know..."

Piper glanced at her from the corner of her eye. A mischievous peek through long lashes that let Victoria know exactly how Julian had come to be wrapped around his wife's pinkie. "It's quite beyond the pale. Outside the bounds. Vulgar. Isn't that how an old crone sitting in a Mayfair townhouse would describe it right this very minute? Who do you want to side with, Victoria, that withered shrew or the eccentric daughter of an esteemed American actress and a debauched viscount?"

"When you put it that way," Victoria murmured and grazed the back of her hand across Piper's stomach, as cautiously as she'd touched the butterfly that had landed on her arm earlier. During the charged instant when she'd felt Finn's focus seize her as surely as his lips had. When she'd begun to sense him tap, tap, tapping on the entrance to her mind.

"Here," Piper said, and repositioned Victoria's hand.

The kick against her palm was harder than she imagined it could be, and she sucked in a breath, releasing it with a marveling sigh. "My, how remarkable."

"Isn't it? Lucien was the calmest thing, a little gentleman like his father, so this baby's vigor has been a surprise. A girl I'm guessing, the tiny imp. I sound proud, don't I? Which proves why I should live very far from the decorous inhabitants of London, that withered shrew included."

"A tiny imp like her mother," Victoria concurred and shyly removed her hand. She'd never had a friend to discuss female things with. No sister, and a rather taciturn mother. No family to speak of in any way that counted aside from Aggie and her brother, and Charles was gone. This intimacy, while delight-

THE RAKE IS TAKEN

ful, was also distressing, sending a pulse of longing through her.

One that made her feel lonelier than she had in ages.

A shout from the house sounded, dispatching a flock of starlings in the alder tree above them. Piper wrestled to a sit with an oath no respectable woman would ever utter. "That's Humphrey's bellow. We'd better go, or he'll come looking for us. Should he find me down in the dirt in my delicate condition, he won't be happy. You think Julian is protective, my word, is that man dictatorial. We're like his fledglings, everyone on the estate. He needs his own family to worry about, but that is a project for another day."

Victoria scrambled to her feet and held her hand out to assist Piper, again wondering where that field cart might be. But they got the job done without issue, the two of them in minutes headed back with the sun sliding low and throwing subdued shadows across their path. There was a decided chill in the air as they lost the light, and Victoria shivered. She'd left her shawl and her spectacles in the library—and she might never be able to return to that room, a space Finn had taken over with his language books and his ledgers and his kisses.

As they started up the pebbled path leading to the front door, Piper halted her with a light yank on Victoria's wrist. Again, a sense of peace overtook her, and she could see why someone would long to have Piper work her magic and make the chaos slip away. The understanding sent a chilling pulse of recognition through Victoria. Someone could also, she was beginning to see, long to have *her* block their gift. Or block another's gift—with very despicable intent.

Victoria turned to find the viscountess gazing at

her with an expression solemn enough to have her taking an apprehensive step back. "What you said earlier, about Finn, isn't quite true. He has his pick of women if you believe the broadsheets. And the gossip." She laughed softly, her eyes glowing the color of the grass beneath their feet. "Has his pick because he's near the loveliest man in England. But I know him better than anyone, or I used to before he grew up and starting hiding things from me, and those women he has his pick of are for one night." She shrugged a slim shoulder beneath soiled, wrinkled silk. "Men can't always resist the tempting offers thrown their way. But he doesn't want that. Finn wants someone for a lifetime. Wants a love to last a lifetime because that's what he's seen his brother obtain happily with me. Someone to match him in intelligence and wit and kindness, someone to deal with his temper because he has one though he hides it well. Someone to help navigate the mystical world he's been unjustly forced into, a world he paid a horrific price as a child to enter."

Victoria glanced at the library window, the feeling of someone watching—though she couldn't see clearly without her spectacles—shooting a dart of unease through her. She didn't need to picture him as a child, abandoned and abused, to make her want him more. Her yearning was a vibrant entity all on its own. "There's no need to tell me this," she replied in a terse tone she wished she could sweeten like one of her confections, "when I'm going to marry the Grape and live happily ever after. Or not. The end of the story isn't always a love to last a lifetime. I've never seen it done in such a fashion. Not necessary, is it?"

Piper sighed despondently and trudged up the path. "*That*, my new friend, is exactly why I told you. Finn knows what love is like. He's experienced it every day since Julian and Humphrey pulled him out of Seven Dials, when you, sadly, have not. You're the one we'll have to fight harder for."

Victoria stumbled to a halt, Piper's words stinging like she'd walked through a patch of nettles.

With a choking sigh, she realized she'd not had anyone fight for her in a very long time.

CHAPTER 10

*T*he dream tore through his night.

Victoria. Light from a blazing hearth washing over her, hair loose, an amber shroud about her face. He peered through the dense shadows to see she clutched a tarnished chain, the ends dangling from the crease in her fist, the clasp slapping her wrist as she gestured. An appeal. Imploring. Not in fear but frustration.

He moved closer, heat from the fire stinging his cheeks. *Que voulez-vous de moi?* What do you want from me?

Victoria shook her head and pointed to the darkened corner...and it was then he noticed the other woman. The filthy tip of a worn slipper, the ragged hem of a nondescript gown. She tilted her head into the meager light—revealing eyes the exact color of his.

The smile that captured her face was golden, as earnest and radiant as the sun. The answering dash of love to his heart, instant and spontaneous recognition, nearly brought him to his knees.

Finn wrenched from sleep and dragged quivering fingers through his hair, the ends blunt and shorter than they'd been in many a day. That damned haircut. Backhanding sweat from his brow, he slid from the bed on unsteady legs. Rage was carving him up, as was the memory of that kiss, the most erotic he'd experienced in a lifetime of experiencing them.

She'd touched him, ferocious, lips and tongue and teeth, scorching him with her hot breath and even hotter skin, making him consider a future he'd never before considered while knowing her dreams were more than she'd implied.

Personal. To *him*. A piece of his *life*.

Victoria Hamilton had made him, for one imprudent moment, feel things he'd never hoped to feel. To him, as potent as a first kiss, a first tup.

The sense of betrayal, a sensation he'd not suffered since those appalling days in Seven Dials, drummed through his body. Stealing his breath and his restraint.

Yanking a shirt and trousers on, he was out his bedchamber door and down the hallway before he'd put his thoughts in order. Muddled, mixed with the scent from the dream—lemon and linseed—a fragrance that called to him from long, long ago. Victoria's room was on his floor, second door, left. He'd known but tried not to imagine her nestled beneath a silk counterpane, her long legs twisted in damp sheets. His body covering hers, pressing her into the feather mattress. Those amazing eyes of her lighting up as he wrapped his fingers around hers and slid inside.

He'd imagined everything. And more.

How dare she, was all he could manage, knowing full well talking to her in this state—with fury making his hands shake until he had to curl them into fists to steady them—was not the smartest plan. An experienced swindler, he rarely showed even the slightest whiff of irritation or let anyone see what he thought of them, even when dealing with the mindless procession of titled idiots who frequented the Blue Moon. Anger was the biggest tell. He'd never encountered anyone who, with a simple snap of their fingers, made him so furious he wanted to put his fist through a wall.

Until *her*.

When he reached her bedchamber, he cursed soundly to find it empty, those tangled sheets he'd visualized highlighted in a streak of pale moonlight. The room smelled of her, that slightly sweet, appetizing, entirely too tempting fragrance that only kicked his resentment a notch higher. Well past midnight, the house was silent, at rest, her long-suffering maid sleeping belowstairs. He strode to the window, knocked the drape aside. The lawn was deserted except for a footman he could see patrolling the parameter. *Julian and his security*. Though it looked like they would need it.

Where could she be?

He closed his eyes, concentrating on the thoughts flowing in and out of his mind like a gently-drawn breath. Only a faint flicker of recognition not his own, so she was close. Close enough to block, or he'd have been privy to every opinion in the house. Rolling his fingertips together, he searched the lowest level of his consciousness. Deliberate, patient, until he caught her.

One teaspoon vanilla extract, he heard her say as clearly as if she stood next to him.

Snapping his eyes open, he left the chamber at a run, barreling down the narrow servant's staircase that led to the kitchens in a reckless sprint. He halted in the arched doorway, stunned to truly find her there, spreading blueberry jam onto flat squares of dough he suspected were the delightful pastries he'd eaten for breakfast the past two mornings, better even than Cook's crumpets. He'd been late to Julian's meeting for the bloody crumpets when he'd sever an arm for the pastries.

And they'd been hers.

Brilliant.

The woman could break his gift, kiss him until he almost passed out, *and* cook.

One more moment, he decided as he stood there, indecisive and unsure. To allow his boiling blood to settle, to allow yearning to tighten his chest. Then he was going to get the information about the dreams and be done with this. Done with her. Let Julian record a thousand pages of notes in the chronology about the blocker, test Victoria with every talent on the estate, marry her off to Ashcroft if he so desired, but *he*, Finn Alexander, philanderer, mind reader, thief, would be finished. He couldn't trust her. Obviously could never trust her. And he didn't know her —and without his tricks, he didn't know how to *get* to know her. Get to know any woman.

This feeling of helplessness was intolerable.

"Too thin, Tori," she murmured and rolled a length of dough between the wooden chopping block and her palm, back and forth until he imagined both the dough and her skin were warm and sticky.

"Tori," he whispered, his heart breaking all over again, knowing she'd taken his nickname and claimed it as her own. *Fuck*, this friendship business was killing him.

She brushed her wrist across her brow, trying to contain the wisps of hair that had escaped her chignon and clung to her moist skin when she only succeeded in sending a streak of flour across her cheek—adding to the one on the tip of her nose. His gazed lowered to her breasts, straining against the bleached apron she'd slipped over her dressing gown as she coaxed the dough into submission. Lowered again, all the way down, his body heating to the tips of his toes to see hers peeking from beneath fluttering silk, wiggling in time to her movements. Lovely ankles he would give a year of his life to press his lips against as he worked his way north, not stopping until she begged, and he meant *begged*, him to. Loving this idea, his cock sprang to life, a painful press against his trouser close.

A bit of boredom.

That's what he'd told Julian, and he needed to guarantee the sentiment stayed true. It usually was. But his fierce desire for this woman wasn't easily defeated. There was a way to have his mind overcome his longing, he realized. He had only to think about the secrets she—*Tori*—had been keeping from him for fury to deflate his erection like a needle stabbed into a balloon.

"Who is she?" he asked, pleased his voice sounded wrathful rather than wistful because his mind wasn't quite sure which path to take.

Victoria startled, the dough in her hand flopping to the wooden block and sending a cloud of flour into the air. She coughed, dragging her hand over her chin, leaving another tantalizing trail on her skin as her eyes made a lingering sweep from his tousled hair to his partially exposed chest. In his haste, he hadn't completed buttoning his shirt, and it hung open, the wrinkled ends batting his hips. Her gaze caught on his scar—he just knew that's what she was looking at—before skipping away. "I had trouble sleeping and baking…it, I…it calms me."

He stepped into the room, the scent of vanilla and butter rolling over him like a wave. So this is why she always smelled like biscuits. Halting at the chopping block, he mocked his spineless character. It didn't matter if he was vexed as all hell, knew her to be a swindler, a charlatan, he still wanted to shove her against the wall and lick flour from her skin. Wrap her legs around his waist and get as close as he possibly could while standing up. He also wanted to dash from the room and never see her again. Each an avenue of escape. *"Who is she?"* Gripping the block, he leaned in until he could make out the flecks of green in her eyes, golden brown in the hushed gaslight. A mix of colors magnificent enough to adorn one of Julian's canvases. "The woman in the dreams. Yours and now mine."

Her chest rose on a stunned breath. "I didn't lie."

"You didn't tell, either," he said between clenched teeth. His cheeks heated, and he knew everything was spilling like ink across his face while she stood there, pressing her knuckles into the dough and looking good enough to eat. Like her blasted pastries. "When you knew it affected me quite personally. Knew for months, I'm guessing, while you let me rescue you from one debacle after another, as I tried to gain insight into my dreams about you. Mine brought me to you when yours pushed us away."

"That's not—"

"Who, Tori?"

Victoria blinked at his harsh tone, her lashes staying low to hide the changes her eyes would make, coloring to her mood. Sadly, he'd never look at her again and think of her as anything but Tori, a nickname he'd created on a whim. Not when she'd repeated it to herself in that soft, dreamy voice.

Tori worked quite well with Blue, should it have come to that.

"I'll wait another minute, then I'm coming around

this battered slab of wood, and you may not like the result. We haven't tested what happens when I touch you and very diligently try to steal your thoughts. I'm willing to take them by force if I have to. I've scrambled minds when I've pressed too hard, left people in a state for days, and I would hate for that to happen to you. But as I see it, how I, in truth, saw it this evening, your dreams are rightfully *mine*."

Her head lifted, her gaze scalding him where it landed—belly, chest, shoulders—before settling on his face. Hers was dusted with flour and flushed with remorse. "I didn't know how to tell you. What to tell you. This dream interpretation business is more involved than a simple parlor trick where I make someone forget a foolish thing I've done behind a potted fern. I'm still feeling my way here, whether I'm given leave for that or not."

"Who is she?" The whisper was low and furious. One second. He was one second away from demanding she release his life to him, demanding she kiss him as she'd done in the library. As if it were the first of her life, the only that had ever mattered to either of them.

Get the information and be done with her, push her away, stay safe.

He held up a finger. "One." Another. "Two."

"Your sister! I think she's your sister!"

The kitchen fell deadly quiet, apart from the ragged breath he took and the clipped one she released. "I don't have a sister. I have no one from the past."

"Did you see her eyes, Finn? And how young she was? There could be no one else in the world with eyes exactly like yours so close to our age who is haunting our dreams."

"I don't have a sister," he repeated in a gruff voice,

the words sounding like they'd been rendered on the edge of a blade. His heartbeat gained speed, cracking against his ribs until he feared pitching to a lifeless heap at her feet. There was no sister. There was nothing before Seven Dials. Before Julian and Humphrey. Piper. Simon. Ashcroft. Harbingdon. And if he'd once recalled a girl reaching for him as tears streamed from eyes exactly like his, he couldn't endure admitting it.

"I'll tell you everything," she whispered hoarsely. "I've seen enough, perhaps, to find her. She has a slight accent. French? Light hair—and those eyes. And she's in London. This I have witnessed. This I know."

Finn stumbled back, out of reach. If Victoria touched him, he would go up in flames. Turn to ash and blow away in the breeze, an eloquent end to the Blue Bastard.

Sister.

A headache had started to thump, and he pressed his hand to his brow in agony. Victoria's answering look of pity shot a crimson haze across his vision.

Her fingers grasped his sleeve as he stormed past, out the servant's door, and into the walled side garden. The grass was damp and chilly beneath his bare feet, a crescent moon casting muffled light and shadow across his path—and before he had time to formulate a plan he was running. Past the clump of unpruned rose bushes, past the gardener's cottage, the conservatory, the potter's shed, the lake. Running until his lungs burned and his skin stung, until sweat coated his face and trickled into his eyes, through fields and forest he'd traversed as a young man, every nook and valley as familiar to him as the lines on his palm.

He ran until he got far enough away from Victoria Hamilton for his gift to return in full force, bringing with it the torment of his life, hearing too much.

When his legs finally gave out, he locked his hands on his knees, hung his head, and gulped in sputtered breaths, stunned to find he'd made it to the Stone Fortress, the dwelling receiving its name when the Duke of Ashcroft lived there when he first joined the League, the lone structure on the estate impervious to fire.

The sound of the front door opening didn't shock Finn.

On this night, nothing else *could* shock him.

Slowly rising, he swiped his hair from his eyes to find Humphrey lounging in the entranceway, hands in his pockets, a golden flood of gaslight spilling around him.

"Come in, then, as you look in the middle of a first-rate sulk. Unless you'd like me to come out there. We can crack each other's teeth until your fury's got nowhere to hide. Sometimes that makes a man feel better. Crude, but efficient."

With a grimace, Finn crossed the yard and shouldered past Humphrey and into the cottage, never once considering the brutal offer. He'd no desire for a man Humphrey's size to 'crack his teeth' when he quite liked them. Too, he already had the chip from his fall off his mare. His smile was almost as noteworthy as his eyes, and one had to protect one's assets in an uncertain world.

The Stone Fortress was modestly furnished, rustic, and cozy, which suited the hulking man currently perusing the collection of bottles lining a rough-hewn sideboard. A fire was crackling in the hearth, but the open window allowed a bracing draft inside, opposing sensations Finn let swirl and settle. He had no fight in him at this point, even to decide between being cold or hot.

Humphrey held a bottle aloft. "I'd go with Ireland, as you look like you've been pulled through a keyhole. Scotland requires more soothing contemplation."

Finn grunted and collapsed to a brocade sofa that had seen better days. He poked his finger in a hole in the faded upholstery, remembering Humphrey had moved to the cottage once Ashcroft found reasonable control over his fiery talent, and Julian no longer feared letting him reside in the main house when he visited—because the main house certainly better suited a duke. But stone walls better suited a man known to start fires.

Humphrey retreated to a chair across from him, a bruised leather piece that looked like a castoff from the servants' quarters. He offered a glass—filled to the brim, thank God. "Go easy," Humphrey advised, "this is the strong stuff."

Finn winked, saluted, and drained the glass in one shot. His eyes watered, and he coughed, the whiskey burning a path from his lips to his heels, just what he needed to incinerate the vision of Victoria's ashen face and the dark blue eyes from his dream.

A sour smile crossed Humphrey's face, and he shoved to his feet, bringing the bottle back and pouring another draught for Finn. "One of those nights, is it? Going to have to hold your head over a rubbish bin, I'm guessing. The anticipation of *that* is killing me."

"It's one of those months, Rey. And never fear, I'll puke outside in your azalea bushes. I'm a gentleman."

Humphrey took a leisurely sip, gazing at Finn over the crystal rim. Patient, almost as patient as Julian, when Finn had little of the skill himself. Twitchy when he was a boy, full of verve and arrogance as a young man. Reckless. Even a mite demonstrative, something a lad wasn't often allowed to be in an aristocratic household. Julian's words sounded in his mind, about Humphrey comforting him during the night terrors, and he wondered why the hell anyone, a young man himself, would have accepted this responsibility? Why would anyone want to be surrounded by the occult and the danger it presented? Especially when you weren't cursed yourself.

Besides a family, what was in it for the pensive man sitting across from him?

But there it was. *Family.* Which answered Finn's question.

"Powerful thoughts churning through that hard head of yours." Humphrey tapped the crystal against his temple. "Almost afraid to ask. Your smile usually provides good cover. I'm not sure what to think about this pathetic display."

The whiskey had done its job, chasing away some of his apprehension, and Finn slid into an answering sprawl, balancing his glass on his belly. "It's a woman."

Finn watched Humphrey catch himself before the grin broke free, the rotter. "Which one? According to the chattering snits, more of those than you can count on both hands."

"There's only one, I'm afraid. The rest are immaterial." He tipped his glass and peered into it. "Which does present a problem, one I've never had to deal with."

Humphrey's eyes widened at the admission.

"Did I mention she's betrothed and an earl's

daughter, therefore untouchable, as well as being one of the most powerful beings in our mystical universe? Remember her?"

Humphrey took a deliberate sip. "I remember."

"Julian's so eager to fill pages of the chronology that I'm panicked to admit housing Lady Hamilton is becoming an issue for me and a reputational danger for her. Leave it to me to find myself captivated by the rarest find in three hundred years in our strange little world." He finished the second whiskey and poured a third, certain both decisions were going to force him to bed down on Humphrey's battered sofa —after, as promised, he left his dinner in the shrubs surrounding the cottage. "The kicker? She's dreaming of someone she swears is my sister. And you know what?" Finn laughed, a serrated sound with all the buoyancy of a pillar stone. "I believe her."

Humphrey paused, his glass arrested halfway to his lips. Finn was delighted to finally crack his composure. "Sister? *What* sister?"

Finn slid low, until his head rested on the back of the sofa. Closing his eyes, he let the world tilt. Not the heaviest of drinkers, as mind reading didn't tolerate drunken comportment, he'd pay dearly for this indulgence. As it was, Humphrey's thoughts were intruding, and the whiskey was making it hard to fight them off. "Tori's been dreaming, and of course, with the number of fanciful ones I inspire, I assumed they were about me. Ro-man-tic even. Embarrassed to tell me and all that. Sounds plausible, doesn't it? But they're about someone with eyes exactly like mine. A woman with an accent."

In a language that had come easily, too easily, to him when he'd first tried to speak it.

"Tori, is it?" Humphrey's glass thumped the table, his boot heels scraping across the stone floor as he inched forward in his chair. "An accent. Interesting, as you've always had a knack with languages."

Finn blinked into the amber radiance cast from the fire, the whiskey composing a delightful musical score in his skull. "Do you think it's possible, Rey? That there's someone out there related to me? Why wouldn't I have dreamed of her? Been able to read *her* mind? Why would this woman, this stranger, be our connector?"

"How the hell do I know? All I grasped was that this summer was going to be anarchy, an itch I've had under my skin for weeks. The insane gods of magic stirring up our lives. Our peace interrupted." Humphrey pointed his glass at Finn. "That's *my* gift, the ability to sense chaos. Let Julian record that in his book."

"I have to find her," Finn whispered.

"You don't have to convince me, boy. Can't have anyone entering our world without finding out why." Taking a considering draught, Humphrey tilted his head. "When we found you, I was so damn reckless. Act first, think never, that sort of thing. Wasn't unheard of, a titled bloke dropping a byblow in a slum, a place no one would ever connect them. So, I broke into the orphanage even though you were by then living in that shack—maybe a month after we rescued you—tore the place up looking for records, papers, something to tell us who you were. There was nothing, but I always wondered. You were filthy, covered in insect bites and bruises, a layer of dirt on your skin it took five baths to wash off, but the moment we cleaned you up, you looked like a little prince. Sounded like one once the cockney slipped away. You came from somewhere, that's all I knew. Because I'd come from the gutter, never anyplace but, and I recognized the difference right off. Julian's creation about you being from his side of the world may not be far from the truth."

"I don't want another story. I'm happy with Julian's creation," Finn murmured and slumped back on the sofa, slinging his arm over his eyes, the whiskey cutting a wide path through him. Oh, was he going to feel wretched tomorrow.

A blanket settled over him as Humphrey loosened his fingers from around the glass and set it aside. "Thank you," Finn whispered, when he meant, for *everything*.

He didn't want his life to change. He wanted the family he'd found, the family who'd found *him*.

Why go and wreck his moderately predictable supernatural existence by falling in love?

With Victoria Hamilton or a long-lost sister.

≈

Piper lifted her finger to her lips as Julian tiptoed into the nursery. "Finally," she whispered, gesturing to their son who lay sprawled on his bed, his favorite bunny, Alfred, tucked beneath his chin, a dabble of spit sticking fur to his cheek. She'd practically had to pin Lucien to the mattress to get him to sleep, a battle of wills that had left them both exhausted. It was hard to be vexed when the little devil looked so much like his father that it made her heart ache.

Moving behind her, Julian wrapped her in his arms, placing his chin on the crown of her head. "Trouble with my beautiful boy? How could that be? He's an absolute angel."

She turned, trying to wiggle close enough to press her cheek to his chest, but it was impossible. "I'm corpulent," she said with a sniffle, "and I still have another month to go. Maybe longer. It went longer than anticipated last time." Pregnancy had left her with the predilection to cry at *less* than the drop of a bonnet, for no reason at all and every reason in the world. A circumstance Julian had handled with the calm self-possession he was known for.

She felt his lips curve against her brow. "You're ravishing, and you know it. So damned beautiful, you take my breath away. How do you think we got into this mess? Twice, I might add."

The babe chose that moment to kick, a jarring thump Julian had to feel even through layers of clothing. The wondrous expression on his face when his eyes met hers was almost as devastated as Victoria's had been when she'd shyly pressed her hand to Piper's rounded belly earlier today. Which brought Piper back to the topic at hand. "Did you find him?"

Julian's arms clenched before he dropped them and stepped back. "He's at the Stone Fortress. Humphrey sent his serving boy with a note. So we didn't worry when he doesn't make it to breakfast. Because it looks like he won't."

"Ah, there's drink involved," Piper murmured and crossed to the settee they'd situated in the nursery for storytime and feedings, settling herself as gracefully as she could, which was not at all. She landed with a soft thud on the velvet cushions.

"That detail wasn't included in the note, but I think it's a sound wager." Julian brought a woolen blanket and tucked her in, his touch gentle, his smile tenuous, his aura speckled with azure and gold. Love and concern. Like a mother hen, he worried incessantly about his chicks. He and Humphrey shared this preoccupation. "That was quite a kiss we interrupted," he noted, taking the empty spot next to her and drawing her into the comfy nook against his chest she'd been trying to locate. Coming at it from the side instead of the front solved the problem. A clever man, her husband, she thought with a smile.

It *had* been a startlingly sensual kiss, Finn pressing Victoria Hamilton to the wall, their bodies so close you couldn't have slipped a feather between them. However… "She's the loneliest person I've ever met."

Julian flinched. "Who?"

"Lady Victoria, silly, who else? I thought I was forlorn until the thunderbolt struck, and you realized I was the light of your life"—she laughed as Julian gave her a teasing shoulder knock—"but the way she looked at me, oh, she's in much worse shape. At least I had a family with you and Finn and Humphrey, even then." Piper ironed the blanket with her fingers and faced his questioning gaze. "The baby kicked, and I let her feel it, which I'm sure goes against every tenet in society's blessed book. But I did it anyway like I always do—and her face just crumbled. She has no one, Jules, no one. Nothing to do with reading her aura because I can't. I wanted to cry, which comes easily as you know, but I held off for fear of embarrassing her. Then I wanted to cry again when I remembered the Grape is going to be her *someone*. She's giving herself away because she doesn't believe in love enough to fight her family for the chance to experience it."

Julian looked to the fanciful mural he'd painted on the nursery walls as if it was suddenly of great interest. "She can't marry Rossby. When it comes to her needing protection, as it did for you, he can't provide it. Someone, someday, will find us again. In my gut, I know this. We've had recent warnings from the continent in the letters Finn is translating. The blocker is too tempting a target. The Duke of Ashcroft would be a suitable choice for her. He's in the League, and being a former soldier, has men at his beck and call. He needs an heir, a wife, even if he wants neither." Julian counted off the positive points on his fingers. "Society placated, Ashcroft not setting fires, Lady Victoria protected, her ridiculous father spared from debtor's prison. Check, check, check, check."

Piper harrumphed beneath her breath. "There's no check for love. Did you not hear what I said? My word, does the woman get any say in her future?"

"Typically, no, they don't. This isn't America, Yank. Consider the dilemma with your suppressed British half."

"If this is about money..."

"It isn't. Thanks to my father's corrupt solicitor, Finn's inheritance is secure, and without a hint of scandal attached to it aside from the malicious by-blow business none of us can change. Better bastard of a viscount than rookery orphan, that much I'm sure of. He has enough to save her family, Piper. It's the societal discrepancy. Which, even with the lies I've been telling since Finn was a boy, is considerable."

"I was a walking scandal, and you married me."

Julian rolled his head to look at her. "You were a hellion but granddaughter to an earl, daughter of a viscount. Finn has no such lineage. This issue will always matter to the ton and be exemplified in the most hypocritical ways. Most ladies in our circle wouldn't dare attach themselves to him for more than a brief time. A liaison, a flirtation. Although we're staunch champions of women's rights in this house, what about Finn? Does he want Lady Victoria for more important reasons than not being able to read her mind? I told him all this, and call me a killjoy, but I'm not sure. Although he did offer to steal Rossby's thoughts for her, which sounds like more than a simple case of desire to me."

Piper thought back to that kiss, the dazed expression on Finn's face when he'd glanced over his shoulder and seen them standing in the doorway. The way his gaze lingered on Victoria after they'd hastily separated, murmuring inane explanations and brushing at their clothing as if a swarm of bees had lit upon them. "I think he wants her."

"Yes, and a thousand others. Or the reverse, I suppose, is the more accurate statement. Blasted hell, if I had a face like his, I'd never leave the house."

Linking her fingers with Julian's, she brought their hands to her lips and placed a tender kiss on his knuckle. Her husband was more than a little handsome himself, and he knew it. "He let her cut his hair."

Julian sputtered a laugh. "He *what*?"

Piper giggled and pressed her cheek to his chest, the steady rhythm of his heart the most reassuring manifestation in her universe. "Love can change him, give him a sense of security and hope. Lead him home in a way we can't. As it did for me, for you. He's smiling for the first time since the accident on the wharf. Writing in his journal. Growing into the man you hoped he would. And, wonder of all wonders, he can't read this lively, fascinating, discarded woman's mind." At Julian's doubtful look, she pinched his arm, then soothed the spot when he growled. "She was the first to reach him when he took that tumble off his horse. Opera glasses to watch the birds, my foot. *He's* her bird, a dazzling azure one! I'm not fooled."

Julian tipped her gaze to his, his grin digging that dimple she so loved deep in his cheek. "I have no idea what you're talking about. You understand that, right?"

"If I say trust me, will you?"

He frowned, his arm tightening around her. "Trust you to do what? That's never worked well before."

"Engineer a little magic?"

"Will you still respect me if I admit I'm scared?"

She slid her hand behind his neck and brought his lips to hers. "Love is always dangerous, darling. Don't be frightened."

CHAPTER 11

The plink of a stone striking her bedchamber window pulled Victoria from a restless slumber. Dazed from half-sleep, she wondered at the hollow ache in her chest. In a flash, the look of stark betrayal on Finn's face returned, an image she'd had no success wiping from her mind, even with the tray upon tray of pastries she'd baked after he stormed from the house. To find that this sophisticated man, admired beyond measure although for wholly superficial reasons, had a heart she could injure surprised her as nothing else this remarkable summer had.

Even with honorable intent, she didn't like knowing she'd hurt him. Banter, parry, thrust, the teasing game of trading insults and innuendo was all well and good, but throwing a dart that wounded was unacceptable to a woman who urged her staff to release spiders into the wild. A killer of insects or feelings or hope, Victoria Hamilton was not. She was, in truth, not quite the misanthrope she portrayed herself to be.

Not deep in her heart anyway. A place she invited no one.

The second dink sounded, and she slid from the

bed, grabbed a dressing gown, and slipped it over her night rail as she crossed the room. Her feet were bare, the floorboards chilled from the draft seeping through the panes, and she shivered as she raised the window high and leaned out, squinting to get a better view.

Of course, she thought, the hollow ache in her chest receding.

Finn stood just below her window, light glinting off the gray streak in his hair, sparking off an expression she couldn't make out clearly without her spectacles. His shirt was untucked, though properly buttoned, his feet bare as they'd been when he left the house. He looked impossibly tall, handsome, young. While she...

Grasping her dressing gown at the neck, she clenched the material tight, confirming her suitability. Covered, albeit not in the most appropriate manner, but covered. While he looked ethereal, a statuette gilded by moonbeams and mist, his gaze chronicling her in fascinated silence.

They *were* fascinated, she realized with a dull thud of dread.

Both of them.

There wasn't cause to admit it, oh, that way lay danger, but she felt comprehension radiating from him and guessed he felt it radiating from her. There was precision in the dictum that you didn't choose who made your heart race, your pulse pound, your skin heat.

Who made you wish for things that could never be.

Breaking the spell, Finn shifted from one foot to the other, tunneled his hands in his trouser pockets and shrugged. As if he'd given himself instructions he wasn't sure he could follow. After a moment, he exhaled and glanced at her, humility curling his lips if an assessment made with less than perfect vision stood correct. An unpretentious smile. Real. Nothing like the fraudulent efforts he showcased in London, intimate disclosures she was coming to covet in a hazardous-to-her-heart way.

He shrugged again, and she almost made it easier on him by diving into the conversation, a typically feminine reaction to ease the tension. Although his discomfiture was utterly appealing, blast the man, she simply raised a brow and remained silent. *This should be good*, she thought with a smile she tried valiantly to contain, wishing she had her opera glasses handy.

He caught her faint grin and laughed beneath his breath with her. "I'm sorry," he finally said. Looking away, he scratched his chin with his shoulder without taking his hands from his pockets. "For my indignant display this evening. And for the kiss earlier today." His jaw clenched; she could see that clearly in the moonlight. "For the *kisses*. I let us fall into a pattern I'm comfortable with instead of striving to establish a pattern I'm not. Which is why I'm standing down here instead of up there. I don't like that you kept the dreams from me, but I accept the reasoning for why you did so. I'm annoyed but..." He kicked at a bramble by his feet with a muttered curse that drifted to her. "I'll get over it."

She slid to her knees, balancing her elbows on the dew-moist ledge. She needed a hushed moment to gather her composure. Her father had never apologized to her mother, to her. Not once. When there were many times he should have. "I'm sorry for keeping the dreams from you," she returned when her voice was steady. *But I'm not sorry about the kisses.*

I will never be sorry about the kisses.

His gaze snagged hers, and she squinted, trying to record his expression. She expected mockery, but he looked frightfully sincere standing there, staring up at her. "Yes, I know." He tugged a hand from his pocket and shoved it through hair already spiked about his head. "That's why I'll get over it. Friends often muddle it up, don't they? Like family."

"I suppose they do," she whispered for her ears alone. Then, louder, a safe topic, "This couldn't have waited until breakfast? I made enough blueberry pastries for everyone on the estate and the village. Penitence brings out the enthusiastic baker in me."

He smiled, another of the authentic ones she was coming to cherish. "I'm still feeling the effects of a whiskey and advice session with Humphrey, liquid courage as it were. Also, I'm leaving for London at daybreak, off to enlist the Duke of Ashcroft's aid as he has endless contacts in Town." He paused, cleared his throat, snaked that hand back in his pocket. "I didn't want to leave without telling you. Apologizing, that is. Until I return, you'll be fine here with Piper, busy fulfilling Julian's grand plan to record your every interaction in the chronology." Seeming to deliberate, he then said in a gentle voice, "There's a perfectly calm but spirited mare waiting for you at the stable. Harmony. It's time to return to doing the things you love, Tori darling. If I may be so presumptuous, I think your brother would want that for you."

Victoria swallowed past the sting of tears, the thought of this complicated man riding down the graveled drive and away from her more painful a thrust than she had any right to feel. A thrust proving how deeply she'd waded into a turbulent sea. On impulse, she leaned further out the window, an errant gust whipping her hair against her cheeks. The horizon was streaking crimson and gold as sunrise closed in upon them. "You're going to try to find her. I understand this, but I haven't told you all I dreamed."

Finn glanced at the sky, the first hint of impatience stiffening his shoulders. "Humphrey will be right on my heels. Tell him everything before he leaves. Once I clear your shielding boundary, I'll read his mind and know everything he knows. Including how far behind me he is." He yawned into his fist. "It isn't even a fair chase."

She shrugged, puzzled. "Why not wait for him then?"

"*Because*," he said, the word shooting from his mouth with an edge that could slice leather. "Julian's high-handed management vexes, as does Humphrey's, so I'm childishly giving them the slip. Jule can't leave Harbingdon with Piper soon to deliver. He won't, that is. Almost any husband in the ton would gladly accept a reason to escape the confines of an expectant wife's clutches, but you've seen them. He can't stand to be away from her. So, he'll send Humphrey trotting after me while I wait in sophomoric anticipation."

"That's ridiculous."

"It's a brotherly game we play. Let us have our fun."

Men, she concluded with a sigh.

He stared for a long moment, opened his mouth as if he would say more, then shook his head, bowed with more elegance than a barefooted, half-dressed man should've been able to, and entered the house through the door located just beneath her window. She heard it shut with a dull thump.

Conversation complete.

Victoria slid down the wall and dropped her head to her knees, drawing a breath to slow her racing heart. She didn't like what Finn Alexander was doing to her usually steady equilibrium. "Fig," she whispered as the image of Lucien wiping jam across his cheek came to her. Gorgeous, infuriating Fig. *Kind*, infuriating Fig. A man who thought to have a horse provided for her pleasure, riding an interest he knew she desperately wanted to do again but was afraid to try. And tormented, by a gift he couldn't completely control. By his past. In some respect, by his bleak future. Whip-smart and sincere and funny—

"I'm sitting here listing the Blue Bastard's attributes when I should be listing the Grape's. If he has any." Lady Grape had to be able to list the positives, didn't she?

The real problem at the moment? Victoria felt outfoxed, skillfully cornered, cleverly maneuvered. Finn expected her to set this bit of fraternal theatre in motion. Alert the house to his departure. Provide details about her dreams. Patiently await his return while he solved the mystery. As if he'd tapped her politely on the head and said, "Be a good girl, and I may come back for more of those tantalizing kisses."

She shoved to her feet with a reckless burst of umbrage, the scheme coming together in her mind.

She was going to alert the house to Finn's departure.

Provide details about her dreams.

Then convince Julian—enlisting Piper's assistance if necessary—that Finn needed his mind free of other's thoughts when and if they found his sister. Keen, Victoria's ability to block and thereby protect him.

She would present it just so.

While hiding her desperate desire to be by his side during what could be the most significant event of his life. She only knew, a soul-deep feeling, that she must be there.

And she wasn't up to talking herself out of the decision.

Which meant she and the long-suffering, sniffling Aggie were going to accompany Humphrey on the chase.

Turning her back on the beautiful man and his beautiful plan, Victoria went to pack.

∽

"Another daft scheme, this one. And I couldn't talk you out of it. The years are catching up with me, it's certain. Absolutely certain."

Victoria turned from her penetrating review of the countryside outside their swiftly-moving carriage to her perturbed companion. Agnes looked as if she'd not only bitten into a lemon but swallowed it whole. "I have no idea what you're referring to."

"Don't try that with me, young lady. Not when I've been around for all your heedless life. I won't be easily fooled." Agnes yanked a handkerchief from her reticule and sniffed into it. "As if discussing your prank with a clairvoyant viscount wasn't bad enough, now we're loping off after his equally-magical brother, a blue-eyed devil who gawks at you like a sweetmeat when he thinks no one is looking. He's not so skillful at secreting, that one, even with all the stories. And the way you look at him"—she jabbed the scrap of lace-edged linen like a sword—"not much better."

Victoria huffed, hoping it sounded like outrage when inside, a warm glow traveled from her chest to her knees. She would like to be Finn Alexander's sweetmeat, which was a hopelessly pathetic aspiration. As for what she'd like to do to *him*, it didn't bear repeating to a woman who'd slept on a cot in her nursery for the first two years of her life. "We're colleagues of sorts. Friends. Research associates."

Agnes stuffed the handkerchief in her reticule and closed it with a snap. "Is that what they're calling it now? I'm not so old that I don't remember those blistering looks. Or the menace they bring."

Victoria laughed and dropped her puzzle book to the velvet squab. She didn't know much, not nearly enough, about Aggie's past. "Care to tell me about that, Aggie? More interesting than the scenery."

Her companion's cheeks flushed the same color as the crooked initials embroidered on the corner of her handkerchief. "Not on your life, missy. I wouldn't want to give you any ideas."

Finn's lips covering hers and setting fire to her body was something Victoria would never forget for as long as she lived. His long fingers curving around her hip and drawing her against him. The stunned look on his face when he finally drew back and looked into hers.

She needed no one to give her ideas when she had so bloody many herself.

"This is against my better judgment."

Victoria peered at her puzzle book without seeing one word on the page. "Understood."

"We could stay with your cousin, Alphonse," Agnes chirped in that way she did when she knew she was fighting a losing battle. Like air was trapped between her tongue and her teeth. "I had no idea your father would let the house in Belgravia the moment we headed to Oxfordshire and your mother to Scotland. The situation must be even more dire than we thought."

Victoria groaned and dropped her head to the seat. "Alphonse pinched my bottom the last time I shared a drawing room with him." The thought of it still made her skin crawl.

Agnes tapped her reticule with a sigh. "He's out then."

"Beauchamp House is fully staffed. Finn doesn't live there. We won't be occupying the same house. It's perfectly suitable." She said the words, having no idea if they were entirely true.

"Doesn't matter where he lives if you plan to run him to ground the minute you get to London."

"You're going to make me wish I hadn't told you about the dreams. I'm not going to let him meet his sister without me there to block the thoughts. I won't make him go through that when I can help."

Agnes gestured to the hulking man riding his stallion alongside them. "What does *he* think of this?"

Not much, Victoria could have admitted. Humphrey had reacted precisely as Finn said he would. Requesting every detail about the dreams, swiftly packing his bag, arguing with Piper and Julian about taking her with him, then giving up with a furious look that said someone—likely Finn Alexander —was going to pay for his predicament.

Finn knew the exact second they caught him.

She caught him.

It was three days later, when he stood on the lawn of Ashcroft House and Lady Parchant-Bingman's lurid thoughts dribbled away like tea through a cracked cup, leaving his mind crystal-clear. He'd only come to discuss his sister's whereabouts with the duke's investigator and had instead gotten coerced into attending a soiree he'd no wish to attend. One he wouldn't have been invited to if not for his unusually close relationship to the host. Now, he could only gulp a breath of night air scented with a wretched combination of lemon verbena and the Thames while accepting that the unstoppable flood of relief and joy at Victoria's arrival meant he was truly buggered.

I've missed her, he realized and threw back the champagne he hadn't wanted and had, damn it to hell, promised himself he wouldn't drink. *And I'm not surprised she joined the chase.*

Incredibly dangerous, the game they played.

One he nonetheless found himself very much wanting to play.

Lady Parchant-Bingman glanced over her shoulder, and upon seeing she and Finn stood behind a fountain that hadn't filtered water in centuries, a nifty distance from the celebratory horde gathered on the lawn, hooked her finger beneath his shirt cuff and tugged him a step closer. He went, well, not willingly, but obligingly. It was hard to break old habits when he had absolutely no intention of doing anything else.

Of course, that's how Victoria found him.

Standing too close to a woman he didn't know in a biblical sense but appeared to. Her greedy finger tucked in his starched cuff, her gaze lifted as if she expected a kiss and wasn't leaving without one. Finn stepped back awkwardly, surprising himself and the lady, while two foreign concepts peppered his unfettered mind. Shame at being caught in this situation when it was what he *did*. And jealousy, a spiky flush that stung his skin as he noted Victoria's fingers resting securely on Ashcroft's forearm as he guided her around the fountain.

Moonlight and mist washing over them, the gorgeous couple, a first-rate example of refinement and culture, all the things he wasn't even though he faked it very, very well.

One look at Tori, and he knew. She would make a marvelous duchess.

It was an odd feeling to shatter inside but remain standing. Julian's words filtering through and making it worse. *Cracks are how the light gets in, boy-o.*

Victoria's eyes were the color of a leaf frozen in ice when they met his.

"Julian worked quickly," he murmured and glanced again at her fingers draped over Ashcroft's elegant linen coat. *Mine*, shot through his mind as he shoved down the savage urge to yank her away from the duke, which would have been entertaining as all hell. A former soldier and chance mercenary when the instance called for it, Ashcroft would pummel him to within an inch of his life if he so much as breathed on him. Finn was an excellent marksman and damn good with a knife but a soldier of fortune he was not.

Ashcroft glanced between them, sensing unrest but looking too poleaxed to do much about it. He rubbed the fingertips of his left hand together, his cheeks ashen. Victoria's gift was blocking his, as they'd expected, as he'd warned the duke earlier in the evening it might.

How long, Finn wondered, before Ashcroft asked for her hand in marriage? Forget love when your duchess could bring *normalcy*.

A talent more valuable than the Queen's jewels for those in their world.

Lady Parchant-Bingman studied each member of the group, searching for a salacious tidbit to impart later in the evening. Ashcroft rose to the challenge, releasing Victoria and turning to the inquisitive lady with a smooth laugh Finn knew to be the height of deceit. Though he considered him a friend, Ashcroft had the temperament of a caged lion and smiled only on the rarest of occasions. Humor was not in his repertoire. "Come, my lady, I have a better spot where you may view the pyrotechnics."

Finn coughed into his fist. It always amazed him that a man consumed by flames wanted to entertain with fireworks. Of course, a passion for them did explain the blazes that occurred rather often at the duke's estates.

Ashcroft threw Finn a droll look. "Mr. Alexander is going to escort Lady Hamilton to her companion, who was taken with a sudden bout of sneezing and retired to the resting room." He slipped his watch from his waistcoat pocket and checked the time. Gave Finn another look, not so droll this one. "Fifteen minutes until the festivities begin if the rain holds off. Lady Parchant-Bingman, will you assist me in gathering everyone on the south lawn? I would appreciate it, and you are well-acquainted with most of those attending, I believe."

Lady Parchant-Bingman preened, flashing Finn a molten look that said, *later, my darling, but I must go, he's a duke!*

He watched them cross the sloping lawn, Ashcroft's head bent toward the lady's in resigned consideration, while the lady at Finn's side stood silent and seething. Knowing no other way to approach the situation, he started with humor and a smile. Idly, he wondered how much the chipped tooth was affecting his presentation. "I neglected to inquire about your travels. Did Humphrey regale you with all the times he's gone haring off after me? Mad dashes in the middle of the night due to my transgressions? How he'd rather discuss the plague than Julian's chronology?" He snaked his hands in his pockets and rocked back on his heels. "When did you decide you'd rather leap from the carriage than listen to him bemoan his torturous fate for another bumpy mile? That usually hits me before we've made it to the end of Harbingdon's drive."

Victoria turned to him then, and he got his first good look at her in seventy-two hours. Enchanting in a lavender gown that flowed over her body like a waterfall, hair tucked in a lustrous arrangement she and Agnes certainly couldn't take credit for, eyes glowing more hazel than green. That star-freckle next to her lip, his weakness, bringing him home like a beacon. She looked young, guileless, a little skittish. More than a shade vexed. Vulnerable, in a way that unwelcomely captured his heart—a verdict that would nurture her ire when she sought to present a vastly contradictory portrait. As he'd come to know her, her troublesome behavior had shown itself to be a way to protect a generous and intelligent heart. A way to prepare for a dismal future, much as he was doing. She was stubborn and impetuous, true, but nothing like Piper's confident, devil-may-care comportment, which he'd confused Victoria's with at first.

How could the mistake be helped when he'd never known another female before Piper? Not really, as his clandestine encounters had involved little actual *involvement*.

Surprising him, as he stood there debating how to lighten the mood since his chipped smile wasn't doing the trick, she slipped her finger in his cuff and made a very unflattering mewing sound. "Oh, Mr. Alexander, you're the most handsome man! Dreamy. Simply enough to make me lose my breath…and the microscopic thought contained in my tiny brain."

Finn stilled, raw heat traveling from the point

where kid leather grazed the underside of his wrist straight to his groin. "You're jealous." He followed this pronouncement with a bracing laugh that had her snatching her hand back and jamming it against her hip.

No need to mention he'd been jealous as well.

"I am no such thing. It's the constant attention that's hard to overlook. At every event you followed me to, my sullied guardian angel, I watched in amazement as people stumbled and fawned and drooled. Not only women mind you. You want to pick out the men with certain proclivities in our society. Simply place you in the room, and it's entirely evident in five seconds." She whipped her hand high, pointing at the blustery clouds above. "I think even the birds are entranced. I'm astonished they don't tumble at your feet, an act of biblical proportion."

Finn brought his hand to his lips to cover the smile, and the dimple Piper said only made women angrier in tense moments. This was delightful. He hoped Tori would tell him more about how she'd watched him those many months—as he'd watched her. Dreamed of her. Began to hunger, without even knowing what her voice sounded like.

What *she* was like.

Now, he knew so many things about her, and his hunger was a raging clamor in his mind. If he could only get it out of his mind that she was made for him. His partner for life, should he find the courage to ask her to give up everything, which of course he couldn't.

"Don't laugh, you beast. You invite the grotesque attention. You wear blue *all* the time."

He looked down at his lapis waistcoat, one that closely matched his eyes, and blinked. *Huh.* Finding her gaze, he chewed on his bottom lip as the expression on her face circled from irritation to suspicion to something he didn't want to define. "One question." Gesturing like a ball bounced between them, he asked with more composure than he felt, "If we're only friends, how could it possibly matter? My flirting? It's like breathing, reactionary and with little meaning, as stalwart and automatic a defense as your behind-the-pillar kisses, but still I ask."

She lowered her gaze, her hands finding her skirt and diving in, twisting the lilac silk into submission. When her shoulders rose with a halted intake of breath and the soft words spilled from her mouth, he was lost. "I don't know…but it does."

Her candor—when he'd found no one in his life except his family to be truthful, worthy, *endearing*— sent a shimmer of fury through him. Catching her around the waist, he backed her into the shadows and brought her up on her toes, tucking her as close to his body as he could without tumbling her to the dewy grass and falling atop her. Where the difference in their height would make no difference at all. Cupping her jaw with fingers that trembled, he tilted her face high. "Is this why you came after me," he whispered, his voice hoarse. *"Pour ce qu'ils veulent tous, ou est-ce plus?"*

For what they all seek—or is it more?

"I return the query," she replied in French. Poorly articulated, badly accented, but understandable. "Is my gift all you want—or is there more?"

"I don't know," he whispered. A lie when he knew damn well. Then he confirmed his truth by cradling the nape of her neck, drawing her into him as he bent to seize her lips. The taste of champagne and strawberries flowed into his mouth, down his body, and out the soles of his feet, grounding him to the earth and to her.

Her arm rose, grazing his waist, ribs, shoulders, reaching past his jaw and sending fingers into his hair, tangling, tugging, creating a jolt of aroused pleasure and a moan he could not contain.

She started at the sound and drew back, her expression concealed by shadow, but her wild eyes were glowing through it. If his groan wasn't enough to tell her he was losing control, the erection pressed against her hip, an awakening he couldn't conceal if his life depended on it, should have.

"Walk away now," he said gruffly, his hands sliding to her shoulders and grasping, drawing her in instead of pushing her away, "before it's too late."

When it was already too late for him.

Shaking her head, she stepped back atop the low row of bricks circling the fountain, slanted her lips over his, and claimed him.

He sighed, giving up, giving *everything* he'd previously withheld.

If she were going to make love to another man, experience pleasure with another man, marry another man, Finn would make sure she never forgot this passionate moment in the midsummer twilight.

This moment when she was *his*.

The bricks made it easy for her to loop her arms around his neck, her breasts settling heavily against his chest. Hyacinth, he concluded after days of questioning, she smelled like hyacinth and vanilla, the unique fragrance unraveling his longing and laying it out like a rug before him. He cradled her head, nipped her bottom lip, soothed with his tongue, then nipped again. Her answering shift, hip to hip, the ragged sound of delight whispering from her throat, telling him all he needed to know.

He didn't have to handle her delicately, like a vase he feared breaking. The woman who he was certain rode a horse like a whip and rolled in the grass with Piper and quarreled with him until he lost the will to conquer her would be an enthusiastic, fearless lover, meeting him move for move, sigh for sigh, pleasure for pleasure.

Unafraid to reveal his yearning, he palmed her hip and brought her gently against his hard length, settling her rather perfectly. Even through layers, he could feel her. Warm and welcoming. "Tori," he whispered hoarsely, "you are magnificent." Her hair was wild, the moist air creating a wealth of riotous curls he longed to see spread beneath him as he slid inside her.

With a stuttered catch of breath, she gripped his shoulders and followed his languid rhythm, their tongues echoing the movement of their hips. It was a dance as old as time...one he'd fantasized about, sweat-slick sheets and flushed skin, the scent of her, him, *them,* capturing the bedchamber and defying his every concern.

Slowing the kiss, she dropped her head to his shoulder, breathless, trembling. She was close, he thought in amazement, and he hadn't even put his hands on her, not truly. He could make her come, right here in the moonlight, while standing on a low brick wall surrounding a decaying fountain on Ashcroft's estate. Make her remember *him* if she were to marry the duke, every time she saw the crumbling monument.

If she were this responsive fully clothed, what would she be like when he stripped her down to nothing, all those silly stratums gone, his lips and teeth, his tongue, covering every inch of her with absolutely no barriers in place?

A lewd impulse, but one he followed, fingers trailing across her belly and up the side of her body to her breast. Cupping the full mound, his thumb found her nipple, pressed, circled, making it harden like the pebbles wedged beneath his boot. Her head fell back, exposing the glorious, arching nape of her neck. Powerless, his lips were there in seconds, kissing, sucking, drawing her skin tenderly between his teeth. Her pulse tapped against his jaw, proof of her yearning, the realization sending a pulse of longing through *him*.

Hell, he could come himself with nothing more than her sighs ringing in his ears, her fingers clutching his shoulders, the sweet taste of her filling his mouth.

Desire was overriding sense, he knew, when he began calculating how long it would take to retrieve his carriage, parked a scant distance from Ashcroft's house to avoid the throng, send a note to Julian's townhome so Humphrey didn't worry, then spend the next two days inside, over, beneath, and behind Victoria Hamilton.

She had no idea how inventive he could be if inspired, which he rarely, if ever, had been.

He might even surprise himself.

He was eagerly reclaiming her lips when an explosion sent them stumbling apart, Finn's quick reflexes, an arm snaked about her waist, the only thing that kept her from tumbling into the bone-dry fountain.

CHAPTER 12

*I*n stunned bewilderment, Victoria watched color from Ashcroft's horribly-timed pyrotechnic display wash across Finn's cheeks and spark off his enlarged pupils. His hand lay on her breast, no longer cupping but still a firm, mesmerizing hold, and their eyes, at the exact same second, dropped to the marvelous indecency.

As she mentally debated the next steps—to the carriage together or apart—many things occurred at once.

A storm. The Earl of Hester. Finn's temper. Observations about her gift.

A lone raindrop hit her bottom lip. Finn's gaze tracked it as he leaned in to kiss it away when the Earl of Hester stumbled through a break in the hedges with a sneering chortle. Without a word, Finn strode directly to Hester and sent his fist into the man's jaw. The earl went down like a carpet had been yanked from beneath his feet, the savage display unlike anything Victoria had ever seen.

She hopped off the wall and went to stand over Hester. He was breathing, air whistling from his bruised lips. So not dead. "Are you daft?" she whispered and turned to find Finn flexing his fingers with a pained expression. The aroma of Hester's drink of choice enveloped them, driving out Finn's enticing scent. Another blasted interruption.

"You don't want to know what he thought when he saw us." He blew on his knuckles and bared his even, white teeth. "He's lucky I didn't kill him. I should carve him up with the knife in my boot. The rotter has no idea who he's dealing with."

"How lethal," she murmured, wondering why seeing Finn's uncivilized side sent heat swimming through her body. And then she realized…

"Finn, you were able to read his mind."

He halted and palmed his brow, his lids fluttering. "Lady Teasdale is looking for Hester. She's crossing the lawn, daring the rain to ruin her rendezvous with him. Apologies, Tori darling, but I think the fountain is a well-used location." Giving the earl's shoulder a nudge with his boot, he flexed his hand again and said, "Can you take care of this? Erase the last five minutes or so? I think it would be best."

As cool raindrops began to pelt her, she squatted beside Hester, circled his wrist with her fingers, and let the sound of his pulse enter her consciousness. She held on until she heard a click, until she'd stolen enough from his memory to secure their safety. "It's done. Perhaps even so much as the entire night, poor Lady Teasdale. I can't control how much. Or how little. We'll hope it worked."

Hester rolled to his side with a loud snore. Laughing, Finn grabbed her hand and yanked her along behind him as the sky opened up in a violent deluge. The storm had sent the revelers fleeing into the house, so Finn and Victoria skidded and tripped their way across a thankfully deserted lawn. Around the house, through a side garden, down an alleyway, through a rusted gate. He obviously knew the estate well, likely had kissed someone, a hundred someones, behind Ashcroft's fountain.

The most amazing experience of her life when it undoubtedly meant little to him.

Foolish to be possessive of a man nearly every woman in London owned a piece of.

A landau was conveniently waiting at the curb, and Finn shoved her into it with a terse directive to return to Julian's townhome shouted to the coachman who sat shivering on the bench. She went to her hands and knees on the velvet squab, expecting Finn to follow. She glanced over her shoulder, got a good look at his face, and realized he had no intention of doing so. His hair was slicked to his head, his skin glistening in the streetlamp's glow. Water streamed into a gaze fixed stonily on her in an impassive assessment.

"The kiss broke my gift," she rushed to say over the rain popping sharply against the carriage's soft top, fearing he was set to send her off without another word.

He dipped his head, but not soon enough to hide his smile. "Yes, love, it appears it did. Although only for a few moments. I'm not that good. At kissing, I mean." He tapped his temple. "Silence governs once again."

Love? Her heartbeat scattered. "If I come to the Blue Moon, will you let me in?" she asked, the last thing she'd expected to leave her lips. She'd never gone further than kisses behind potted palms with anyone else, but with Finn, she wanted to go to the ends of the Earth.

He leaned in, cupped her cheeks, and kissed her. Deeply, tenderly, thoroughly. Finally. "No, I won't let you in," he murmured, releasing her and shutting the door. "I'm ruinous to you, and you're quite simply dynamite in my pocket, deadly to me."

She wanted to fall into him, become part of him, lose herself completely. Risk everything. In that moment, nothing else mattered. "Wait!" she called as Finn tapped the side of the carriage, and it rocked into motion. "Your sister?"

Finn swallowed, his cheeks taking on the pale gray of the foggy night. "You were right. She's in London."

She slammed her fist against the trap, and the vehicle halted. "Tell me," she implored. "You can talk to me, you know you can."

A look of naked agony crossed his face. Indecision and relief and torment. "Ashcroft received your information, and his men found her. I'm going tomorrow morning. All this time and I never knew." He slapped the side of the carriage harder than he needed to and let the coachman know with an ill-mannered directive not to terminate the journey again. No matter what the lady said. "I suppose it's not too late even if it feels like it. When all is said and done, you truly can't outrun the past."

She leaned out the window as the carriage rolled away, bringing more scandal atop her should anyone see the indecorous display. "You'll take me. So you may meet her without her thoughts tainting it. Promise me, Blue!"

He turned without comment, his tall form disappearing into the mist rising off the cobblestones. That melancholy look had flowed right back into his eyes; her touch hadn't kept it away for long.

Again, his words rang in her ears. *No, I won't let you in.*

Collapsing to the squab with a punitive exhalation, she caught sight of her reflection in the rain-streaked windowpane. Touching her swollen lips, it was all she could do to keep from curling into a ball and crying her eyes out.

She looked wholly compromised.

Wild-eyed. Well-loved. Wrecked.

And there was no need to contemplate how she *felt*.

Humphrey and Agnes were not going to believe a single word she said when she lied to them about the evening's events.

~

Victoria barely slept, wrenching awake with every shift and settle of Julian's townhome until she gave up and did puzzles until dawn, then went down to the kitchens to shock the staff and ask to be allowed to bake. They were stunned but cordial—and ungifted, according to Humphrey—likely only thinking how odd the titled class was, working when one didn't have to. Baking, of all things.

She learned nothing new while preparing cinnamon waffles and blueberry scones to accompany the standard fare of kippers, beans, and eggs. Humphrey was respected but solitary, Finn adored but forlorn. Imagine living above a gaming hell when he could reside in Mayfair, where rubbish didn't litter the streets, and the stink of the Thames was beaten down by the scent of lemon and vinegar. The consensus was, with notably engrossed looks thrown her way, that both men needed wives to straighten out their regrettable existences.

Victoria pressed dough and sprinkled spice and slid tray after tray into the oven—only burning herself once—as the previous night rotated through her mind like the wheel of an overturned carriage. Finn's fingers cupping her breast, teeth nipping her bottom lip, hips grinding, pressing his long, hard length against her. Eagerly pleasurable perfection, all of it. Raw and spontaneous, gasping breaths, trembling limbs, moist skin. Amazingly, she'd come close to securing that intense feeling she'd found in her darkened bedchamber, her hand tucked between her legs in exploration.

My, what would it—*he*—feel like if they had greater access? Free of clothing, lying on a bed or a sofa or the floor, where she didn't have to stretch to reach his mouth? Or any other part of his body. She pressed her fingertip to a cooling scone and shivered. The landau she'd traveled home in last night was extremely spacious. The brocade settee in her bedchamber big enough for two if the two were pressed close together. One atop the other would undoubtedly work. Before the hearth, on the sweeping marble staircase, in the linen closet she'd passed this morning.

Her imagination overflowed with possibilities.

However, men didn't crawl into linen closets with women they compared to dynamite.

A statement she had no idea whether to consider a compliment or an insult.

As she was pulling the last of her scones from the oven, Humphrey stomped into the room, took one look at her and snapped, "I'll be damned."

Placing the tray on the metal shelf at her side, she swiped her hand across her brow. "Excuse me?"

Humphrey yanked his hat from his head and beat it against his thigh. "I was worried when I couldn't locate you after last night's fiasco, Ashcroft's piss-poor job of management, you coming back without that crying maid of yours, looking like you'd been tossed over someone's shoulder. Look in the kitchens, Finn tells me when he arrives, flecking a spec from his sleeve, cool that one. I ask myself, how does he get that if he isn't pocketing your thoughts, which we all understand he's not. But here you are—like he knows you better than you know yourself. Like my suspicions about the two of you are on the money, a safe bet I'm feeling close to crying over because it gives me that itchy, fated feeling I haven't had since Julian and Piper got tangled up. But a gentleman is supposed to forego stating the obvious, isn't that the way it works? So I'll be a gentleman and not say what I honestly think is going on here."

Her temper sparked. "As I told you and Agnes—"

"I know what you told me." He exhaled and jammed his hat on his head. "What you told that unfortunate woman whose job it is to corral you."

"But—"

"Listen, princess, are you going with us or not?" He grabbed a scone and bit into it, squinted at her as if doubting she could make something so delicious, then took another bite. "Having Finn's mind on the task at hand and not on the usual confusion cluttering his brain is a crafty idea. Even if you used it as leverage to get to London, you were right to suggest it."

She stilled, her heartbeat tripping into a mad rhythm. "He's letting me go," she breathed.

Humphrey regarded her with a penetrating gaze as he polished off the scone and reached for another. "Only if you want. No one's forcing."

Oh, she wanted.

So many delicious things she'd never get.

CHAPTER 13

*T*he dwelling Ashcroft's investigator directed them to was a hovel.

Located in an area by the docks Finn guessed Victoria had never set foot in. Likely her servants hadn't even stooped to crawling this far down society's ladder, even for blood oranges or Moroccan coffee straight off the boat. He almost laughed when absolutely nothing about this was amusing. They weren't far from where he'd taken a knife in the chest trying to save Freddie. Maybe this woman Victoria claimed was his sister had even scurried by him that day, rushing past another person bleeding out on the wharf.

A putrid gust lashed his back, giving him an unsolicited nudge toward the door he stood before. One knock against pitted wood to change his life. Conversely, he could turn to the woman standing close behind him and change it in another way entirely.

Both choices terrified him.

Drawing an agitated breath, he identified the scent of hyacinth and cinnamon riding above the rank aroma of charred meat and coal smoke. *Tori.* His sweet-smelling companion hadn't uttered one word this morning—the carriage ride had been tense and joyless, propelled by his somber countenance—but he felt what could only be called protective support radiating from her. From Humphrey, which was his norm. Maybe even from sniffling, woebegone Agnes. She likely worried about everyone and then some, the hapless woman.

With a resigned sigh, Victoria reached around him and knocked, her gloves worth more than a year's lease on this dilapidated space. Finn heard the tumblers shift without the occupant asking who stood on the other side of the door, and the questions raced through his mind.

Who am I? What if I can't live with what I find out? And finally...how do I know this is real?

But he knew it was real.

Because he recognized his sister, in a way that went beyond sight and arrived from the heart, the *soul*, the moment he saw her.

Eyes a replica of his widened before the woman gasped and slid into an elegant swoon that in no way fit the dreadful surroundings. Humphrey was there before Finn could react, able rescuer of vulnerable women and orphaned children, lifting her into his arms as if she weighed nothing. Which from the look of her frail form, she didn't.

"Inside," Agnes hissed and gave Finn and Victoria a shove across the threshold and into the dank rabbit hole of a flat.

Except for him, they were a well-organized group. Humphrey settling his slight bundle on a threadbare settee; Victoria prodding Finn into a chair he neither remembered seeing or sitting in; Agnes procuring a moistened rag she placed on his sister's brow. Task complete, Humphrey took one look at him and set to roaming the space, no doubt searching for liquor as Finn had an idea he wasn't far off from fainting himself. Black dots were spotting his vision, and he inhaled sharply, trying to drive them away. Dreams of the past, imagined or real, swirled like mist through his consciousness.

Humphrey pushed a chipped glass in his hand, the first-rate port sliding down Finn's throat and making him choke but bringing heat to his cheeks.

A murmur came from the settee, and the entire room stilled until the only sounds were loud bellows from the street and gusts whistling through the multitude of cracked windowpanes. The woman turned her head toward Finn, her eyes, *his* eyes, locking on him. She gestured limply to his drink. "Your grandfather was born in Portugal. It was his favorite, I was told." She closed her eyes and swallowed deeply. "I kept it, always, for when you finally found me. With your talent, I knew someday you would."

"Can you afford this?" Finn gazed into the glass, asking the most inane question possible and considering if he should finish the dram if she couldn't.

She laughed, a wonderfully authentic reverberation when most laughter in his world was forced. "No, Finley Michel, I can't."

Finley Michel. The name brought forth that memory, faded and indistinct. Racing through grass high enough to whip his knee, giggling, tripping, and someone coming back for him. Tossing back the remainder of the port, he slapped the glass to the table and wrenched forward in his chair. "Had I known, I would have torn England apart searching for you."

His sister elbowed to a sit, her hair, as light as Finn's was dark, flowing over her shoulders and down her back. Her clothing was quality but years out of date, patched and faded. She was petite like Piper but thin, too thin. He was afraid to catalog her features to determine what else they shared outside their eyes, each revelation adding weight to his chest until he felt the room closing in on him, his breath hard to catch.

"Isabelle," she murmured and rose, going to her knees before him. With trembling hands, she drew the locket he'd seen in his dream from beneath the bodice of her gown. Flicking the pendant open, she showed him the painted portrait of two children.

"Belle," he whispered.

"*Yes.*" She reached for his hand, and he let her take it. Offering solace when he felt hollowed out inside. Her palms were chapped and raw, the hands of an older woman. "Our mother was the daughter of a marquis, an impoverished title, meaningless after the French Terror, wealth and lands gone, most of the family killed in the siege. Our father, Tennison Laurent, was a tradesman who died in Lyon just after you were born, and *Maman* had nowhere else to go but the home of a distant cousin in Surrey. She met a man there, married."

"And…" Finn's fingers clenched around hers.

Belle shook her head, shrugged. "*Maman* was stunning, we were destitute, he was wealthy. Simple enough as those arrangements go. But I didn't stop you from telling him what was inside his mind. Even at three years old, you said too much. You dreamed of him, too, so he began not only to loathe but fear you. There's time for me to tell you everything, but know this…" Her eyes glistened, and the tears overflowed, racing down her cheeks and dropping to their linked hands, searing his skin and his heart. "You weren't to blame. *I* was. I could have hidden us, but he took you away the day after she died, the only person I had left, and I've been looking for you ever since."

"How?" he breathed.

"I have no gift, nothing like yours, but I know when others do. I realized the moment you were born that you were different. I can walk a street and tell you who sees things they shouldn't. A serving girl in the Ax and Shield, the bloke who operates the coster cart in Leadenhall. My skin tingles, my brain hums." She glanced about, pointing to Victoria, Humphrey, Agnes. "The upmarket lady, yes, the handsome brute, no. The frightened mouse of a maid, no. "

"The mystery deepens," Humphrey said wryly from his position guarding the darkest corner of the room. "Holy hell, but will Julian love this. Any chance you can locate a gifted majordomo with that humming mind of yours, Belle sweet, as we need one on the estate?"

Belle turned to gaze at Humphrey for a long moment, her eyes narrowing in fascinated study, then she shook herself and circled her attention back to her brother. "I was told our beast of a stepfather dropped you in a London slum. I ran away from him when I was fifteen and went to a smaller village in the next shire where I could afford lodging. Then I took every job an insufficiently educated woman who nonetheless speaks three languages and is willing to lie through her teeth can—seamstress, tutor, shop girl, maid—while I saved money. I arrived in London ten months ago and began to roam the streets, lying in wait for a man with my eyes. I knew you'd find me eventually, with the dreams, but I hoped to hurry fate." She smiled without humor and motioned to his expertly-tailored clothing. "I fear I was walking the wrong streets. I don't often go so far as the West End and the society pages. You're the bounder with the blue eyes they write about." Her lips tipped low, a short sigh slipping from her. "Oh, Finley Michel, what have you been doing?"

As if awakening from a stupor, Finn glanced about the room, recording every tattered piece of furniture, every battered surface. The sound of glass breaking and a hoarse shout in the alleyway running alongside the building only added to his unease. "You're not staying here, Belle. Not another night." With a creak in the floorboard, Victoria stepped closer, reacting to the edge of panic in his voice. That she was so attuned sent an ill-tempered rush through him. "Don't argue with me, any of you," he said in a voice he rarely found the opportunity to use, except when pitching a drunken sod out the back door of the Blue Moon. It was Julian's voice he emulated, a rigid tone offering no room for negotiation. He had learned from a master.

Humphrey stepped into the pale candlelit circle. No gas fixtures in this dwelling. "I'll bring another carriage for the belongings."

"Who are you to order me about? It isn't much, but it's home," Belle said and straightened her slim shoulders in a pitiful show of force. Finn felt a swirl of dread imagining what she'd had to endure without him, without a family, without protection. But those were stories for another day as he was confident his heart couldn't take much more on this one.

Humphrey chortled and scrubbed his hand across his stubbled cheeks, amused by her, Finn could see. "I didn't save his arse all those years ago"—he jabbed his elbow at Finn—"to have his sister spend another second in this squat."

Belle stared, and Humphrey met her gaze without flinching when a woman's fury could be a harrowing thing. Finn wondered if he imagined the spark of awareness that flowed between them. Perhaps Belle found Humphrey handsome. The women in the village trailed after him, chattering about him needing a wife, so anything was possible. He *was* the most protective man Finn knew aside from Julian, and the most caring, though his hulking frame obscured his gentle nature.

It didn't sound like Belle had encountered this type of concern in years, if ever when Finn had been smothered daily.

For the first time since they'd entered the pitiful abode, Finn looked to Victoria. They shared that spark of awareness, too, for some unfathomable reason. It snuck under his skin like a splinter, pain, and pleasure. She returned his regard without wavering, her gaze molten gold in the candlelight, ethereal, haunting, her knowledge of him so absolute he felt naked in a way wholly unrelated to his attire. This was his life—chaotic, bewildering—and she had an uncomfortably clear view of it.

A view he'd never given another. Never thought to give another.

"I'll help you pack," Victoria offered, her encouragement subtle but intoxicating. So compelling a proposal, he turned his head to gaze at the frayed wallpaper rather than watch a woman he was becoming obsessed with bundle a sister he hadn't known existed into her threadbare coat. "You and Finn have much to discuss"—the crash of a cart and human sounded on the street—"but perhaps not here."

"I'll go," Belle finally whispered, "because there isn't any reason to stay. There has never been."

At the softly spoken words, Finn ushered her outside and to the waiting carriage, his heart shattering for them both.

~

Finn had suspected she'd come, hence her protection.

The footman followed at a discreet distance, trailing her through streetlamp-lit shadow and light, across slick, rain-drenched cobblestones. Staying close as she snaked between the carriages lining the street outside the Blue Moon, the men inside them laughing and making ribald comments. Her guard made no effort to conceal his presence as he splashed along behind her. He also made no effort to impede her journey.

Prevent her from making a life-altering mistake.

If giving the man you were falling in love with your innocence was a mistake. She considered it a gift. To herself.

Before marrying one she didn't love, like, or desire to save her family.

This choice was hers. The *only* choice that was hers.

And his, if she trusted her instincts, which she was foolish enough to do.

Tugging her cloak closer about her face, she crossed the thankfully deserted alleyway backing the gaming hell. Shattered glass crunched beneath her boot as a varied combination of foul scents stung her nose. There was no alternative. Not after seeing Finn's inconsolable face before he bolted from Julian's townhouse, Humphrey's grip on her arm the only thing keeping her from running after him.

She and Agnes had tried to make an unorthodox event routine, settling Belle in a bedchamber more luxurious than any she'd previously occupied if her hesitancy to touch the furnishings provided an accurate narrative. Tucked her beneath an overstuffed counterpane with a cup of cocoa and a plentiful fruit and cheese tray while Humphrey closeted Finn away for—what had Finn called it?—an advice and whiskey session.

This sudden appearance of his sister was too much to shoulder alone. She'd known this the moment he left his discussion with Humphrey to find her haunting the hallway outside the study like one of Simon's ghosts. He'd only shaken his head wordlessly and stalked past her, rushing out the door like the devil nipped at his heels.

Swallowing her apprehension that she was intruding where she shouldn't, she halted before the Blue Moon's side entrance. Lifted her hand to smack that silly little bell when the door opened, and Finn unceremoniously yanked her inside. They stood in the entryway, breathing heavily for no reason, tripping into each other's gazes.

"If you turn me away, Blue, I'll find another man at the first opportunity to relieve me of—"

"Oh, no, you won't," he snarled and in a masculine show of fury, tossed her over his shoulder, kicking the door shut, and taking the stairs to his chamber two at a time. She slapped his back and hip, struggling, but he contained her easily, lean muscle concealed well beneath his tailored attire. Her cloak slid from her shoulders, and he kicked it from his path without pausing.

Ruining any notion of romance, he marched into the room they'd clashed in two short weeks ago and tossed her atop the massive sofa. She gasped and went to her knees, straightening her skirts while shooting him a glare hot enough to scorch wood. The overflowing bookcases, artwork-lined walls, and curio-stuffed shelves, evidence of a keen mind and industrious life, were no longer a surprise. She now knew there was much more to him than he cared to show a thoughtless world.

The room was chilled, murky, no fire in the hearth, no glow from the gas sconces. The ideal setting for a brooding bastard who was not a bastard after all. Her gaze fixed on the door to his bedchamber as a sizzling spiral lit her up from the inside out. Jealousy and longing claimed her, and that kiss behind the fountain, *oh*, she could almost feel Finn's teeth nipping her skin. If he somehow guessed the strength of her attraction, she would leap from the window to the bustling street below without a care.

She nodded to the bedchamber. "Any scantily clothed friend in there this time?"

"You're my only friend," he whispered from his vigil by the window, hands shoved deep in his pockets, shoulders hunched as if he stood in a raging storm. His coat and waistcoat were tossed over his desk, his pale shirtsleeves glowing in the slice of light oozing through the grimy panes. His quietness frightened her, his calm before an emotional storm.

"Then talk to me," she said, knowing she'd come for his body. But she'd also come for his mind. Better to admit, if only to herself, that she'd come for *everything*. "Unless you want me to leave." Added because his exacting stillness was sending her courage in the wrong direction.

"That's the problem." Ripping his neckpiece off, he let it flutter to the carpet. "I don't want you to leave, but I can't talk. Not yet. Not when my heart is this bruised. I'm sorry to say, I need a moment. I need *you*, but maybe not in the way you're offering."

She propped her elbows on the back of the sofa and leaned out enough to catch the scent of his him, brandy, smoke, and bergamot. Close enough to see the stubble shadowing his chiseled jaw. Her breasts pressed into the tufted leather, nipples pebbling, more sensitive than they had any right to be. "Careless liaisons are your preference. Mine, too. I can see why. Talking is a tricky business."

He turned, wedging his shoulder against the window ledge, letting her see his bleak, hunted expression. Letting her know more about him. His collar was open, exposing golden skin and a dusting of hair and the angry scar she wanted to press her lips against. She took him in, a gradual perusal from his bare feet to the disheveled strands sweeping his brow. Helplessly, she paused mid-review. His form-fitting trousers did little to hide his reaction to her invading his space. "If you want to arrive at your marital bed untouched, you'd better leave now," he said roughly, and she realized he was as provoked as she was. "It's your choice, it always has been, but friend or foe, if you stay, I mean to have you. I'm being as honest as I've ever been with anyone. I'm tangled up inside, Tori, more than you likely want to witness. I'm not going to make a judicious decision right now. I'm just going to take what I want. What I think might ease my heartache. Or, hell, perhaps it will only make it worse."

She felt an easy smile tilt her lips. *Want*. Yes, that about covered it.

He took a fast step forward, jerking his hands from his pockets. "Don't you dare smile. *This*, everything between us, is an utter disaster. It's going to destroy us."

She started unlacing her bodice, one eyelet, two, three before she looked back at him. He hadn't moved, not one inch, but his gaze was riveted, air shooting from his lips, the hands at his side closing into trembling fists.

She crooked a finger, her smile growing. "Come ruin me, Blue."

Shoving off the ledge, he crossed the short distance, grabbed her hand, and drew her from the sofa. Wordlessly out of the room and down the hallway, his stride urgent, his grasp firm. Faintly, she could hear the clamor from the gaming hell, a muffled shout, the clack of dice, loud laughter. Up another flight of stairs until the sounds trickled away. Everything trickled away but the muted rasp of their breaths and their soft footfalls. Halting before a paneled walnut door, Finn tugged a key from his trouser pocket.

"*This*," she breathed—a space she recognized as his upon entry. Stacks of books, modest furnishings, subdued colors. An unassuming iron bedstead covered in twisted sheets, battered chest of drawers, escritoire desk. Simple, well-ordered, unadorned.

The room below was where he pretended.

This was where he *was*.

She opened her mouth to ask him why he was showing her this when he cradled her jaw with his long fingers and captured her lips with his.

And her world compressed to nothing but their kiss.

CHAPTER 14

$\mathcal{F}$inn kissed her to shut her up.

To keep her from probing him like a fresh wound, making him bleed more of his life out for her. He'd never brought anyone to this chamber, never even considered it. This space was personal, dreary, but snug, precisely what he needed when other's thoughts were creating a painful drumbeat in his head and behind his eyes. *He* was often dreary; only no one knew it. Except, maybe she did.

Victoria was already so firmly embedded he didn't know how to get her out. Or even what parts of him she hadn't seen yet.

Extreme confusion on top of raging lust made for an inelegant partnership, he decided.

He also kissed her to assuage his feral compulsion. To touch, to savor, to *possess*. His longing had teeth when it usually contained as many sharp edges as a cake of soap.

Victoria bounced up on her toes to deepen the kiss when he set her back. Her eyes met his, dazed amber in the silvery light reaching them from the lone window. Her lips were moist, plump, inviting. Before she could argue, which she looked set to, he brushed his thumb across the bottom one and let his hand fall to the eyelets of her bodice. "Easy," he murmured, "I'm not going anywhere. And neither are you."

He'd once been very good with his hands, nothing like Simon, but a rather proficient cutpurse, and he made quick work of her clothing, trying to ignore the enthusiastic effect exposing her body to his hungry gaze was having on him. Laces, ties, hooks. Fewer layers than he'd expected, and he raised a brow when, except for her chemise and gloves, her clothing lay in a neat puddle of silk, linen, and lawn at their feet. A smaller puddle than it should have been. Not a silk stocking to be had.

Her cheeks tinted, the first blush he'd ever seen on her. "I took the liberty of leaving some pieces behind."

Of course.

So, she wanted to seduce *him.*

He was charmed, troubled, reluctantly agreeable. He lowered his lips to her shoulder, creating a decadently moist abrasion through the thin cotton. Her breasts were straining against the material of her chemise, and he brushed the back of his knuckles across them. She smelled of hyacinth and nutmeg this time, sweet and spicy. His cock was hard, his body hot, his intellect aroused, his resolve weak. She was the most beautiful thing he'd ever seen standing there in light that lit her up and hid her all at once. And he couldn't read her mind, not one thought, not even a glimmer. This level of intimacy was unfamiliar, completely foreign. Joyful and erotic.

He'd never touched a woman without thoughts tainting the experience.

My God, he marveled and skimmed his mouth

along the nape of her neck to her jaw, *this is how it feels to truly love someone.*

He made to remove her chemise, but she halted him with a low hum, knocking his hand aside and beginning work on the buttons of his shirt. When she fully exposed his scar, she pressed her lips to the mottled ridge, bottoming his heart out where he stood. "I'm going to ask about this," she whispered, watching his shirt flutter to the floor, "but not now."

He gripped her wrist when her focus slid lower. Took her hand and tugged her glove off, finger by finger by finger. Then repeated the process with the other hand, letting the gloves tumble to the floor. "Are you looking for a way to bring a man to his knees, Tori darling? I'm fearful that with a little exploration, you'll figure out exactly how to do it."

In answer, she placed her mouth over his nipple and sucked, lightly, gently. He shook his head, implying absolutely nothing, unable to banter if she was going to do that.

She laughed and freed her hand from his grip, hesitated, then covered his hard length. "Ah," she murmured as if something surprised her. He was beyond asking what.

With a muffled groan of surrender, he backed up until his hip met the wall. By that time, she had most of his trouser buttons undone, his drawers down enough to free his cock. Tipping his head back, he closed his eyes, ceding any plan to manage the encounter.

She wanted to explore, he gathered, from the fingertip cautiously tracing his rigid length in a leisurely, wonderfully awkward circuit. *Okay*, he decided and blew out a breath. He could allow this for one minute. Maybe two, if he kept his eyes closed and avoided studying her luscious body concealed only beneath a thin chemise. He wasn't going to embarrass himself by not making it to the finish line. Not with *her*.

The only woman who would ever matter.

Going up on her toes, she resumed the kiss, tentatively stroking her tongue against his in the same rhythm as her hand caressed him. Moaning against her lips, he revised his calculation because her technique, surprisingly suitable for a beginner, was bringing that shiver to the base of his spine that meant his body was on a countdown to release.

Moving in, slowing down, he tangled his hands in her hair and walked her back. The mattress hit her mid-thigh, and she sprawled across the bed, her curls an ebony spill across the pale sheets. She rose to her elbow and flipped the jumbled strands from her face. "You liked it?" she asked with a half-smile.

He tilted his head, considering. *God, yes.* But he wasn't about to admit it.

"What's that look about?" she murmured, her gaze running the length of him as it had earlier. Like she was sketching him, one languid stroke at a time, setting him aflame with her earnest regard.

He flicked open the last button and stepped out of his trousers, kicking them aside. His drawers soon followed. Her eyes were dazzled, vulnerable, captivated. "Skin to skin will change everything," he whispered in French, knowing it was probably a more complicated statement than she could translate.

A realization only devastating experience would bring.

She pinched the material of her chemise between her fingers and let it flutter back to her breasts. "There's still this."

Leaning over her, he grasped the neck and ripped it down the middle, exposing her magnificent body

TRACY SUMNER

to the meager light. Light as starved for her as he was. Crawling over her, he braced himself on his forearms, letting his weight settle atop her in slow, tantalizing degrees. Trying to conceal how entranced he was by everything about her. Her quiet beauty, the intelligence shimmering in her eyes, the courage, the keen interest.

The innocence he was set to take.

One more moment, he thought, before I give you my heart.

Skin to skin indeed changed everything.

"Now, there's just us," he whispered and let himself fall.

~

He moved over her in the darkness, shifting and settling between her legs as his lips captured hers.

His sleek body was as beautiful as his face, and she memorized, her exploration unskilled, ravenous, daring. A silky sprinkling of hair trailing to his waist, lean hips, muscular legs. The hard length of him digging wonderfully into her thigh.

She wanted to disappear into him and become one. The end goal, she understood and arched her hips against his in invitation.

More. Now.

Pressing her lips to his neck, she sucked on a patch of skin and verbalized the demand in a hoarse whisper. He responded with a low groan, a nip to her cheek, her jaw. Lowering his head, he circled her nipple with his tongue, then moved his lips fully around the sensitive nub and drew it between his teeth. Pleasure, pain. *Pleasure.* She came off the mattress with a husky cry she'd never heard herself utter, her hand tangling in his hair and bringing him closer.

"The lady likes," he murmured, his breath washing over her, bringing another fissure of delight. Continuing his assault, he caught her other nipple between his thumb and finger. Her thoughts dissolved, leaving nothing but desperate need, yearning, *sensation*. Seeking to ease the fierce pulse that had settled between her thighs, she ground against the leg he'd so cleverly maneuvered into place between them.

It was enough, this movement combined with his taste, scent, touch to send a tiny, explosive ripple through her. Skin aflame, limbs tingling, logic evaporating until she was left a powerless, writhing muddle.

"That's a start," he whispered against her lips and trailed his hand down her body. She felt the moisture on her thighs and thought to warn him, embarrassed and unsure, when he recaptured her lips and slid a finger deep inside her. Then he pressed his thumb to the spot she'd come to find, through her exploration, held the most pleasure. *Oh.* She dragged her hands down his body, scraping her nails over his skin. The slopes and ridges of his back, the rise of his buttocks. He was glorious, and she was going to record every inch of him while she let him turn her inside-out.

An apt pupil, she caught the rhythm of his finger, two when he added another, realizing they were acting out what would happen later. Soon, if his rushed breaths, the sweat slicking his skin to hers, the trembling arm braced by her shoulder, meant anything. Her head fell back, her back arching as she gasped, overcome by sensation, unable to maintain the kiss. In reply, he circled her waist, pulling her up and into him, devouring her.

"Come for me," he whispered roughly against her cheek, his damp hair clinging to her skin, his body shifting as he sought to move closer. "Next time, I'll use my mouth...make you shatter in seconds." He sighed, long and low. "For now, this will have to do. I'll come in seconds if I go there."

The thought of his lips pressed to her core, of his release, sent her over the edge.

She could only lie back and disintegrate, weakly registering every thoughtful, resolute caress. Fingers stroking, thumb circling, teeth marking her shoulder, the nape of her neck, his exhalations harsh against her flushed skin. The weight of his body forcing hers into the mattress, a delicious, unexpected benefit.

Bliss. Waves and waves of it, stealing the air from her lungs and thought from her mind. "I can't," she panted with a shaky effort to push him away. "Too much."

She felt his lips curve against her cheek, his fractured breath whispering past her ear. He uncurled her hand from where she gripped the counterpane and drew it down between their bodies. "Feel what you do to me."

He was hard, incredibly so, which had shocked her earlier. And smooth, sleek, just like he was. A drop of liquid rested on the tip, and she smoothed it over his skin. "Perfect," he murmured and captured her lips. Wrapping his hand around hers, he moved into position at her entrance, gradually, letting her feel their joining, control the speed, the depth. "This is what we feel like."

"Yes," she whispered raggedly, lifting her hips as he edged inside.

Then he began to thrust, slowly, allowing her to accept him. The pain was minimal, a sharp pinch that quickly faded, leaving only a feeling of abundance between her legs, an unfamiliar yet fascinating fullness inside her body. Pleasure simmering beneath her skin, Victoria locked her arms around Finn's shoulders. Her hips bumped his as her hunger rose, their movements awkward until, with a sudden agreement, they found each other's rhythm.

Then it was magic.

Angling her bent leg against his thigh, he slid deeper, sending a blistering tremor through her. She must have made a sound because he shifted, going again, harder, the dart of delight increasing.

There, that spot, *yes*. "Blue."

He answered with another stroke, tip to base, and another until she had no words left to utter. His speed increased, his exertion pushing them up the bed. He switched between bottomless kisses she struggled to match and gasping, labored breaths released against her neck. His hands were restless, caressing her hip, her breast, her face.

At that moment, they were one.

For the first and perhaps the last time, she wasn't alone.

It was then she noticed the squeak of the bed, louder even than the sound of their bodies moving together. Finn grasped one of the coiled metal slats and braced himself. Her eyes helplessly followed the flex and twist of his bicep—as if she needed additional incentive to catch fire and turn to ash. "This bed," he said in a gravelly voice as he dashed a bead of sweat from his jaw, "is not meant for activity of this consequence."

She stilled, her eyes racing to his. "Here, you've never…"

He shook his head, sending damp strands as dark as the sky beyond the bedchamber window skating across his brow. "I'll slow down." He rocked his hips against her, his lids fluttering. "We have hours."

The pleasurable peak she was *so* close to reaching wouldn't allow for hours. "I have another solution," she said and gave him an unanticipated shove that sent them tumbling off the bed in a tangle of slick skin and bewildered awareness, the wrecked scrap of silk that had once been a sheet wrapped around them. She ended up on top, sprawled across him, hands still clutching his shoulders.

He knocked the sheet aside as she blew her hair from her face and met his bemused gaze. "Although I would honestly delight in having you ride me, seeing as you're impatient…" Without another word, he had her on her back, reclaiming her with a hard thrust that stole her breath and sent a sizzle of ecstasy scorching through her body.

Closing her eyes, she gave herself to him completely, wondering if she'd survive this onslaught.

They regained their flawless rhythm within seconds. Skin flushed, bodies trembling, breathing stuttered, a well-coordinated, feverish dance. Colors burst behind her eyelids as a wave of pleasure rolled from her toes to her knees, pulsing higher with each stroke of his body. She writhed in his arms, biting his shoulder, his neck, to strangle her cries. She was marking his skin, she knew, but she was powerless, nothing but a pounding heart and the roar of blood through tight veins. He whispered something harsh and unintelligible, snaked his hand between their grinding hips, touched her once in that lovely, secret place and sent her to paradise.

She closed her eyes as wave after wave broke over her, her shudders turning to low cries as he kissed her. His body wracked by tremors, he surged a final time, then rolled away at the last moment, disengaging, protecting her when she wanted him *there*. Surrounding her.

With a hushed groan, he tucked her against him, her head finding an ideal nook on his shoulder. His heartbeat skittered beneath her ear, matching the wild pulse of hers. She wanted to capture him like one of Julian's paintings, lovely and dazed and content. A lazy panther lounging by her side. She didn't want to think about sharing this incredible intimacy with another man, one she didn't love—while wondering if *this* man felt connected to her simply because he couldn't read her thoughts.

"Quit thinking," he murmured in a sleepy voice. "Because right now, my mind is as sharp as a melon. And I hate losing arguments." He smiled softly, his dimple pinging to life. "Christ, that thing you did with your hips, most inventive and appreciated."

Flattered to the tips of her toes, she rolled atop him, recalling his comment about *riding*. His lids fluttered, revealing a heated gaze filled with sudden interest. "I guess we can argue since my chances are good." She shifted her body against his. "Or..."

"I'll take 'or,'" he said and grasped her hips, letting the passionate debate begin.

CHAPTER 15

A vivid nightmare wrestled him from sleep. One mixed with images of the past and the present. Of the danger surrounding Victoria should her existence come to light. Of his helplessness, his fear.

He woke fully to find the knife he kept beneath the mattress in his hand, and Victoria curled against him, her shallow exhalations skating deliciously across his chest, their fingers linked atop his stomach. Replacing the knife in its hiding place without jostling her, he lay back with a tormented sigh, his thoughts in absolute turmoil. Glancing to the window, he judged it to be just after midnight. Twenty-four hours. They'd spent twenty-four hours exploring each other's bodies in ways he'd never hoped to explore. Free from the prison of recording his partner's thoughts, it was as if he'd never tupped anyone, never given of himself—because half of him, more than half, had always been fending off what were wholly awkward intrusions. Embarrassing intrusions. Unfulfilling intrusions.

Truthfully, he'd felt as virginal as she was going into this.

He palmed the hollow twinge in his chest, a rare burst of insecurity hitting him. Perhaps Victoria's interest was only carnal—that's what women wanted him for—when his interest in her was centered deep within, nothing he could shift or change or remove.

Devastation, just as he'd promised.

Love if he judged correctly.

Letting that awful declaration circle for a long breath, he then sent it from his mind like he did the errant thoughts that consumed him as he walked the city streets.

Settling Victoria on her side, he tucked the sheet around her shoulders and rose from the bed. Food. He needed food. Victoria needed food. They would share a midnight repast, his first experience of an 'after' with anyone, then he would return her to Julian's townhouse before the servants were up at dawn. He'd sent a note to Humphrey—*she's safe*—no doubt infuriating him and the always lovable Agnes, but there was no need to push the issue more than he already had.

Not when he'd gone and done the silliest thing imaginable. Fallen in love with a woman rightfully set to marry another man. A woman far above him in both gift and station.

Pulling on his trousers, he tiptoed down the steep back staircase to the kitchens, where he pilfered a round of bread, quarter wheel of cheese, three slices of ham, and a bottle of wine. He encountered no one employed at the Blue Moon on the journey. He had an exceptional manager in Benjamin Squires, a former rookery sharper who handled the day-to-day supervision with largesse and the occasional ruthlessness. He wasn't sure if Benji even knew he was in the building, and for another hour or two, he wanted to keep it that way.

She was awake when he got back, standing solemnly before the window, the decimated counterpane gathered around her shoulders, her hair a molten river down her back. He *loved* her hair, had delighted in tangling his fingers in the silken strands while wrapping himself around her. Dropping his edible bounty on the bed, he noted that the sky over London's rooftops was beginning to rotate from ebony to a bruised violet, meaning it was later than he'd calculated. Victoria knew he was there but didn't turn, so he stepped up against her, unable to keep from touching her. When he didn't need to make this evening more romantic, an occasion harder for either of them to forget.

But she made it harder, melting into him with a surrendering, flawless fit.

He propped his chin atop her head, breathing in her scent. Breathing in his scent on her. The night rolled in the open window, tasting of coal smoke and the river. If he closed his eyes, he could pretend they were older, pretend he'd been able to keep her, pretend they'd made it through this strife. Made it past their disconcerting gifts and his humble status. Made it past the betrothal he suspected she'd toss aside if he asked her to, and the incredibly fortuitous one Ashcroft was possibly set to make. Swallowing regret there was no use voicing, he pressed his lips to a love mark on her neck. She'd marked him as well, scratched his back, bitten his shoulder.

Nothing compared to the damage she'd done to his heart.

"Please tell me that's food you dumped on the bed." She turned in his arms, the counterpane fluttering to the floor.

He glanced down at her, stilled. She'd slipped his shirt on and fastened two of the buttons, leaving it to drape and part delicately over her slim frame. "Yes, food," he said distractedly, wondering why he'd once preferred women with generous curves when the willowy nymph standing before him was simply perfect.

Grabbing his hand, she tugged him across the room, scrambled atop the bed, and lit into the food, attesting to her hunger and confirming she was wearing nothing *beneath* his shirt. She patted the spot next to her, chewing furiously. Leaning, he yanked the knife from beneath the mattress. With wide eyes, she watched as he jammed the blade in the cork, gave it a good twist, and wiggled it free.

"You like the rough side of me, don't you?" He skimmed the blade down her arm in a teasing sweep, observed her responding shiver. "I'll have to remember that." Then he frowned, thinking, remember for *what*? This affair ended at dawn.

Propping against the headboard, she stretched out her long legs, smiled widely as his gaze took a sluggish path to her face. Just a few short hours ago, he'd started a deliberate journey at her ankles and worked his way up. It had been a *very* thorough trip.

"Are you ready to tell me?" She gestured with a hunk of cheese to the scar on his chest.

He climbed to the bed and rested back against the bedpost, facing her but apart, worried he'd not be able to tell her if she touched him. "There's not much," he said, his voice raw, invalidating the assertion. "We found a boy with a tremendous gift. A runner assisting ships docking at the wharf. Freddie told the wrong people what he could do, and I didn't get there in time when a group of sailors decided to brutally test him." He took a weary pull from the bottle and circled his gaze to the ceiling, not ready to accept the sympathy he'd find coloring her eyes. Not prepared to let her see the guilt that surely lay heavily in his. "You know, the rookery where Julian and Humphrey found me isn't far away. Part of the reason my living here vexes them. Why return to a slum once you've managed to crawl out of it?"

"It's a good question," she whispered.

He closed his eyes. Let the sound of her breathing, a shift in a floorboard belowstairs, the rustle of silk against her skin settle in his mind. "I was an undisciplined hooligan with a nasty mouth, spewing threats I couldn't possibly defend. Beatings were routine, even expected. Learning my lesson, as it were, was out of the question. Not when I couldn't reconcile my despair, not while being dipped in everyone else's. Walking through the market, down the alleys, the fateful stories, the private misery revealed to me. The cloistered thoughts rushing through my mind were consuming me. And then there were the men." Tilting his head, he opened his eyes to find the pitying expression he'd hoped to avoid paling her cheeks. He shrugged though the pain was still intense after all this time. "It's what happens to the beautiful boys."

She swallowed, her throat clicking. A tear streaked unchecked down her face, and she scrubbed it away. "But they...Julian, he saved you."

"They mostly saved me, yes." He took another sip, the wine storming his empty stomach. "Never fear, Humphrey's punishment when he found them was brutal. In all honesty, it made me realize what crimes I hadn't been born to perform. A shock to the system about how unprepared I was to live my life in a rookery. Though I was a very skilled thief, a decent enough lockpicker, I was no killer, and to survive, with this gift, one needed to be. Or standing behind someone who was. Anyway, that was that. I was removed from the vicinity. Finley Michel, unknown grandson to a marquis, became Finn Alexander, beloved half-brother to Viscount Beauchamp."

He flinched when she leaned in, seeking to comfort. One touch and he would shatter. "The only person to truly suffer was my sister. Belle lost everything while I gained. A family, wealth, even if I stepped down a few levels societally, unbeknownst to me."

Victoria ran a knuckle beneath each eye but had the sharp insight not to approach him again. Then, with a drawn breath, she stilled, her brow pulling in thought. "Ashcroft is downstairs," she said, smoothing her fingertips together as if they'd just gotten hot.

Finn took another drink, the wine beginning to slacken his awareness. "The troops have arrived. I suspected Humphrey would ferret us out at some point. Ashcroft is a bit of a surprise."

Victoria scrambled to his end of the bed, her hands going to cradle his jaw, drawing his somber gaze to her frantic one. "I can't do this with someone else. I *won't*. You're happy to bed every woman in this city but I—"

"Do you think this is like anything I've ever experienced?" He shoved to his feet, wine splashing down his arm and to the faded carpet. At her weak smile, he growled, "I don't know why my anger always seems to goddamn amuse."

She scooted to the edge of the mattress, her adorable body covered by almost nothing, sending his thoughts in a stupendously lascivious direction. "Because it's real, Blue. Not that tedious mockery you show the ton." She wiggled her elegant little toes and cast a shy glance his way. A tender look that melted his heart right where he stood. In a puddle with the bloody wine.

He found himself saying in desperation, "If Ashcroft offers, accept." Ignoring her startled gasp, he stepped back, creating distance in the only way he knew how. "You would make a wonderful duchess and instantly decrease the odds of Mayfair going up in flames. It's a win-win, as they like to say on the gaming floor two stories below. Earlier, I woke from a nightmare with a knife in my hand, Tori, which should tell you all you need to know about how far apart our worlds are."

She shot to her feet and caught him in the shoulder, a glancing blow that nonetheless sent him stumbling. "Oh, you would love to fob me off on the Fireball Duke, wouldn't you? Tie everything up in a tidy package, no remorse, no bother. Victoria placed in a proper, agreeable situation and everyone's ecstatic!"

He smacked the wine bottle atop the sideboard and grasped her shoulders. "Actually, I wouldn't."

"It's my choice who I give myself to. Not in marriage, perhaps, but in *this*."

She didn't realize. Much of anything.

That her family had more control over her future than she would have liked. That he'd never been able to play in bed. Be spontaneous. Be himself. Laugh, smile, tease, *enjoy*. She didn't realize how awful it was going to be to watch her marry someone else. The Fireball Duke, the Grape, anyone but him. "I want you," he growled and shook her to help the words sink in, "but you're not mine. I want to spend the next year inside this room, inside *you*, discovering every hidden piece of you, body *and* mind. Talking and touching and baring my soul. But I'm not changing who I am, not taking the potential avenue of escape that's been offered by claiming the Laurent name, grandson of a marquis, which would never be accepted anyway. The byblow of a viscount I'll remain, untouchable for you. Let's be clear on this point. I'd be untouchable no matter the circumstance."

As tears flooded her eyes, he pressed his brow to hers, so he didn't have to see them shimmer and flood molten gold. "You don't understand the level of ruin you would face should you link yourself to me. You can't possibly imagine what it's like to be an outcast in every room you enter."

"Was this"—she gestured to the rumpled bed— "because you can't read my mind?" He felt her tears dampen his skin, the faint hiccup as she tried to hold them back wrecking him. "Is my blocking the attraction, a talent I don't want or know how to use?"

He wanted to lie, it would be the easiest way to push her in the right direction, but he couldn't do it. "No," he whispered and curled his hand around the nape of her neck, bringing her lips to his in a graceless kiss born of all the things he couldn't admit. Offer. *Do.*

She was crowding him into the wall, arms rising to circle his shoulders, deepening their exchange and weakening his resolve, when the knock sounded. Very light, more of an announcement than an interruption. Finn turned to see an envelope sail under the door and skate across the floor. With leaden steps, he stepped away from her and went to retrieve it.

La fin de l'amour, the end of love, Finn thought as he read the note.

"Finn, for pity's sake, tell me what it says."

"You were seen kissing Ashcroft at his summer party. The Earl of Hester stumbled upon the two of you behind a fountain, and he couldn't help but share the scandal—though he fingered the wrong man, the senseless bloke—and it ended up in the gossip sheets. Which had Rossby notifying your family posthaste that he wants to move up the wedding date."

"Move up the date," she whispered, her hand going to her throat and holding tight.

"Despite the scandal, he still wants you. Knowing that a duke mightily trumps a baron should you feel the need to amend your selection, Rossby sent a rather threatening note to Ashcroft telling him to back off, or he would make things exceedingly difficult for your family. If he cares for you, don't make this scandal worse seems to be the extract."

It was insanity that Finn felt a hot lick of rage because *he'd* not been the man Hester connected Victoria to. The man who'd kissed the life from her behind that damned fountain. When his name had been splashed across those sheets more times than he could count, and he'd never cared about misrepresentation before. "If we only knew what Rossby held over your family, we could easily clear the path for Ashcroft."

He glanced up to find Victoria clinging to the bedpost, her fist clutching his shirt to keep it from sliding off her shoulder. Fury stained her cheeks a most becoming shade of cherry as her lips drew into a fierce line he'd come to know well. "Even if you clear the path, I won't do it," she vowed, her words dropping like stones in a still pond. "I won't marry either of them."

"Yes, you will," he said quietly and crumpled the sheet in his fist. "Because I'm not offering another option. Not when a bloody dukedom, the most secure future imaginable, is possible with a little reconnaissance. You'll be safe from anyone who hoped to find you, respected, secure. With the most impressive title in the ton. Deep down, you know I'm right."

"You mentioned secure twice, Blue, while forgetting an important element. Happy. Which I realize I'm senseless to envisage when I could be what every girl dreams of being, a duchess with a husband who doesn't love her."

"Then we understand each other perfectly," he returned while his mind screamed, *don't do this, Finn, don't let her go.*

She rocked back on her heels, her gaze leaving his, being torn from his. She waved him away, his shirt slipping down her arms and sending a sizzle through his belly. "If you'd be so kind as to secure a carriage while I dress, minus that chemise you destroyed, I'll ride gracefully into my future. Leave you to ride gracefully into yours. How about that for understanding each other?"

Finn turned and walked from the room with a force of will he hadn't known he had in him, although he hardly felt his feet hitting the floor. Mechanically, he resumed his life in measured degrees as he located transport, as he bundled Victoria into the dim confines of the carriage, as he watched it roll down a filthy alley six streets from the appalling hovel Julian had rescued him from, his sorrow backlit by nothing but a brilliant sunrise and an unsteady heartbeat.

He could quickly return to the women and the gambling, he decided as he smashed the wine bottle against his bedchamber wall. To the idiotic horse races and the leaps from widow's balconies, he resolved as he stripped sweat-streaked sheets from his bed and took his knife to them until they lay in tatters.

To waking alone, wondering what it would be like to share his life with another person.

He brought the torn chemise to his nose and inhaled a last, lingering breath. As Victoria had so eloquently put it, he would return to the tedious mockery of a man he presented to the ton.

~

Finn made an agile leap from the oak branch to the sloped roof of Rossby's townhome, landing outside his bedchamber window if the kitchen maid whose mind he'd read had provided proper information. His grief was a living thing, making his skin raw, and his breath painful to catch. He was looking forward to taking out his sorrow on someone. His aura would present a nightmare of color, he suspected, should Piper be able to see it.

He slid the already open window high enough to slip through, landing on the carpet with a dull thump. The room smelled of cigar smoke and port, and a choking, sweet fragrance he didn't try to name. Maybe opium, which was interesting. The lights were dim, the furniture heavy, the form huddled beneath the coverlet still. Finn had been watching the house for hours, waiting for Rossby's return. The baron had stumbled from his brougham less than an hour ago, in precisely the state Finn wanted him to be in for their discussion.

The sharp point of his knife was against Rossby's neck before either of them took another breath. The baron wrenched awake, his bloodshot eyes widening as he scooted up in the bed. "Alexander. What...what the devil are you doing here? I don't owe the Blue Moon. I paid the note months ago."

Finn hadn't tried to disguise his identity. Even

with a mask, his eyes would show, and everyone knew those. "Another matter, sorry. I'm here to insist you compose an exceedingly humble missive telling Lady Hamilton's father you're respectfully stepping aside so she may marry the Duke of Ashcroft. Because you believe in true love, etcetera, etcetera. It will overflow with positive intention, and I do mean *positive intention.*"

Rossby laughed and wiped his wrist across his lips to contain the spittle. "I've wanted the girl since I first saw her when she was no more than sixteen. If you think I'm letting her go after all I did to secure her, you're suited to a spot at Bedlam."

Finn's hand twitched, the blade digging into the baron's fleshy, moon-pale skin. He watched the trail of blood race down Rossby's neck to mingle with the spun cotton of his nightshirt with absolutely no feeling. "My God, are you making this bad on yourself."

The baron slumped against the headboard, his hand rising to cover the wound on his neck. It was then he realized this was a game he might not win. "What's this? Why do you even care about my marriage? About the girl? You're known to be close to the duke, is that it? Did he send you?"

"Don't worry about who sent me. Worry about waking to take your daily jaunt through Hyde Park tomorrow."

"You vile bastard." Blood seeped through Rossby's clenched fingers, dribbling to his wrist.

Finn released a measured smile, delighted when Rossby's skin paled. "Is that the best you can do? Disappointing."

"You won't get away with this."

Finn wasn't sure he would, either, but for Victoria's sake, he was willing to risk it. Leaning down until Rossby's fetid breath struck his cheek, he ran the stained blade beneath the man's chin. "Oh, yes, I will. Because I know what you have on her father. I know *everything*."

Rossby's gaze darted around the room, frantic, before circling back to Finn. His body spasmed beneath the sheet he'd drawn to his chest in defense. "You couldn't. No one would talk. We have an agreement." And then, of course, he started thinking about everything Finn could know, what might have been said because you couldn't *fully* trust anyone.

Having never been more appreciative of his gift, Finn closed his eyes, brushed the tip of his pinkie over the ticking pulse beneath the baron's ear, and let the man's thoughts tumble through him. Finn shuddered because mixed in with a detailed account of certain reprehensible and quite illegal business dealings, were images of what Rossby had been hoping to do to Victoria.

Finn swallowed hard and removed the blade from beneath the baron's chin before he made a snap decision and gutted him in his bed. Stepping back, he wiped the knife on his trousers, metal glinting in the moonlight spilling in around him. "I want the file. And don't argue, because I'm either leaving with it or with a man's death burdening my conscience." He shrugged, meaning his next words with every beat of his heart. "It's completely your choice."

"You can't do this," the baron whispered, but he was rising from the bed, and Finn had ascertained from his thoughts that he was going to retrieve the file.

"I already have," Finn said with a sigh, snagging his hand through his hair with a dull pulse of misery. "But don't despair, she's gaining a duke. An incredibly high step from a lowly baron. Such a benevolent decision you're making."

"I suppose you feel good about this," Rossby snarled and yanked open a drawer on the escritoire desk just visible in the shadowed corner. He pulled a file out and crossing the room, thrust it at Finn. "Helping the duke marry his ladylove. I'd heard you were friends. And everyone knows the Alexander brothers think themselves noble. Tell Ashcroft I won't forget this."

Finn grasped the file and turned to the door. He wasn't leaving through the damned window, he didn't care how many servants saw him. He held all the cards now. "Remember what you will, Rossby, just know I have this information, and it implicates you in a very damaging manner should I decide to throw you to the wolves. Next week, next year, in ten years. What you'd best understand is that *I'll* never forget."

Exiting the townhouse, Finn closed the door behind him and sagged against it. He tipped his head to stare at a festal sky filled with winking specks of silver and a low, velvety gray haze. He gulped a breath of the river and coal smoke and the scent of fear lifting from his skin, carriages and people and even a stray dog moving past him, unconcerned with one man's marginal island of desolation. He felt disassociated from the sounds of life around him. His heart was racing, his skin chilled, his mind teeming with unwanted images. A blinding headache was sitting just behind his eyes, and he brought his hand to his temple to push it away.

If he could only push *her* away.

Rossby had been dead wrong. He didn't feel good about this.

He only felt his bloody heart breaking.

CHAPTER 16

There were traces of Finn all over Julian's townhouse.

If one looked closely. Which, during her extreme and deadening misery over the past two days, she had.

Russian language texts, puzzle boxes, a handkerchief hidden in a desk drawer that carried his scent as solidly as her clothing did the faint zing of nutmeg. The *pièce de résistance* was a small portrait of him Agnes found her standing before, Victoria's gaze likely as lost as it was enchanted. When she walked down the hallway the next day, the painting was gone, only a whitish mark on the wall to show where it had previously hung. Like Finn leaving her life with only a bleached mark staining her memory.

And just yesterday, she'd received a fateful memorandum from Rossby, brief but respectful, stating he couldn't stand in the way of true love and would allow her to break their betrothal agreement. She could only stare at the missive in dry-eyed wretchedness while wondering how much Finn had to do with it. He'd removed the Grape from her life's equation, and for this, she owed him.

THE RAKE IS TAKEN

But she was still stuck marrying a man she didn't love.

Humphrey, Aggie, Belle, and the servants were handling her like someone being dispatched to the country for a recuperative period instead of what she was, a forthcoming duchess who'd yet to have a conversation with her duke. On the streets of Mayfair, the rumors connected her to Ashcroft, but inside these fashionably stenciled walls, everyone knew it was the endearing half-brother of the viscount who'd…

Victoria slumped to the marble bench hidden amidst a thicket of lilac bushes in the townhouse's walled garden. Gazing at a turbulent sky the color of wet ash, she searched her mind, her breath scattering.

What, exactly, *had* Finn done to her?

Shown her a side of herself, a wanton, unaffected side she quite liked. Forced her to question her commitment to her family, to blind obedience, to sacrifice. Caused her—for the first time—to consider what *she* wanted from her life.

Did her happiness mean less than her father's because she was a woman?

Were her options limited by her sex?

Everyone in her world certainly thought so. Without batting an eyelash thought so. Ashcroft had sent an admittedly agreeable message stating he'd visit her at three o'clock to discuss the details of their arrangement as if this expressed all that needed expressing.

A done deal. Which she supposed it did, and it was.

Finn understood what living on the fringe of society was like and had impressed upon her the certainty that securing her heart's desire meant being banished to the nether reaches.

She didn't care about being banished.

But *he* cared.

Enough to push her away, enough to turn his back when she'd gotten closer to him than anyone ever had. When, maybe, just maybe, he loved her, too. A flush lit her skin as she recalled the glorious things they'd done to each other in his stark bedchamber above the Blue Moon. True love or brief liaison, she couldn't end their story for him. Not if he'd regret it every time they entered a shop, and someone gave her the cut direct.

And it appeared as if he wasn't going to offer a way out when Ashcroft could provide everything she allegedly needed—security, wealth, standing.

Everything except love. Happiness. Contentment.

She wanted Fig Alexander's children, not the Fireball Duke's.

Drawing her slippered feet to the bench, Victoria dropped her cheek to her knee, cried out, hollow, absolutely empty inside. She sniffled and breathed in the overwhelming scent of lilacs, proving there were more tears in there somewhere. *Finn Alexander, you coward.* Except he wasn't. He was an honorable man intent on doing the right thing, and she loved him for it. His bloody sincerity. His exemplary kindness. His sincere concern that someday she would need protection only a duke could offer.

Victoria stilled, her fingertips tingling.

Ashcroft.

Rolling her head to the side, she watched the duke cross the terrace with a purposeful stride, saddened that she felt nothing for the tall, menacingly handsome man. Not a single burst of heat, not even one goosebump. Enigmatic and intimidating, he would be hard to tame.

Victoria liked puzzles.

And, heavens, he was a *duke*.

An interesting man if she were interested.

Maybe she could pretend.

Until she figured out how to get Finn to run away with her.

Ashcroft bowed before her, flexing his hands, the look on his face one of bewilderment. Her gift still seemed to astound him. "May I?" he asked and gestured to the bench.

She gasped and yanked her feet to the ground, smoothing her skirt. "Of course, Your Grace." The man must see she was no one's idea of a suitable duchess. Incorrigible. Hadn't Finn called her that with no small amount of admiration, his words muffled against her moist skin? He liked her passionate nature when the austere duke looked like he favored obedience.

"Ashcroft, please. We needn't stand on such rigid formality." He smiled, though no warmth reached his eyes. "Lady Hamilton, may I ask what you did to poor Hester at my summer party? We found him stumbling around the lawn, clutching his head and stammering about my kissing you. Which"—he coughed into his fist, his brow winging high—"I think I'd recall."

"Along with my slight gift…" She chewed on her nail and gestured inanely. "I'm able to erase the recent past from someone's mind, a parlor trick I've mostly used for my own trivial benefit. To avoid scrapes, that sort of thing." Scandals her guardian angel had saved her from when her gift had not. The realization made her chest ache, her hand curling around the stone bench and sending the jagged nicks into her skin. At that moment, she missed Finn so much, she wondered how she'd get past it.

"My dear, your ability to blast the heat from my

fingertips is demonstrated whenever I'm within a hundred yards of you. Nothing slight about it." He stared wonderingly at his scarred hands, and she recalled the stories about his many military escapades. "It's bloody remarkable."

Her breath seized, the illumination in her heart dimming to a tiny, wretched dot. He would marry her for her gift while Finn pushed her away despite it. She picked at a loose thread on her skirt, gathering her courage. She and Ashcroft couldn't build a relationship, even one as associates in the League, based on lies. "I have to be honest…"

"Let me guess. You're in love with young Finn, you and half of England," he muttered, issuing a sound somewhere between a laugh and a snort. As if she'd chosen to place her money on the horse everyone expected to win. "I noted the way you looked at each other standing by my fountain, even if you were both trying mightily to stamp out the fire. I imagine he's the man Hester observed kissing you, but your mind-scramble rendered him a faulty witness."

Relieved to have her secret revealed, she steadied herself on the bench, her gaze catching his and holding. His eyes were stunning. Warm honey shot through with streaks of amber. Now she knew why some in the ton referred to him as feline. "Yes, I'm in love with Finn Alexander, more the fool, I know."

"That makes one of us. About love, I mean. It isn't on my agenda. But if it's on yours, as it appears it is, you can keep him. Once the matter of an heir is settled, of course, because a bloody duke has to have one and if the first babe comes out looking as exquisite as your erstwhile love, that would be a problem." He frowned suddenly, again doing the hand flex. "You don't want to know how many times Mayfair has almost gone up in smoke. This entire city breathes a sigh of relief when you sit next to me. Thanks to Viscountess Beauchamp, I have more control, but still. You're my good luck charm."

Arrogant male, she reflected with a grimace. She'd love to tell him what he could do with his good luck charm, but one didn't often say to a duke what one *thought.* What a constricting marriage that restriction would create. "Finn would never share. I don't know how I know this, but I know this."

Ashcroft blew out a breath, gave the midnight-black strands hanging in his face a swipe. "His brother has given him the mistaken notion that marriages are created for love when they're business arrangements. Julian and Piper are an exceptional example. We'll be a transcendentally exceptional example in our way, aside from my saving your family from financial catastrophe, which is commonplace." Closing in on her, he tipped her chin high. Impersonal and emotionless when she wanted no one's touch but Finn's. At least she didn't flinch. "Let's not let dust gather on this conversation. Do you need words of love? Is that what's missing? I apologize, I fear I'm going into this too brusquely when I usually exhibit marginal charisma. Your gift rattles me to my bones when I'm normally steadfast. Humble apologies all around."

"Finn never gave me words of love, Your Grace." But he'd shown her in other ways.

As she'd shown him.

Ashcroft frowned and let his hand fall to his lap. Victoria was glad she didn't know him well enough to read the look on his face. "Oh, that hardly signifies. For a man, at least. We're not good at admitting our feelings."

"Young Finn," she whispered and laughed, a rigid, harsh sound. "Are you so much older? May I ask?"

A world-weary mien crossed Ashcroft's face. "Seven years, I believe. But my experience as a soldier and this blasted gift have aged me beyond what's presented." He massaged the back of his neck and exhaled softly, seemingly torn between sharing what he must with the woman who would be his wife versus keeping his own counsel. "Let's just say I feel a *hundred* years older."

"When should we...the marriage?" she murmured as a raindrop struck her cheek. Helpful that, so the commanding man next to her wouldn't notice her tears mixed in. "Your gracious offer is much appreciated. My family's situation is perilous. I'm being childish. Ridiculous to feel anything aside from relief and gratitude. I humbly thank you."

Ashcroft tilted his head, a penetrating study she'd no idea how to interpret. "I'm on the way to my solicitor to obtain a special license. We can discuss details over a late breakfast tomorrow if that suits."

She heard only the wind whispering through the lilac bushes and the stalks of grass stirring beneath their feet. And her heartbeat, telling her with a decidedly swift rhythm to forget Finn Alexander. Forget his kisses. Forget the words he'd whispered in her ear when his body surrounded hers. Forget the dimple that lit his cheek when he smiled. Forget how tenderly he'd touched her, held her, *listened* to her when she told him about her brother, her loneliness, her isolation. Forget the despair on his face when he'd told her about Freddie. The adorable wonder when he'd expressed his profound desire to establish a relationship with Belle.

"It suits," she said and rose to her feet.

Ashcroft followed her move, drew her hand to his

lips, and pressed a kiss to her gloved fingers. He turned to walk away, then halted, and glanced over his shoulder. "Don't look so forlorn, my dear. The future has a way of correcting course."

With that perplexing statement circling the walled garden, her future husband left her to the impending storm and her immense sorrow.

～

He couldn't let this dog lie, Sebastian Fitzgerald Tremont, fifth Duke of Ashcroft determined as he climbed into the unmarked carriage and thumped the trap to alert the coachman. A crested conveyance presented too much temptation in the lower reaches, which is precisely where he was headed. Also, he appreciated the anonymity of racing through London's streets without acknowledgment.

Until he stepped from the coach.

Then, the acknowledgment was ghastly.

He liked Finn, had been in the supernatural trenches with the Alexander family for going on seven years, and if the boy loved, genuinely *loved* Victoria Hamilton, Bastian couldn't stand in the way. Even if his offer was the best she'd ever receive. The smartest decision she could make if one didn't factor affection into the mix.

Her heartbreaking expression came to mind.

If those morose looks were a common occurrence, Bastian questioned being able to perform his husbandly duty. Her misery would color every facet of her life *and* his, he knew this well enough from a mother who'd been categorically miserable. How could he bed a woman who looked as sad as the dowager duchess always had? Wasn't an heir, aside from the lady's amazing ability to filch heat from his fingertips, the reason he'd agreed to this?

There was the added benefit of Victoria Hamilton being quite lovely.

Quite lovely and in love with a friend.

What a muddle, he decided, and leaned as his coachman took the curve too quickly, which Bastian had instructed him to do. He had a reputation for navigating London's streets at a breakneck pace, and he saw no reason to adjust course. Firestarter, scoundrel, soldier. He'd thought to add husband to that list and occasionally relieve himself of the first, but that intention was looking bleak indeed. To make matters even more wretched, Angelica, his current paramour, had heard of the impending marriage and reacted badly. So, he had the choice of letting that relationship cool or swinging by his jeweler to purchase a suitable apology.

Bloody hell, he thought, tugging at the leather ceiling strap as the coachman made a move that had the carriage springs squealing. Perhaps a period of celibacy was a good idea. He could retreat to one of his country estates, that utterly remote, crumbling one in Scotland, catch up on his reading and his many business obligations, and set fires at will. Or he could spend the rest of the summer at Harbingdon and work with Piper on controlling his gift. Maybe Lady Hamilton would assist in a strictly platonic capacity, once he gave young Finn the swift kick it looked like he deserved.

Viscount Beauchamp's repeated advice about happiness being possible for people cursed with mystical abilities had not only influenced Finn, it had also made Bastian consider if he *was* as lost as his friend alleged. Observing Julian and Piper's hushed communication and glowing looks over the years had polished him to a high sheen when he didn't want to shine. He was surrounded by former soldiers from his regiment. Women. Supposed friends. Sycophants, servants, solicitors, tenants, beneficiaries.

As if a duke could ever be lonely.

When he arrived, the Blue Moon was a disaster, men spilling from the entrance, the night's winners striding down the street to the next adventure, the losers slumped against the bricked stoop looking as if a fierce wind would send them tumbling. Coaches and hacks lined the road, waiting to discharge more into the mayhem. Two hulking porters stood by the baize-covered door, a crimson beacon winking in the night, admitting only those on the membership list. The activity reminded Bastian of a swarm of bees, a sting the one thing in the world he was fearful of— and deathly allergic to—so he left his carriage a block away and circled around, arriving at the gaming hell's back entrance. He made quick work of the padlock, thinking to alert Finn to how easy it had been to pick. He'd spent many an evening here, often while praying a streak of good fortune wouldn't have him accidentally setting the place ablaze. There'd only been the one instance, minor destruction to a velvet drape and window frame a quick-acting croupier had extinguished.

When he entered the main salon, ribald laughter, drunken shouts, the clack of dice and shuffle of cards swept over him, as did the scent of macassar oil and burnt tobacco. He wove between tables offering hazard and *vingt et un*, lifting his hand in greeting to those who called out but not halting, working his way to the back parlor, a private room that held other, more delectable, enticements.

That jackass, Bastian deduced the moment he laid eyes on the boy—his heart taking a little dive as he said goodbye to Lady Victoria Hamilton and her ability to erase his curse.

Because Finn was a rake on all counts, true, but a reserved one most of the time.

This was a show.

Bastian sighed and crossed the room. He's as in love with her as she is with him.

Finn had a cheroot anchored between his teeth, long legs unfurled before him, a woman of indiscriminate everything draped across his lap, and a circle of saccharine admirers surrounding the table where he held court. "That face," Bastian groused beneath his breath, "is more trouble than it's worth." As he approached, the indiscriminate everything's hand snaked up the back of Finn's coat, and Bastian could only think he'd arrived in the nick of time.

"Alexander," he said and slipped into the empty chair that had materialized with his arrival.

Finn blinked drowsily, a challenging smile twisting his lips. "Your Grace."

Bastian rolled his eyes. Foxed and belligerent. This endeavor promised to be amusing. "I thought you and I might have a little run on the hazard table. I'm feeling lucky."

Finn gave the woman in his arms a suggestive wink. "I am as well, Ashcroft."

"May I say, I think your current predilection is a mistake."

Humor sliding from his face like mud down a slippery slope, Finn gave his temple one hard tap. "I *know* she wants me to stay. My mind is full, nothing blocking if you grasp my meaning. So stay I shall."

"What's it to you, your bleeding grace," a man across the table that Bastian believed to be a baron of considerable ill-repute but significant wealth mumbled. His clothing was rumpled, his hair disheveled, his face bloated. Unsteady hands, weak posture. The soldier in Bastian, even if he'd left those rigid mores behind long ago, was disgusted. "Don't be ruining our fun because you had to go and muck up yours with that Hamilton chit. Not worth the trouble, that one, if what I've heard is truth. Too bad she outwitted you, the conniving she-devil."

Bastian had little time to react as Finn vaulted over the table, scattering glasses and conversation, the indiscriminate everything's ample bottom plopping to the floor amidst a shower of brandy and silk. Without hesitation, Finn launched his fist into the baron's face, sending the man sprawling and the table flipping, which allowed for another explosion of liquor and crystal.

"Holy hell," Bastian growled and stumbled back in time to avoid the baron's badly-thrown return swing, which, even in its inaccuracy, clipped Finn's jaw.

Grabbing Finn by the collar and dragging him out of the fray, Bastian shouted orders to the men, who jumped into action like they were members of his regiment. *Escort the baron to a carriage. Help the lady to a resting room. Return the parlor to rights.* His fingertips tingled throughout, leaving his skin moist and his breathing shallow. "Control," he repeated, hearing Piper's soft voice ringing in his mind. This was not the time, not the place.

"Oh, that would be rich," Finn laughed as Bastian wrestled him from the room and down a darkened servant's hallway, "if the place went up in flames around us."

"Shut up. Would you rather deal with Humphrey? I can arrange that." He released Finn at the bottom of the stairs, taking them two at a time and expecting the boy to damn well follow. Once again, he could look forward to his transgressions being featured in tomorrow's broadsheets. While Finn was accustomed to publicity, Bastian was not. If he didn't consider the man to be the younger brother he'd never had, he would kick his arse from here to Westminster.

When they reached the landing, Finn brushed around him and, using a key procured from his waistcoat pocket, opened the door to his suite, his movements steadier than his behavior below would forecast. "Are you coming in, or was this simply an escort? A bit hypocritical, your disapproval," he added with an indignant side-glance. "How did Angelica react to the news of your betrothal, by the way?"

Bastian gestured to the chamber. *Insolent pup.* He wasn't going to get angry when that was unquestionably what Finn wanted right now, another purgative brawl when the fight would be most inequitable, and they both knew it. "I think you and I should have a little chat."

Finn peeled himself off the doorframe and strolled inside, only a rapidly ticking jaw muscle revealing his temper. The man hid his true nature better than anyone Bastian had ever seen.

With a groan, Bastian collapsed on the sofa, giving in to the urge to let his exhaustion show. The boy was poised as all hell, he would give him that, while Bastian felt as if he'd been shoved through a crack in a windowpane. Blast, did those seven years difference in age feel like seven *hundred*. He was getting too damned old for this business.

"A wise man once recommended going to Scotland for occasions such as these." Striding to the sideboard, Finn splashed whiskey in two tumblers, took a fast sip from one, then delivered the other to Ashcroft. "When you leave, how do you know I won't go down and find that willing creature? Do everything I was thinking of doing before you so hero-ically popped by. You've only given me time to sober up, more the enjoyment for her."

Bastian took a thoughtful drink, let the excellent Scotch skate down his throat and warm his belly. This heartfelt camaraderie with those who knew *what* he was, is why he'd joined the League in the first place—and why he feared it in no minor measure. "Because if you do, she won't forgive you." He eyed Finn over the crystal rim. "And you won't forgive yourself."

Finn cursed soundly, threw himself in a leather beast of a chair, and drained his glass, as sufficient a reply as any to being in love, Bastian supposed. As he'd told Lady Hamilton, men weren't comfortable expressing emotion. Finn, even with the tender heart he hid from the world, was no better. Why he'd been placed in the role of matchmaker, Bastian couldn't say. Sometimes one had to roll with life's little detours.

At least he wasn't setting the building aflame.

"I offered," Bastian murmured, watching closely enough to see Finn's fingers tighten around the tumbler. "I'm guessing it was your intervention that had Rossby graciously stepping aside."

After a charged moment of silence, Finn whis-pered so softly Bastian had to strain to hear, "A cour-teous overture after Hester's blunder, and I thank you for it. I brought Victoria to the attention of the League, but that doesn't mean I own her, despite how possessive I may feel. After all, what man wants to lose not only the woman of his dreams but the one *in* them?"

Bastian shook his head, having no reply as he'd never desired a woman in this manner.

"I understand the situation. An irresolvable societal dilemma for a baseborn man. Perhaps even a trite one, falling for a woman above your station."

"There are ways around any dilemma. Or rather, ways to soften the impact."

Sliding low in the chair, Finn's posture was uncaring, but his gaze alert. "I can't protect her. A gift this powerful won't be concealed for long. Our enemies are as desperate for relief from their mystical abilities as we are, they're just willing to injure to obtain it. It's a slight difference but a critical one. She needs you when I'll do nothing but destroy her. In more ways than one." He rotated the tumbler in a gradual circle on his belly, the gaslight bouncing off the facets and throwing silver slashes along the floor. "I hope you didn't foster hope that there's another choice. Why your actions this eve are almost fraternal."

"Therein lies the issue, because she didn't accept. And I'm not even sure how solid I was on the offer."

Finn jerked to a sit, blinked, raised the glass to his lips only to find it empty. "Didn't accept," he echoed as if this possibility had never occurred to him.

"Let me set the record straight for all men given an unenthusiastic rejoinder to a sincere but loveless proposal. She thought she did, but she did not." Bastian took a delaying sip set to extend Finn's discomfort, beginning to enjoy this. He deserved every bit of pleasure he could wring from this quixotic venture. "Claims she's in love with you."

Ah, that got through as the whiskey had not.

Finn's gaze heated to a fierce, concentrated blue. No wonder women dropped like flies when the boy looked at them; Bastian had trouble looking away. "She told you that?"

Bastian sighed, nodded, praying he never loved someone enough to sit there looking poleaxed by an admission of love. Horrifying thought. "She said she wanted to be *honest*. What woman in the ton, in the world, wants to be honest? No wonder the girl never seemed to fit in. All this time, swimming with scrupulous intent in a sea of sharks."

Finn rocked forward, placing his glass with great care on the table at his side. "I would be the end of her. She'd be shunned in every shop, on every street corner. Invitations to events would immediately terminate, except for the events where we were unknowingly part of the entertainment. And there's nothing *I* can do, that *love* would do, to change that."

Victoria Hamilton didn't care about being shunned on bloody street corners. This was Bastian's verdict after witnessing the feral emotion in her eyes. So he addressed the problem he could solve. "We'll increase security, as we did with Piper. Wherever you choose to live, a private detail will be attached. It's a simple arrangement. She goes, they follow." Ashcroft began compiling a list in his mind. As a former soldier, protection was second nature. Fires were, unfortunately, first. "It will cost you, but I have the men. Returning soldiers who need employment. Very loyal, to the death loyal. And you have the resources, or am I mistaken?"

Finn nodded absently. "Money's not the issue, has never been the issue."

"Does she know that?"

Finn glanced up, dazed as if he'd arrived at the conversation after fighting his way through a river of pea soup. "Victoria?"

"If there was any hint of resignation in her reply, it was in her ability to save her family. She's sacrificing her love for you by doing her duty to them. The threat to her person is not a real concern for her yet. That will come with more understanding of the League."

"But, I'm flush." Finn struggled to his feet, swayed, paying dearly for that guzzled glass of Scotch. "The gaming hell alone brings in enough to shelter ten families. Before my dismissal, I wasted half my selections at Oxford on economics and finance because Julian thought to have me start investing. And I've done really well, a surprise to both of us. Marriage to me is not a financial risk, it's reputational. Sound logic, every point I presented, and she understood. She agreed. She knows I love her. I made it clear. I *showed* her." When he noticed Ashcroft's sour look, he added, "I'm trying to do the noble thing here. At great sacrifice, I might add, so get that acerbic scowl off your face."

Bastian polished off his drink with a snort. "Christ, Finn. Did you think to *tell* her you love her? I'm no expert, that's undeniable, but even I realize it's the starting point."

"If she knew, I couldn't have dragged her away, no matter the miserable future I threatened her with. You don't know her. Stubborn doesn't begin to cover it."

"I have a partial solution. Not flawless but achievable. Though there's little I can do about your illegitimacy, with my support of your marriage, Lady Hamilton will survive being given the cut at every millinery and haberdashery in town. Considering she's choosing the comeliest man in England, most will understand her selecting him, even over a duke. I'll start by throwing a celebratory ball, which as the person who's betrothed was stolen from beneath his regal nose, showcases my incredible benevolence and our remarkable friendship. Imagine the sympathy I'll receive as I publicly concede to true love and brotherhood." He slipped his watch from his pocket and checked the time. He was set to meet with his solicitor, and one of them was going to need a special license. "Talk about noble."

Finn turned from the window and his study of the turbulent crimson and gold sunset flowing like crushed velvet over the horizon. "Is the most distinguished rogue in London suggesting happiness is possible for people like us?"

Bastian scrubbed his hand across his face to hide the flush. He rarely suffered from discomfiture. "You and your damned brother are rubbing off on me. You see, at my core, I'm a humble man. I was a lowly third son who, against my family's wishes, bought an army commission to try and escape a supernatural curse, only to find much of that family wiped out by cholera when I returned. A dukedom I was ill-equipped to manage landing like a boulder on my chest. You see, I'm still adjusting to this life." He coughed, shrugged, not any better at sharing his emotions with men than he was with women. "Maybe I'm stepping in where I'm not wanted, but if you love the lady, I want you to have her. If she'll have you."

Finn released a fetching smile, both bashful and insufferable. "You think she will?"

No one denied the Blue Bastard. Bastian would wager a gold sovereign that Victoria Hamilton wasn't going to be the start.

"Tell Lady Hamilton to make the retelling of her rejection of my offer tragic. I want the ton in tears, absolute despair." With a yawn, Bastian stretched out on the sofa and laid his arm over his eyes. "Women love consoling a heartbroken man. They can all step in to comfort me."

"Thanks, my friend," Finn said as he sprinted from the room. "I'll never forget this."

A matchmaker, Bastian thought with a sigh. How peculiar. How interesting.

A singular feeling of satisfaction flooded the often-subdued Duke of Ashcroft as he fell into a dreamless, contented sleep.

CHAPTER 17

$\mathcal{F}$inn smoothed his palm over his rumpled waistcoat and drew a nervous inhalation through his teeth. It was just after midnight, and Julian's townhouse was hushed, the only sounds a ticking clock somewhere down the hallway and the creak and shift of an aging domicile. The liquor he'd shared with Ashcroft had worn off hours ago, leaving his belly empty and his hands trembling. *Slightly* trembling. Who could judge harshly? After all, it wasn't every day a man professed love to two women.

One he felt sure would accept his offer, the other he wasn't so sure about.

He decided to start with the easier sell.

Stubbing the toe of his boot against the polished plank floor, he raised his hand, grazed the door with his knuckle, then shot another breath from his lips and knocked. Soft footpads sounded from within the bedchamber. The squeal of an unoiled doorknob broke the silence, then she stood before him. And his heart—recognizing her without any provocation, without any true memory, their eyes and a past he couldn't recall the only thing connecting them—gave a firm, vigorous thump.

"Finley Michel?" Belle whispered through the crack between door and frame. Her smile growing, she brought it wide and motioned him inside, her flaxen braid swinging. The locket around her neck glimmered in the dusky gaslight. "What are you doing here? At this time?" She reached to touch his cheek, brushing a strand of hair from his eyes. "You look flushed. Are you unwell? There's a bruise on your jaw."

He pressed her hand to his face when she would have pulled away, closing his eyes to capture the sensation of someone of his blood, for the first time, touching him. The sting behind his lids was one of happiness, but he fought the reaction, nonetheless. He didn't want to scare her with overly emotional sentiments on what was turning out to be the most emotional day of his life. "I'm fine. More than fine." He opened his eyes, his gaze catching hers. "I'm resolute. Determined. Certain."

Her brow knit in confusion, but she tugged him into the bedchamber by his sleeve and closed the door with a soft snick. Leaning against it, she watched him prowl the small but luxurious space, accepting of the time he needed to resolve his dilemma. His mind was clear of stolen thoughts, proving Victoria was in residence a floor below, but the words he wanted to utter were tangled in his throat.

Halting by the settee Piper had placed in the room to fashion a modest sitting area, he yanked his gloves off and slapped them against his thigh. "Belle, I'm going to do everything in my power to make sure you're happy, protected, loved. You'll never want for anything ever again. And…where I go, you go. No matter the changes coming up in my life, you're my family." He exhaled through the tension contracting his chest. "If you want to live with me, that is."

He hoped one proposal this eve was going to be accepted without a fight.

Belle pushed off the door with a graceful move reminiscent of one he would execute. As she crossed the room, he studied her. He could see a resemblance in the shape of her face, her mouth maybe, and yes, the eyes. Most assuredly the eyes.

"I'm sorry," he said when she got close enough for him to see her tears, "for things I couldn't possibly have changed. I'm sorry, but I *will* make up for it, I promise you this."

She bumped against his shoulder, and his arms opened, his gloves falling unnoticed to the carpet. "We have a future, Finn. A real one this time," she whispered as he hugged her tight. "I'll go where you go. You need not ask. I cannot be more grateful because I have my brother back."

He settled his chin atop her head and sighed out the past. Remorse, guilt, fury. There was no place for these emotions in his new life. He wasn't going to be held back by fear or uncertainty or even goodness of heart. He was the bastard son of a viscount *and* the grandson of a French marquis—and he was going to marry the woman he loved.

The bloody aristocracy better learn to stay out of his way.

"*Le début de l'amour*," Belle said.

Yes, it was the start of love.

$\sim$

The air in Victoria's bedchamber was stifling, her moist skin sticking to the sheets. Restless, she turned one way, then another, rolling across the mattress. Her mind was humming, the way it had that time at Harbingdon when she'd been knocked off her feet while blocking Finn. As if he was close and either trying to read her mind or keep her from his.

But that couldn't be. He'd left her life.

He'd left *her*.

With an oath, she kicked the sheets aside and vaulted from the bed. The Duke of Ashcroft was arriving in a few short hours to settle the arrangements. If this *suited*.

What suited was a future of her choosing.

What truly suited was a future with the Blue Bastard. With Fig.

Victoria strode to the window and wrenched it high, allowing a humid gust to rip inside, bringing with it the scent of blooming lilacs and coal smoke. The gross disparity that was Mayfair. Leaning her head against the shutter, she sighed. Blinked. Straightened. Cursed for real this time.

Finn stood on the veranda below, a cheroot anchored neatly between his lips, the tip shooting a crimson glow across his clenched jaw. Moonlight glimmered off the streak of gray in his hair as he yanked his hand through it. He seemed lost in thought as he paced, an occasional tug on what she would guess was a pristine waistcoat his only tell. If she weren't so lost over him, she might find his obvious apprehension endearing. As it was, and for a myriad of reasons, some as half-baked as the Bakewell tart she'd completely ruined this evening, she wanted to punch him in his gorgeous face.

The vase was in her hand before she quite knew what to do with it. Going strictly on impulse, she tossed its contents out the window like she would an overflowing chamber pot, an adept pitch. Fragrant water and roses petals and hydrangea blossoms landed on his back and shoulders.

His gaze shot to the window, then to the floral waste on his clothing. He didn't hesitate but took off at a sprint into the house. She heard his heavy footfalls along the landing, slapping the stairs as he climbed them. With a stuttered laugh, she raced to the door, unsure if she planned to lock him out or welcome him in when he slammed inside, saving her from having to decide.

Without a word of greeting, he hauled her into his arms, walked her back five steps to the bed and pushed her down on it. The vase dropped from her hand and rolled across the floor. Her muffled protest, token at best, was vanquished as he fell over her, tangled his hands in her hair, and set his mouth to hers, kissing her with all the desperation she felt. He tasted of brandy and man, dark, spicy, Finn Alexander. The best taste in the world. With a low moan, she twined her arms around his neck and gave herself to him. Her legs fell open, and he slipped into place, nothing but a thin nightdress covering her, his hard length rocking against her, pressing her deep into the mattress. Lighting a fire more potent than any Ashcroft could start.

It was then she got a whiff of him. Lavender. Feminine but cheap, not a fragrance she'd ever worn. And not one of the flowers she'd doused him with. Pushing against his chest, she noted the bruise on his jaw, his bloodshot eyes. He braced his forearms next to her shoulders, lifting his head just enough for a shaft of flimsy moonlight to reveal his tormented expression.

"I missed you so much I ached," he whispered without prologue. "I love you. And I think we should get married."

"I'm not marrying a man who comes to me smelling like a trollop," she returned, her mind going wild with possibilities as jealousy scorched a path through her. She gave him another shove and tried to roll from beneath him.

He replied by grasping her shoulders and giving her the lightest shake as if trying to wake her up. "I'm finished with that life. I'm done playing the role of the fickle wastrel. The bruise was gained by acting the heroic knight. For you." He kissed her brow, her ear, her lips, silky strands of his hair sliding across her cheek as his lower body moved into an even deeper press against her. "Nothing happened. *Nothing.* There is no one else for me. There'll never be anyone else, Tori. I haven't touched anyone since the dreams started, not even that night in the Blue Moon. She was uninvited, and I sent her away after you left. Once you were in my mind, there was no room for anyone else. I told Ashcroft that I don't own you. But you own *me.*"

Victoria sank to the mattress and closed her eyes. Finn's staggered breath streaked her cheek, her collarbone as he laid his brow on her shoulder in defeat. His arms came around and under her, drawing her into his body, letting her feel the rough pounding of his heart through her nightdress.

She had a choice.

She could trust a man who'd never shown her he was anything *but* trustworthy. A generous, patient, intelligent man, one who secreted his true self from the world; a man who was temperamental, arrogant, even obnoxious on occasion; a man who liked to laugh, sometimes at her expense. An impish charmer. A false-bastard who, because of his profound love for his brother, wasn't going to try to change the ton's impression of him. Not even for her.

With this choice, she would gain a new family in Julian, Piper, Humphrey, Simon, and Belle. Be able to join the League fully and put her gift to use. Learn to manage her talent, maybe even learn to control it.

With this choice, she'd be accepting the love of a man she didn't want to be apart from for one moment for the rest of her life.

So, there *was* no choice.

Cradling his face, she directed those astounding eyes to hers. "What were you doing down there on the veranda?"

He blinked, nonplussed. "I'd just let Belle know what I was planning to ask you. Since I can't discuss it with your father, your family, as tradition demands, because they'll toss me out on my arse, I wanted to discuss it with someone in mine." A slow flush crept across his cheeks, and he ducked his head to keep her from seeing it. "And I was nervous. Trying to figure out some brilliant thing to say when a floral arrangement landed on my head. Then I just blurted it out anyway, the most graceless proposal imaginable."

"Oh, Blue," she whispered, her heart breaking. "You don't have to convince me."

"That I love you? Want you? Need you?" His hands slipped low, bringing her hips against his with a shift and rock that sent stars spinning through her universe. "That you'd be crazy to turn me away when you're my world? Yes, I do. I will. I'll spend every day for the rest of my life convincing you. Because you're going to give up so much if you decide to keep me."

She'd already decided to keep him, but *after* would be an excellent time to tell him, she thought with a smile. She was burning up, the pulse between her thighs so constant it was making her entire body tremble. Visions of everything they'd done before shimmered through her mind like light through a frosted pane. Pulling his mouth to hers, she soothed his bottom lip with her tongue because she knew he liked it. Knew this would make him put his hands on her that much faster.

His response was swift, her nightgown flowing up and off her body to float to the floor. His waistcoat and shirt soon followed, his boots, trousers, drawers, until their bodies were a naked, molten press, air ripping from their lungs, hands seeking, caressing, delving. The kiss he pulled her into was ferocious and uncontrolled, deep-throated, glorious. They fit, knee to knee, hip to hip, chest to chest, finding a blinding, blissful cadence as they sharpened each other's need to a fine point. She gasped, taking a harsh breath to find the sheets in a damp tangle, the pillows and counterpane in a wad on the floor.

"I've never felt what I feel with you," he murmured as he took her nipple between his teeth and sucked hard, drawing a pleasured cry from her. "I never imagined."

Body shaking, she followed the hair trailing his chest, drawing circles over his flat belly, his hip, his thigh. He lifted slightly to encourage more. She took him in hand, smoothed her thumb over the silky tip and stroked his length, slowly, then with greater speed, just as he'd shown her. His mouth fell away from her breast as he rolled to his back with a hushed groan, the most arousing sound she'd ever heard come from him.

"There, love, ah, yes." His head tilted, neck arching, lids fluttering. His fingers burrowed into the sheet, curling into a fist as he tried to control himself. She stared, enthralled, about to arrive herself just from watching him. She didn't know how to do what raced through her mind, so she simply obeyed the compulsion. They'd whispered about it in the still twilight that first night as he patiently answered her questions about lovemaking but...

Slowing her touch, she dragged her lips down his neck, traced his collarbone, licked his hardened nipple, shadowing that crisp path of hair she so loved down his body. He gasped, his belly tightening when she pressed a hard kiss to his navel. He was trembling, his skin flushed, his hands rising to settle in her hair. His low murmur of agreement gave her courage.

It stunned, she thought as she sank her teeth into his hip, that she could draw such a fevered response from him.

When he could have anyone, he wanted *her*.

"I won't be able...to last..." He caught her wrist as she took him in her mouth, trying to stop her. But the effort was half-hearted. "Christ, I can't," he moaned, hips rising off the bed.

He tasted wonderful. Like soap and the slightest tang of salt. Rigid but his skin so smooth, a remarkable contrast. He was lost, his words unintelligible, his breaths stuttered. And she was lost in *him*. Her peak close, she kissed her way down his length. His hand came around hers, guiding her strokes. Fast, fierce, tight. His other found its way between her legs, and with a delicious twist, he slipped a finger inside her. His thumb settled over that lovely hidden spot, the dual assault all it took to push her over the edge.

"Finn, oh, Finn," she murmured, dropping her head to his thigh as the explosions rocked her body. Wave after wave, pulsing, pounding. *Blinding.* Until she was boneless, her muscles lax and uncooperative, her carnal task forgotten.

With what sounded like laughter, he took control,

pulling her atop him. She gazed down at him, skin tingling, dots spotting her vision. "Where am I?" she asked and braced her hands on his chest with a hitching exhalation.

He smiled wickedly, cupped the nape of her neck, and brought her lips to his. She felt him move into position and with one gentle push, thrust inside. Settling his hands on her hips, he helped her establish the rhythm. It felt much different than having his weight atop her. Amazingly different. In control different. With an empowered sigh, she released him from the kiss, rose high, and moved with him. Rode him with long strokes, a languid rhythm, until he was close to leaving her, then back. Again and again.

She felt wanton, animalistic, bared to her soul. Mindless, dazed, frenetic. There'd been no way to anticipate how this sensual, intimate act would bond them.

"Now," he urged and slipped his hand between them, touched her once, lightly, and she knew nothing but astounding pleasure. Closing her eyes, she let him lead her as body and mind parted. Colors burst behind her eyelids, her sensitive skin stung. With a wanton moan, she collapsed, and he rolled her over without missing a beat, his thrusts frantic, his lips, his hands, his teeth, all over her.

He whispered a harsh string of French as he shuddered, his arms closing around her. Falling to his side, he brought her with him, kissing her cheek, her shoulder, her collarbone. After a delayed moment filled with only their terse breaths permeating the room, he reached to tuck the destroyed sheet around her, smooth the hair from her face. Such a thoughtful, compassionate man. Even when she opened her mouth to speak, and he rejected her with an outstretched hand. A tender, tolerant, exhausted gesture.

"Sleep," he mumbled, his voice muffled by the pillow. "Food." He yawned and hauled her closer. "Once you've decided."

She tugged at his chest hair. "Oh, I've already decided."

He blinked, the one eye not swallowed by the pillow sliding open. "You have?"

"Finley Michel Laurent Alexander, I think it would be best if I make an honest man of you." She gestured to the disturbed bedchamber. "Seeing as you can't keep your hands off me. And seeing as I love you more than anyone I've ever known."

Finn's smile was beatific. "One less thing to worry about in the grand scheme. Except for your expulsion from society, which I'm warning you, will be severe."

She closed her eyes and took him in, his scent heaven, his touch *everything*. He wouldn't believe how little she cared about being expelled from a group she'd never admired in the first place. "I'll like living on the outside edge. It's the finest place to be. Not too close to the sun."

"The glorious middle," he murmured, sounding sleepy again. "We shall muddle along. We have support. A viscount who touches objects and sees the past, and a duke who starts indiscriminate fires with his blazing fingertips."

"Ashcroft," she breathed, "I forgot all about him."

A choked laugh escaped Finn at her admission. "*Good*. Though he's offered to throw us a magnificent celebration complete with pyrotechnics because he's known to fancy them, playing the rejected suitor to the hilt, of course. The women will swarm him. And Julian"—Finn snorted softly—"believes wholeheartedly in love. A romantic if there ever was one. He'll be blinded by excitement over our marriage. You'll be joining the League in an even greater capacity than he'd hoped. Blocker extraordinaire *and* sister-in-law."

He rose to his elbow, leaning over her, his smile dimming. "There is one thing I must ask for. Or two rather. You see, I have a modest estate just down the road from Harbingdon that Piper gifted me on my twenty-first birthday. Brook Cottage. A gift to *her* when Julian stupidly thought they'd never marry. It's quite lovely. And easily protected. There's a small conservatory, a stable. Enough chambers for Belle and Simon, who's as much a son to me as my own could ever be—"

"Yes," she whispered and brushed the hair she'd trimmed when they were falling in love from his face. Cupping his jaw, she felt his pulse jolt beneath her thumb. "They should live with us. Since my brother's passing, I haven't had a family, Finn. Charles was all I ever had. I want one with you. With Humphrey, Piper, Julian. Belle and Simon and Lucien. I want the League. I want to find my place."

Sinking to the bed with a sigh, he tucked her into the curve of his body. "Simon needs me, and I need him. I need Belle. I don't know why, exactly, but I do. As much as I need you. And if not for you, I'd have never found her. The dreams make sense now." He swallowed, the click of his throat echoing in the room. "With patience, some things in life do come full circle."

"You love me," she marveled, recalling he'd said it more than once while he moved inside her.

He hummed beneath his breath, his breathing slowing as he slipped into sleep. His voice was soft. "*Tu m'aime.*" You love me.

She did, with everything in her. Heart, mind, soul.

And she was never letting him go.

Because this rake was taken.

EPILOGUE

In a very charming part of the country...
Oxfordshire, Six Months Later

Snow battered the charming cottage by the brook, pristine white drifts edging past the windowpanes, the raging storm trapping the inhabitants inside. Victoria shifted her puzzle book into the firelight and bit into the treacle tart she'd baked earlier today. She'd fallen in love with the cozy manor with a fierceness and speed that surprised her, having never felt possessive of a dwelling, cherishing it like she would a member of her family. But cherish Brook Cottage she did.

After all, it was her first real home.

She was surrounded by all the things she loved, a faultless moment in time. Occasionally, she reflected with a warm curl in her belly, her happiness was near to overflowing.

She sat before the hearth, back against the brocade sofa, Finn asleep beside her, his chest rising and falling in a contented rhythm, one of his language texts still clutched in his hand. Simon lay half-on, half-off the sofa, his gentle snores the only sound in the parlor beyond the clack of Belle's knitting needles. Her sister-in-law was a horrendous knitter, as the unusually-shaped hats and scarves she'd gifted everyone attested to, but she said it kept her hands and her mind occupied. Occupied from what, Victoria wasn't sure but thought she might be able to guess.

Covering a smile behind her tart, she watched Belle glance toward the door with a troubled expression. Humphrey had gone out to secure more firewood and check with the sentries who patrolled the cottage, and despite what the two of them said when asked, which everyone had gotten around to asking in the past months, he and Belle sparked off each other like wood in a hearth. Hissing and spitting. One moment friends, the next enemies.

Passion moved slowly—or sometimes not at all. Victoria only hoped, if Belle was falling in love with the handsome, hulking, overly-compassionate-though-he-tried-to-hide-it man, she'd be courageous enough to fight for him. Humphrey, for his part, when he wasn't trying to ignore her, treated Belle like she was breakable.

When love often demanded rough handling.

More a battle than a dance, at least in her experience. But, oh, those longing looks Humphrey threw in Belle's direction, they smoldered.

"There's the smile that makes me nervous."

She turned to find her husband—*husband*, she repeated with an ecstatic internal giggle—blinking sleepily, his cheeks rosy from the fire. "I have no idea what you're referring to. None of my smiles should make you nervous."

He yawned, his lids drifting low. "I couldn't sell that lie on a rookery street corner for a halfpenny. Would not wager one on it in the Blue Moon."

She reached, unable to keep from touching him, her fingers finding his and lacing tight. He returned the caress, drawing a slow, sensual circle on the inside of her wrist, a move that made her want to strip his clothing from his body and climb atop him.

"This is my favorite spot in the house," he whispered for her ears only.

She felt her face heat. They'd made love here many times since moving into the cottage. Last night, in fact. She well knew it was his favorite spot. He said the firelight made her skin glow like he'd dusted it with amber.

His hand tightened around hers, a fast, agitated clench. "I had another dream. About Ashcroft. About the girl. I could almost see her face this time. She was surrounded by books, I think. They were annoyed with each other, nothing friendly about the interaction. It almost looked like Oxford's library, though I can't say I visited that often during my tenure."

Victoria tensed, then made herself relax. The love of her life was like no man she'd ever encountered, and the danger surrounding him, surrounding her now that she was a part of their supernatural community, was something she had to learn to live with. Work with, grow with. This new, welcome life of hers was changing everything. "I'm sorry I can't block those. Julian is trying to understand why my interference with one of your gifts only seems to make the other stronger." She chewed her lip in thought, thrusting aside her angst. She couldn't solve every challenge Finn faced, more the pity because she'd have given her life to protect him. "The dreams coming more often and more intensely."

"Julian is an able taskmaster. He closets you away for hours a day pouring over that dusty chronology. You're the League's, *his*, newest pet project. He so wants to have a firm grasp of your gift; it *is* hard to deny him. He's even recruited Agnes to help with the research, poor woman." Finn lifted their joined hands to his lips and placed a delicate kiss on her palm, his tongue tracing a pulse point with calculated finesse. "I wish I was as interested in the occult when I simply want to live my life and lessen the damage. I want my children to be liberated from this burden. God willing, our talents skip a generation or leave our family completely. Find a way to solve that dilemma in those damned pages, and I'll get excited about the process."

Children. She desperately wanted Fig Alexander's children. He was so good with Lucien, and Piper and Julian's new baby, Emma.

As the jolt of awareness from Finn's touch danced along her skin, she wondered, with a quick look around the room, what Belle would say if she dragged her husband from the parlor and didn't return until morning. "Are you going to tell Ashcroft about the dreams?" she finally asked, her voice breathless, wanting, something her husband would notice. And hopefully, take delicious advantage of.

Finn rolled to his side to face her. Still, she found herself arrested by his beauty, his intelligence, his kindness. "I am. He's coming for Christmas as I suppose we're his only family, our delightfully mystical clan. Worse, I have to tell Julian. I've only delayed because once I do, we'll be off on the chase. Who is she to Ashcroft? Why am I dreaming about her? What's her bloody connection to the League?" He closed his eyes, his frown sending that adorable dent between his brows. "Truthfully, I'm exhausted by these campaigns. I want them to *end*."

She leaned in to smooth her lips over his cheek. "Well, now, you have me to lean on. I'm quite strong, you know. Let your wife shoulder part of the burden. Make use of my willingness."

Easing his hand behind her neck, he shifted her mouth to his to initiate a kiss. "Didn't I embrace your willingness last night? *And* this morning?"

"Oh, bother, you two need to find a chamber," Humphrey snapped as he entered the cottage on a rush of frigid air and swirling snow, juggling an arm-load of firewood, and awkwardly kicking the door shut. He'd escorted Belle home just as the storm began to rage, and he was none too happy to be stranded at Brook Cottage. Victoria had a sneaking suspicion being held hostage with Finn's enchanting, quick-tempered sister was the reason for his pique. "Isn't the honeymoon long over?"

"I'm trying to sleep," Simon groused, curling his arm over his head, and turning his back on the room. He was, by all accounts, a typical, irritable adolescent. They never knew if he was talking to them or one of the recently-deceased people who inhabited his world. Although Victoria's blocking seemed to keep the haunts at a slight distance. Peering in the windows of the cottage, according to Simon, which did send a vague scamper of unease along Victoria's skin.

"*Lune de miel*, a marriage's sweetness, can last for years. Or so I've been told," Belle murmured with a clack of her knitting needles. "Such a romantic, Ollie. It inspires, truly."

Humphrey dumped the firewood in the log holder and turned to her with a muttered oath everyone heard quite clearly. "We've discussed the nickname, missy. It's Humphrey. I don't go by Oliver, I never have. Who the hell even told you my first name, I'd love to know." His hot gaze fell to Finn, one of only three people, before one of those three disclosed the secret, who'd known.

Belle smiled but didn't look up, the needles speaking for her. A formidable opponent for the gentle giant if Victoria had ever seen one.

"Don't go getting ideas," Finn whispered with a grin, though he tried to flatten his lips to hide it. "I don't think Ollie is ever going to marry. And Belle…" He shrugged with another of those frowns pleating his brow. He worried about Belle finding her own life when she seemed content to mother every lost soul Julian dragged to Harbingdon until it was hard to remember when she wasn't there to nurture, console, placate.

Victoria leaned to kiss Finn, willing to suffer Humphrey's wrath.

Children with her beloved. Marriage for Belle and Humphrey.

She would pray for two Christmas miracles.

~ END ~

THANKS!

Thanks for reading *The Rake is Taken*.
I so appreciate it and hope you liked Finn and
Victoria's love story!

Ready to dive into Sebastian and Delaney's sizzling
romance? Get your own copy of *The Duke is Wicked*
or read on for an excerpt!

Happy reading!

"Sparks fly in this sultry Regency romance!"
—*Kirkus Reviews*

THE LEAGUE OF LORDS
SERIES

THE DUKE IS WICKED

AWARD-WINNING AUTHOR

TRACY SUMNER

ABOUT THE BOOK

Victorian historical romance with a sexy splash of the supernatural.

Leagues and lives apart, Delaney and Sebastian navigate a world they're not destined for together. Can she let down her guard and learn to trust a WICKED Duke?

He's harboring a fiery secret....

The Duke of Ashcroft is determined to keep the League of Lords under wraps. After all, the group's supernatural gifts brought the mystical misfits together and nobody is going to tear them apart. Intelligent and wily, Sebastian knows better than to trust anyone--especially an impulsive and intrusive American woman.

She's looking for answers...

Competitive and confident, Delaney Temple is hellbent on uncovering the truth about the League. She'll stop at nothing to unearth the secrets they're

burying. But when Sebastian is in trouble and Delaney comes to his rescue, their contempt turns to a
burning desire. Suddenly, with their passion ignited,
they can no longer deny their attraction.

A forbidden love...

PROLOGUE

A Wretched Ducal Home
Mayfair, London
February 1848

Dying was going to be easier than he'd imagined.

Sebastian Fitzgerald Tremont plunged his hand through the thin layer of ice and into the frigid fountain. Biting his lip until he tasted blood, he closed his eyes to the pain, his body shifting from hot to cold and back again so quickly he felt faint. He'd long ago surrendered to his skin going numb, rain and mud seeping through torn buckskin where he rested against the fountain's rough stone. Long ago surrendered to wondering when, exactly, his father would succeed in killing him.

Long ago yielded to his hatred.

"This time, keep it there. Even if your skin turns blue," the Duke of Ashcroft snarled. "And then we'll see about these bloody fires you're starting. The third one this month, my boy, and the third is going to be your last. With her death, I promise until mine, it's your *last*. No son of mine will suffer this misfortune."

Sebastian lifted his head, focusing a gaze close in

color to the inferno that had ripped through the gamekeeper's lodge two hours ago on the duke. He'd only gone there to mourn his mother in private, to rage over what could not be helped. As if he would suffer this *misfortune* if there were any option not to. "Don't make me think about the fires, Your Grace," he forced past lips clenched tightly to contain the tremors rocking his body, his vision spotting at the edges. If he passed out, his threat would go unheard. "You know what will happen if I do. I can see your coat going up in flames. Your bedchamber." He jerked his shoulder toward the magnificent dwelling behind them. "This entire estate."

His father gasped and stumbled back through the slush, filth splattering his fine woolen trousers. He pointed at his son, the ruby in his signet ring glinting in the moonlight, the crest of a lion with bared teeth leaping into the night. "*No*, you little spawn, you won't touch me. You won't! You killed your mother this very morn with this alchemy, put her in an early grave. Weak from dealing with your curse, she couldn't survive. She nor the babe. Both lost to me." He pounded his chest, three hard pops. "She loved you more than life, shielded you to the end. When I should've shipped you to the estate in the Highlands the moment I realized what you were. Somewhere so remote you'd never make it back."

In a fury, Sebastian yanked his hand from the fountain and closed his eyes, let his fingertips heat, his mind sizzle. Fires raged in his dreams and out of them, smoke choking him, flames licking his skin. Forests ablaze, the world one fierce, glowing ember and him, the speck of life within it. Ribbons of crimson and gold and indigo flooded his vision. With his father's wail, he blinked to find flames ripping across the fountain, water bubbling and churning.

The rain had turned to snow, sticking to his lips, melting when it touched his cheek, an arctic slide into his collar—when all around him was blistering heat.

It was hell on earth in the middle of a Mayfair winter.

Hell on earth in his mind.

Hell on earth in his *life*.

His father backed up, tripped on a tree root and tumbled to his bottom. "You'll die alone, do you hear me? Like I will, without my beloved. *Alone*. A lowly third son. I'll make sure of it. No one can love a devil, Sebastian. Destroying everything he touches. No one can be expected to." Scrambling to his feet, he backed away as if singed, when the fire was confined to the fountain, as Sebastian had intended.

Exhaling sharply, he cleared his mind and the firestorm faded. Only air thick with the scent of charred stone and despair lingered. And in the distance, the piercing fragrance of the Thames and the city he loved. He *would* die alone, he agreed, and slumped to the frozen earth, watching his father stagger down the gravel drive and into a home in which Sebastian suspected he'd no longer be welcome.

Maybe he had killed his mother. Not a breech baby, as the doctor had suggested.

Tears leaked from his eyes, and Sebastian scrubbed them away. He'd live a solitary life, he vowed, mired in misery and mud, the chill in his heart penetrating deeper than winter could.

A humble third son. A firestarter. A demon.

Cursed. Unloved. Unwanted.

A horror, all told.

But at least he wouldn't add the burden of being a duke to that life.

ABOUT TRACY

Tracy's story telling career began when she picked up a copy of LaVyrle Spencer's Vows on a college beach trip. A journalism degree and a thousand romance novels later, she decided to try her hand at writing a southern version of the perfect love story. With a great deal of luck and more than a bit of perseverance, she sold her first novel to Kensington Publishing.

When not writing sensual stories featuring complex characters and lush settings, Tracy can be found reading romance, snowboarding, watching college football and figuring out how she can get to 100 countries before she kicks. She lives in the south, but after spending a few years in NYC, considers herself a New Yorker at heart.

Tracy has been awarded the National Reader's Choice, the Write Touch and the Beacon—with finalist nominations in the HOLT Medallion, Heart of Romance, Rising Stars and Reader's Choice. Her books have been translated into German, Dutch, Portuguese and Spanish. She loves hearing from readers about why she tends to pit her hero and heroine against each other from the very first page or that great romance she simply must order in five seconds on her Kindle.

Connect with Tracy on http://www.tracy-sumner.com